"DIE, HUMAN!"

Merikur squeezed the trigger, turning the scream into a death gurgle as a stream of microbeads buzz-sawed the APE. Its upper torso hit the ground with a meaty thump and a navy-issue repulsion pistol skittered across the ground. Merikur dived for it—and rolled away as plasma beads chewed their hungry way across the pavement to where he'd been.

Shit! They were behind him!

Still on his back he blindly sprayed the shadows, aiming low. Two APE's fell as the superheated rounds blew their legs out from under them. Down but not out, they kept on firing, spattering Merikur's face with bits of pavement and bulkhead.

He dropped one of his pistols and popped out a minibomb from his chest dispenser: squeeze, squeeze again, throw! Close eyes against the flash.

When he opened them it was to see three hundred pounds of APE plummeting straight at him. . .

W.C. DIETZ
DAVID DRAKE

CLUSTER COMMAND: CRISIS OF EMPIRE II

This is a work of fiction. All the characters and events portrayed in this book are fictional, and any resemblance to real people or incidents is purely coincidental.

A Baen Books Original

Baen Publishing Enterprises
260 Fifth Avenue
New York, N.Y. 10001

First printing, May 1989

ISBN: 0-671-69817-6

Cover art by Paul Alexander

Printed in the United States of America

Distributed by
SIMON & SCHUSTER
1230 Avenue of the Americas
New York, N.Y. 10020

To absent friends.

Chapter 1

Merikur flinched as the glass bead whapped by his ear. He ducked around a corner. Damn! Since when were APE's equipped with repulsors? Well, it couldn't be helped. Merikur tightened his grip on his own pistol. There were at least five of the damned things, maybe more. The light was poor and the APE's had a maze of passageways and corridors through which to make their approach.

Leathery skin scraped against the bulkhead behind him. Merikur whirled, bringing his pistol up in the approved two-handed grip.

This one was big even for an APE. Seven feet tall and more than three-hundred pounds. Tiny red eyes glared from under a prominent supraorbital ridge, and high cheekbones framed a scaly face. A row of three nictitating nostrils marched down the center of its face rippling open and closed in endless sequence. It opened its wide thin-lipped mouth and screamed, "Die human!"

Merikur squeezed his trigger, turning the scream into a death gurgle as a stream of glass microbeads

buzz sawed the APE. An energy pulse converted each
bead's aluminum skirt into a plasma as it accelerated
up the repulsor's bore. The beads snapped out at
hypersonic velocity and exploded as they hit. Huge
holes appeared in the APE. It fell face downward
and hit the ground with a meaty thump.

A navy-issue repulsion pistol skittered from its
dead fingers and slid across the ground.

Merikur dived for the loose pistol and rolled away.
Glass beads crashed across the pavement where he'd
been, blowing out chunks of concrete. Shit! They
were behind him!

He fired while on his back. He didn't have a target
so he aimed low and used both pistols to spray the
shadows. Two APE's fell as repulsor beads cut their
legs out from under them.

They kept on firing. Their rounds spattered Merikur's
face with bits of pavement and bulkhead.

He dropped one of his pistols and ripped a mini-
bomb from the dispenser on his chest. Squeeze twice,
throw, and close your eyes to protect your night
sight. The mini-bomb went off with a loud boom.
Bits of APE splashed the walls, ceiling and Merikur.

He opened his eyes to see three-hundred pounds
of APE hurtling straight down from an overhanging
roof. He rolled to the right and heard the APE grunt
as it hit beside him, knobby knees bending to absorb
the shock. Splayed toes kept it upright as muscular
arms brought its huge broadsword up and back.

Merikur fired point blank, blowing the APE in
half. Coils of blue-black guts spilled over his legs.

Then the entire body toppled forward and fell
across him. He tried to push it away. It wouldn't move.

The body started to jerk spasmodically as another APE fired into it with a repulsor. The surviving APE was using its weapon to cut through the body to Merikur.

Merikur shoved his pistol between the warm slickness of the APE's digestive organs until it couldn't go any further and squeezed the trigger. Individually the glass beads had very little penetrating power but the stream of them blasted their way out through the creature's lower back and sprayed the corridor with death. Outside an APE staggered, screamed, and died.

Merikur used the APE's bodily fluids to slide out from under. He stood, eyes roaming the surrounding shadows, waiting for the next attack. A white hot ball of pain exploded between his shoulder blades. He felt his face hit the pavement.

Damn. A sniper.

As Merikur got slowly to his feet the lights faded up.

With that the APE's began reunitting themselves even as they were shuffling off towards their maintenance bay, while a host of vagrant gobbets inchwormed in the same direction. They would never make it, but they had to try.

Behind the maintenance bots came Warrant Officer Nister, a wizened little man, with the crossed daggers of a Weapons Master decorating his shoulder tabs. He had a swagger stick tucked under one arm and a clipboard in the other hand.

Nister wore his uniform cap tipped back on his head, but he was otherwise regulation all the way.

His crisp uniform crackled as he moved. He'd already served a hitch in the Marine Corps on the day Merikur was born, and what he didn't know about personal combat could be written on the head of a pin. He had bright little eyes, an oversized nose, and a mouth which had gotten him into trouble more than once. "Messy, Commander Merikur, very messy."

Merikur smiled. "Messy? Since when did you people start scoring on neatness?"

Nister smiled in return. "Well, we don't actually score it, but messy kills take more time, and that can cost you. Like this one, for example."

He toed the body of the last All Purpose Enemy (APE) Merikur had killed. "Once you got trapped underneath him, you did the only thing you could, and blasted your way out. Nice bit of work that, you picked up a lot of points for keeping a cool head, and a few more for dexterity."

His smile went hard. "But you also got dead. You gave a sniper enough time to get into position on a nearby roof. You stood up and he nailed you. Simple as that."

Merikur shrugged. "I can't argue with your assessment, Warrant. But damned if I know what I'd do differently next time."

"Well sir, practice makes perfect, and if you don't mind my saying so sir, you deck officers don't run the course as often as you should. Now let's add these up." Nister's practiced fingers tapped away at the keys on his clipboard as the warrant gave grunts of disparagement or chuckles of approval. "Well sir, things could've been worse."

Merikur smiled tolerantly. "So what's my score?"

"Eighty-six out of a possible hundred, sir. You picked up a lot of points the way you dealt with the unexpected. We kinda slipped you the big one when we gave some of the APE's repulsion weapons instead of swords, and then you really racked 'em up when you grabbed that loose handgun. Course you cost yourself a lot of points when you let 'em gang up on you and were forced to use the mini-bomb. God help anyone else who happened to be in the area."

He shrugged. "Still, eighty-six is pretty good for a deck officer."

"A dead deck officer," Merikur replied lightly.

"Commander Merikur?" called a weapons tech who'd stuck her head in through a side door.

"Over here," Merikur answered, wondering who was looking for him.

"A message from base HQ, sir. You're supposed to report to the Naval Appointments Board at 1500 hours."

"I'll be damned." Merikur glanced at his wristwatch. He'd been bugging them for weeks without success, but as soon as he decided to requalify on the personal weapons course. . . .

It was almost 1400. He looked down at his filthy camos. If he really hauled ass he could take a shower and break out a Class A uniform with about ten minutes to spare. Ten minutes would get him from Bachelor Officer's Quarters to HQ with about thirty seconds left over. He waved at Nister and headed for his quarters.

Grand Admiral Oriana leaned back in his chair,

put his hands behind his head, and stared at the bas relief of Athena springing from the head of Zeus which decorated his ceiling.

He was a handsome man, slim, and long limbed. He wore his kinky black hair short and flat on top in the style currently favored by naval officers. He had glossy black skin, high cheekbones, and an expressive mouth which at the moment was formed into a hard thin line.

He'd made his choice, but was Commander Anson Merikur the right man for the job? The board thought so, but all they did was make recommendations.

The record said Merikur was a solid, dependable officer who'd made each rank as he qualified for consideration. Nothing flashy, nothing brilliant, just a good, competent officer.

In short, just the sort of person Oriana and his superiors wanted.

There was one out-of-the-ordinary notation from when Merikur was a junior lieutenant. He'd deserted his post off Alexis II to chase a pirate raider. The sort of thing that ended your career if it went wrong.

But kids will be kids, and Merikur *did* nail the bastards. There's an unwritten law in the navy which says you *can* disobey orders and get away with it, *if* you're right, and *if* you're real lucky. Fortunately for him, Merikur had been both.

The raider had a hold full of hijacked weapons, and more importantly for him, a vice-admiral's daughter. She'd been captured in a raid and held for ransom. As a result the young lieutenant received a public wrist slapping and the private thanks of some very powerful people.

There'd been no further incidents of that kind, and that was just as well; it wouldn't be a good idea to assign an unreliable glory hound to Senator Anthony Hildebrant Windsor. The senator was unreliable enough. Anyone who believed all that "alien equality" crap was a few planets short of a full system. In Oriana's view the senator was a serious threat to Harmony Cluster—and the Pact itself.

A soft chime sounded. Oriana stabbed a button in the armrest of his chair. "Yes?"

"The board is seated. Commander Merikur is present, sir."

"Thank you, Perkins. I'll be right there."

Merikur tried to relax. He'd been through it before, but each Appointment Board was a roll of the dice. Sometimes you got something good . . . and more often than not you didn't.

"Admiral Oriana will be here in a moment, Commander Merikur. Can I assist you with any administrative matters? Some coffee or tea perhaps?" asked the alien steward. He was a Dreed, tall willowy humanoids with a talent for languages and an instinctual understanding of administrative procedure. They had become widely prevalent within the Pact's sagging bureaucracy.

Merikur smiled politely. "And you are?" Merikur wasn't especially soft on aliens, but he tried to remember their names. Sometimes it paid off in information.

"Humans call me Snyder, sir. It's as close as they can come to the actual sound of my name." The alien's heavy lips curved upwards in a smile, and his liquid eyes glistened.

"Thank you Snyder. A cup of coffee would be nice." As the alien scurried away, robes dragging on the floor behind him, Merikur took the opportunity to look around.

Light streamed in through high, arched windows to splash walls and floor. The chambers were large and richly furnished as befit a sector headquarters. Merikur sat on a chair with intricately carved legs. Facing him was a dais supporting a semicircular table. It was carved from a wood so dark it was almost black. Behind the table sat six senior officers, whispering to one another, and sometimes laughing.

Most likely comparing Nolo scores or some other equally important matter. A seventh chair stood empty.

There was only one observer in the small sections of comfortable seats to the right and left. She was beautiful and doubtless well aware of it, but by no means self-consciously sexy. Rather, she wore her looks like a set of clothes, useful but not essential. She was thirty-five or forty. He saw no rank of insignia on her naval uniform.

But he sensed the aura of power around her. It was visible in her relaxed posture, her sardonic smile, and the slight nod as their eyes met.

Who was she? She had to be here because of him. Merikur stirred uneasily.

"Here you are, sir. Cream or sugar?"

"No thank you Snyder, black is fine." Bowing slightly, the Dreed backed away and disappeared into the service corridors which surrounded the chambers. Merikur took a sip and looked up as a chime sounded.

"All rise," announced another Dreed, this one attired in Admiral Oriana's livery. Shoes shuffled and papers rustled as everyone stood and turned towards the center of the room. A door opened and Admiral Oriana entered the chambers. A few quick steps and he was at the table, nodding to the other officers, and taking his chair.

"Please be seated."

Oriana watched Merikur. Were there flaws there? Weaknesses hidden from the computers but visible to the naked eye? Merikur's hair was prematurely white without even a trace of darker color; he wore it short and flat on top.

In contrast to his hair, Merikur's face was darkly tanned. Not surprising since he'd just completed a tour of duty on Calvin, a desert planet in the Omega Cluster.

He'd seated himself with a certain quickness and grace. Not a born desk jockey, then. Good. He'd have damned little time for sitting at desks in the Harmony Cluster.

"Admiral?" prompted Perkins, his Dreed assistant.

Oriana waved a negligent hand. "Let the record show this session of the Naval Appointments Board is hereby called to order and all that other stuff."

He smiled towards Merikur, as if to say, "It's a lot of bureaucratic nonsense, but what else is new?" What he did say was, "Welcome Commander. After so many weeks spent badgering my staff for an appointment, I imagine you're happy to be here."

"It's always good to get back to work sir," Merikur replied straight-faced.

"And work you shall, Commander." Oriana looked

down at his comp screen, cleared his throat, and read the official text. "Commander Merikur, you are to embark immediately for Harmony Cluster. Upon arrival there you will assume command of all Pact forces, and report to the governor of said cluster, Senator Anthony Windsor. You will obey Governor Windsor's lawful orders, consistent with, and pursuant to, the laws, regulations and operating procedures set forth by Pact Command and known to you." Oriana looked up and smiled. "Do you understand?"

"Yes sir."

"Good." With just the ghost of a smile, the Admiral continued: "In keeping with your appointment, and its responsibilities, it is my pleasure to announce your promotion from Commander, Pact Naval Forces, to General, Pact Marine Corps. The full text of your orders is being downloaded to your AID."

Like all officers, Merikur carried an Artificial Intelligence Device, (AID) in his belt pouch. Besides the standard programming provided them at "birth," AID's could learn from experience, and sometimes developed rudimentary personalities. Merikur's was almost fifteen standard years old and a bit irreverent. Annoying though it sometimes was, and rather too revelatory of some aspects of his own personality, Merikur's AID was also very perceptive, and he couldn't bring himself to wipe it and start all over. Besides, he liked the little bastard. Hearing itself mentioned, Merikur's AID buzzed his auditory implant and said, "Orders received, your Generalship!"

Admiral Oriana was like an echo. "Congratulations, General Merikur . . . and good luck with your new command!"

Merikur felt all sorts of conflicting emotions. The switch from Naval to Marine rank didn't bother him, it was common enough, but from Commander to General in one jump! That was damned unusual and there was nothing in his record which would persuade a board to jump him an entire rank.

There was no time to think. The admiral was waiting. "Thank you sir. I'll do my best."

"I'm sure you will son, I'm sure you will," Oriana said cheerfully. He stood and made his way down to the main floor. "Before you strap on those comets, there's someone I'd like you to meet."

The woman Merikur had noticed earlier approached and held out her hand. "Allow me to add my congratulations to those of the admiral. I'm Megan Ritt."

"Yes," Admiral Oriana added awkwardly, as if suddenly unsure of himself. "Citizen Ritt came all the way from Terra to brief you."

Something cold settled in Merikur's gut. Kona Tatsu. The Pact's security service. And this one was working out of Terra HQ itself. He should have guessed from the uniform. The Kona Tatsu wore military uniforms without badges of rank, and went by the title "citizen," although it understated their power.

Merikur felt a soft buzz in his ears and heard his implant say, "She's toting enough shielded electronics to open a store. Chances are you're being recorded in stereo."

"Thank you. It's an honor to meet you, Citizen Ritt. I trust you had a pleasant trip?"

"Quite pleasant, thank you. The navy was most accommodating."

Merikur could imagine some poor captain sweating out the days and minutes until the spook left the ship. Was she really in transit to sector headquarters? Or was that a ploy? A cover story allowing her time to ferret out that equipment inventory the captain had fudged last year. Yes, most captains would be quite accommodating.

"Well then," Admiral Oriana said with a conspiratorial wink, "I'll leave you two alone. I'm sure you have all sorts of state secrets to discuss. Good luck, General. Wish I could go out and bust a few heads with you . . . but there's damned little chance of that. Too much data shuffling to do. Citizen Ritt, it's been a pleasure. Let Perkins know if I can help."

"Thank you, Admiral, I will."

"Very good." With that, the admiral departed.

Merikur felt abandoned. Oriana represented the military, which Merikur understood and liked; Ritt represented other things, dark and political. State secrets? What the hell was going on?

"If you'll follow me, General, I took the liberty of reserving a conference room."

Ritt made no attempt at polite conversation as they walked down the gleaming hall. Was it intentionally disconcerting, or just a natural expression of her personality? Either way he grew more worried with every step he took. Like most line officers, Merikur distrusted spooks.

"Here we are," Ritt said, motioning him through an open door. "Please take a chair."

Merikur gave the conference room a quick once over as he did so. The room was paneled in richly-waxed wood, and outside of the circular table and four chairs which floated at its center, the room was empty.

Once they'd both taken their seats Ritt looked at him and smiled. Suddenly he realized her eyes were very, very blue. "I hope I don't scare you," she purred.

"Not at all," Merikur lied.

"I'm glad to hear it. If you don't mind I'll get right to business. Time, as they say, is short. By now you've figured out that your situation is somewhat unusual."

"Yes ma'am." *Even before the Kona Tatsu started to brief me.*

Through steepled fingers she said, "Tell me, general: how would you describe the Pact's overall political situation and prospects for the future? And please, be frank. This conversation is completely off the record."

Merikur felt his implant buzz softly. "Her AID is jamming my scan mode. Assume she's recording every word."

Merikur wasn't surprised. Since his opinions could easily be ferreted out, he decided to be frank; his views were widely held and far from treasonous. He shrugged. "The Pact stopped expanding hundreds of years ago. Entire clusters have slipped outside of Pact rule. Multi-planet conglomerates, corporate combines, and aliens are all vying for power. In a few hundred years, a thousand at most, the Pact will collapse into anarchy."

Ritt nodded, regarding him from under long lashes. "Succinctly put, General; and in the opinion of many social and political scientists, absolutely correct. The question is, what should we do about it?"

Merikur decided to take a chance. "Things seem pretty stable for the moment. Why not just do our jobs and hope something better rises from the ashes?"

Ritt leaned forward. "It's a possibility. But what if something ugly rises from the ashes instead? And what about the pain and suffering while the Pact slowly disintegrates into chaos?"

Her blue eye sparkled. God help him. A fanatic as well as a spook!

"The Pact *can* be saved," she said, "if we have the courage to do so.'

"I'm glad to hear it," Merikur answered. "I've devoted my life to its defense."

Her features softened. "It was never my intention to imply otherwise, General. Forgive my display of emotion. As you can see I feel quite strongly about this subject. Tell me, what do you know about Senator Windsor?"

Merikur tried to think. Senator Windsor. The man whose orders he'd obey in the Harmony Cluster. Things had moved so fast he hadn't had time to think about his new boss.

The name was vaguely familiar. From the news no doubt, but Merikur couldn't remember more than that. "Nothing much. By definition he's a member of a senatorial family and therefore rich and powerful."

"Quite correct," Ritt said. "He's also young, handsome, and something of a radical."

Did Merikur detect just a trace of wistfulness as she said the last? Maybe not, she was dry and matter of fact when she continued. "It's that last quality we're here to discuss, General. In most things you'll find the senator is quite conservative. Most agree that he's an excellent administrator. It's in the area of human, or should I say non-human relations that his ideas become radical."

"Radical? In what way?"

Ritt smiled and examined a perfect nail. "Senator Windsor believes in full equality for aliens."

Merikur was astounded. Senator Windsor an alien sympathizer? Damn! How was he supposed to work for a man like that? Aloud he said, "*Full* equality. "Why would anyone advocate full equality? Especially a senator. Even if it's legal isn't it political suicide?"

Ritt looked toward the ceiling for a moment. "That's a good question. If Senator Windsor were here, he might answer this way."

Now she glared at the naval officer, angry perhaps, certainly hard and determined. "For the last few hundred years we've used aliens to prop up our economy," she continued. "First as a market for our goods, and then as cheap labor to produce those goods. Increasingly they do the jobs we won't. The hard, dangerous jobs and the jobs we regard as servile. Meanwhile we think we're on top, in control."

"We *are* in control," Merikur said, too amazed to let it pass.

"We are *not* in control," Ritt snapped. "With each passing year we become more and more dependent on their knowledge, their skills, and their numbers. So dependent that many economists wonder if we could survive without them. Meanwhile we deny them home rule, representation in our senate, or any other participation in government."

She paused, but her eyes continued to hold Merikur.

"Yes, citizen," he said calmly, embarrassed by his previous outburst, and more than a little concerned. Even generals couldn't contradict the Kona Tatsu. Not safely anyhow.

Ritt relaxed a little. "So if he were here the senator would say we have two choices. We can either reduce our dependence on the aliens, removing them from every aspect of our economy, or we can grant them full citizenship. And that's what Senator Windsor thinks we should do. In order to revitalize the Pact he believes we must fully integrate human and non-human races."

Aliens, no matter how smelly or ugly, as *equals?* It went against everything he'd been taught, but Merikur had to admit there was a certain logic to the senator's position. Military officers weren't encouraged to question the status quo; but Merikur had a good mind, and the senator's arguments, at least as presented by this deadly woman, meshed perfectly with his own observations.

"I presume," Merikur said, choosing his words carefully, "that others disagree. What do they say?"

"That the senator is a fool," Ritt replied coolly. "Many won't even admit there's a problem, and those who do would rather dismantle the economy than share power with the aliens. They point out that many alien races have higher birth rates than we do. If we grant them full citizenship today, they'll take over tomorrow; and *we'll* be the oppressed minority."

"So which viewpoint is correct?"

Ritt shrugged. "I don't know. No one does. But the consensus is that Senator Windsor should be allowed to experiment. If his theories work in Harmony Cluster perhaps the senate will follow. Ironic name, that. Harmony."

"Yes," Merikur replied thoughtfully, "it is. A lot of people won't like this experiment."

She nodded soberly. "That's why we gave him a general. A *reliable* general."

"But that's not the only reason, is it?"

Ritt shook her head. "No, it isn't. We want Senator Windsor to have his chance, but there are potential problems. There are a lot of Cernian laborers in the Harmony Cluster, and the Cernian Federation has taken an 'interest' in their well being. That interest has increased along with the size of the Cernian fleet. What if they assault the cluster? Will Windsor order you to fight? Or would he try to let them take it in an effort to further alien-human 'equality'?"

Merikur suddenly found himself faced with the prospect of every officer's nightmare: conflicting orders, with treason or mutiny the only options.

The Cernians were a powerful race whose homeworlds had been able to fend off the Pact during its expansive phase. So far they'd avoided an out and out challenge to Pact forces, but what if they chose Harmony Cluster as the place to test the Pact's strength and resolve? After all, Windsor was a nut who *liked* aliens. He might hesitate to fight, or worse, order Merikur not to while he pretended to "negotiate."

To disobey Windsor could end his career, and given what Ritt had just said, the reverse was also true. Pact Command was using him as a safety, a means of making sure that Windsor wasn't allowed to do irreparable damage while carrying out his social experiments. "You realize this places me in a very difficult position."

"Yes," she replied without a trace of sympathy. "I do. But I agree with Admiral Oriana. You're the right man for the job. And things aren't as bad as they seem. Once Windsor gets to know you, he'll keep his enthusiasms under control. With an entire fleet at your command he'll have little choice."

Merikur knew he was being had, but he felt complimented just the same. "Well, that remains to be seen, doesn't it, Citizen Ritt? In any case you've been frank, and for that I thank you." He cleared his throat. "I assume that's all?"

"Well, there is one other thing," Ritt said, leaning back in her chair, and allowing an amused expression to play across her lips.

"Oh yes? What's that?"

"The senator's niece."

Merikur looked a question.

"You're going to marry her."

Chapter 2

The moment Merikur and Ritt left the conference room Snyder opened a rear service door and slipped inside. If someone was still there he'd offer them coffee and tea. But the room was empty so his cover story went unused.

The Dreed's long robes swished as they dragged across plush carpet. Running a spatulate three fingered hand across the underside of the table he found a tiny bump. The small recording device had gone unnoticed. It was just as the voice said it would be. The woman was so confident of the anti-bugging devices hidden beneath her clothing that she hadn't even bothered to search the room.

Snyder popped the little device into a pouch and zipped the pouch into an inner pocket. He sometimes wondered who his employers were. Since he was never allowed to meet them face-to-face, he'd never know.

The shuttle pilot gave Merikur a clean lift and a smooth ride but the general was too angry to notice.

Merikur's family had money, but he was a provincial, and therefore conservative. He knew political marriages were common enough among senatorial families; but didn't approve of them, and he damned well wanted no part of such a relationship himself. In fact, he'd said as much to Citizen Ritt.

"This is outrageous! You can keep your comets. I refuse!"

"General Merikur," she replied sweetly, "refusal to comply with an Imperial Decree, *any* Imperial Decree, is treason."

At least that had told him the level at which Windsor's theories were being discussed.

Already furious with Ritt, Windsor, and Pact Command, he'd returned to the BOQ and found Lisa gone. Ordered out with the same military efficiency which had sent over a complete set of marine uniforms and an orderly to pack his personal belongings.

Theirs had been a contract friendship with only light option, but still, it wouldn've been nice to say goodbye. The only bright note was the set of gold comets in a little black box.

So, as General Anson Merikur stepped out of the shuttle lock, he wasn't in a good mood. His reception did nothing to improve it. Instead of the twittering pipes, and double row of gleaming uniforms to which he was entitled, Merikur was greeted by an ensign with acne, a prominent Adams apple, and the look of someone sentenced to death. Two ratings stood behind him, their faces professionally blank.

"General, ah, Merikur?" The ensign checked a note in the palm of his hand.

Merikur was seething, but he did his best to hide it. "Yes?"

"The senator sends his respects sir, and asks that you join him in the wardroom as soon as possible."

"Oh he does, does he? Well, you tell the senator something for me. With his permission I'll receive a report from this vessel's commanding officer, visit my stateroom, and maybe even take a shit before I join him. Have you got that, mister?"

"Yyyesss, sir. I think so, sir. Is there anything else, sir?"

Merikur saw the two ratings were about to explode into laughter. The story would be all over the ship within an hour. "Yes. Tell one of these ratings to carry my gear and show me to my quarters."

"Yyyesss sir. Nolte, you heard the general. Help him with his luggage and take him to his cabin. It's number four on B deck."

Merikur felt his implant buzz. "The *Bremerton* is a standard Port Class Cruiser. For full schematics, plug me into any printer." Well aware of the ship's layout right down to the smallest crawlway, Merikur ignored his AID and asked, "Your name, Ensign?"

"Polanski, sir."

"Thank you, Ensign Polanski. Dismissed."

"Sir." Polanski did a smart about face and hurried off, an amused rating in tow.

Merikur wondered how Ensign Polanski would handle it. Unless the boy was a complete idiot he'd take the edge off. Senator Windsor would get the message nonetheless. It was a calculated move. To do his job with some chance of success Merikur would need a measure of authority and independence. Being abjectly at Windsor's beck and call would serve neither purpose.

"This way sir." The rating, a young woman with the badges of a weapons tech, nodded towards a bank of lift tubes. She had his bags, his attache case, and a big grin on her homely face. "If you don't mind my saying so . . . welcome aboard, sir."

Merikur smiled. Some officers felt any sign of humanity fostered familiarity, and that once begun, familiarity inevitably led towards contempt. Merikur knew better. Familiar or not, the enlisted ranks knew the good officers from the bad, and no amount of bullshit would fool them. Besides, how the hell can you lead people you don't know?

"Thank you Nolte. It's a pleasure to be here."

As she followed him into the lift tube, Nolte put a bag down long enough to touch the letter "B." "I'm sorry about the way you came aboard, sir. Normally we run a tight ship, but the senator and his party docked half an hour ago and things are a bit hectic."

The platform came to a smooth stop. "Right this way, sir."

Merikur considered Nolte's comments as he followed her down a gleaming corridor. If Nolte was any example, morale was good, and in spite of his reception, that reflected well on the commanding officer. A woman named Yamaguchi, if he remembered correctly. It was equally clear that Windsor and his party had completely disrupted military routine aboard the *Bremerton*. That would have to stop.

"Your quarters, sir." Merikur stepped through the open hatch and into a spacious stateroom. Spacious though it was, the huge pile of baggage in the middle of the cabin made it seem small.

He looked at Nolte. She shook her head and said, "This is number four on B deck, just like the ensign said, sir."

Merikur nodded and circled right. Working his way around the baggage he came to another hatch. Sticking his head through he saw only rounded buttocks, a smooth back, and a mop of hair. Moonstruck, he could only stare.

The woman caught sight of him at the same moment and stood, turning towards him with hands on shapely hips as she did so. Her beauty hit him like a physical blow. Long brown hair swept down to frame an oval face. Her breasts were small and pert. White skin curved down to the darkly-tangled triangle between long slim legs. "General Merikur, I presume?"

He nodded dumbly.

She nodded in return, as if he were confirming her worst fears. Her voice was calm but icy cold. "I see. An officer but no gentleman. Well, we're not married yet, General, so I suggest you come back and inspect your property after we are!"

She stabbed a button, and the hatch slid closed in his face.

Angry and humiliated Merikur stormed out of the cabin, past Nolte and up the corridor. By tomorrow *that* story would be all over the ship too.

Merikur instinctively headed for the bridge. Perhaps up there he'd find something that made sense. Startled crew members scrambled to get out of the way as the new cluster commander stalked down corridors and climbed up ladders.

By the time Merikur reached the bridge the worst of his anger had passed. He was still upset and ready to take it out on anyone who gave him half a reason.

Like a commanding officer who wasn't where he or she should be, for example.

Fortunately Captain Yamaguchi had arrived seconds earlier and knew Merikur was upset. Having heard Ensign Polanski's report, she also knew why. Merikur's reception, or lack of one, constituted a serious breach of military courtesy.

It all started when the duty officer mistook Merikur's shuttle for a supply lighter. By the time he'd realized his mistake, and informed Yamaguchi, it was too late and Merikur was aboard. No matter that the shuttle was a supply lighter, commandeered at the last moment, and that the pilot must have failed to identify his new status properly.

It was a silly mistake, but one which could seriously impact her next fitness report, if Merikur wanted to be that way. In fact if Merikur were *really* angry, he might relieve her of command and order her off the ship, probably in the same supply shuttle which had brought him.

She could have dumped the whole thing on the duty officer, and many commanding officers would have, but that wasn't Yamaguchi's style. She'd have a private heart to heart talk with the duty officer later.

If she still had a command later. She just wished to hell that the Senator, who must have gotten word direct from groundside, had deigned to inform her as well as the ensign that the cluster commander had come aboard.

In the meantime she did what she could: "Attention on deck!" Those members of the bridge crew who were standing came to rigid attention and those who were seated froze in place.

As an ex-naval officer Merikur knew that even in orbit it was unusual, even potentially dangerous, to call the bridge crew to attention, but he also knew what Yamaguchi was trying to do. She was simultaneously paying him the respect denied him on boarding while also demonstrating the readiness of her crew.

Still the point made, there was no reason to have a dysfunctional bridge crew. "*As your were*. Thank you, Captain . . ."

Yamaguchi's body was no more than five feet tall but her personality filled the bridge. "Captain Marie Yamaguchi, sir. I apologize on behalf of myself and the ship for my absence when you came aboard. Shall I summon my first officer?"

Merikur smiled. Yamaguchi was offering to relinquish her command. Someone had screwed up and she was accepting the responsibility. His respect for her went up a notch. "That won't be necessary, Captain."

From the corner of his eye Merikur saw the tension drain out of the crew members near enough to hear. The crew liked Yamaguchi and was pulling for her. Better and better. "I could use a cup of coffee though."

In spite of her best efforts to look impassive, Merikur saw relief in Yamaguchi's eyes. She'd met the general and survived. "Of course, sir. My day cabin is right this way."

As in every other Port Class Cruiser, the captain's

day cabin was just aft of the bridge. As he entered, Merikur noticed a transparent display case filled with sea shells and stopped to admire them. Another side of Yamaguchi's personality. "Pretty."

"Thank you, sir. A hobby of mine."

As she ordered coffee Merikur took a chair. He'd hardly settled in when the coffee arrived and was served by a Cernian steward. Like most Cernians this one was short, no taller than Yamaguchi, and olive green in color. Many humans called them trolls. Short and squat, their heads seemed to merge with their torsos, and at first glance their features seemed coarse and ugly. A closer inspection revealed intelligent eyes, an expressive, remarkably human-looking, mouth. Like most Cernians, this one wore a short jacket and skirt combination.

Remembering Ritt's comments about possible conflict with the Cernians Merikur made a mental note to find out how many were on board. He blew the steam off his coffee and took a sip. "Good coffee."

"Thank you, sir."

Merikur found himself looking into bright brown eyes. He could see the wheels turning. Yamaguchi's actual rank, commander, was the same as his less than a day ago. Obviously she'd heard about his double jump to general and was wondering what made him so special. Well, he couldn't answer that one, because he didn't know himself. But he could clear the air. "Let's clear the deck, Captain."

"I'd like that, sir."

"I'm going to need all the help I can get to carry out my orders. That includes straight talk from my senior officers. So when we're alone let's cut all the 'yes sir, no sir' crap and just talk, My name's Anson."

She grinned. "And mine's Marie."

"Good," Merikur said. "O.K. Marie how's the ship? Can she run? And more importantly, can she fight?"

Yamaguchi took a sip of coffee. "She's as good as any twenty-year-old ship can be, and in answer to your questions, she can fight better than she can run. Newer hulls can run circles around us."

"Fair enough. Now the senator. Is he pissed because I didn't come running?"

Yamaguchi laughed. "No, he's not pissed, not according to what my ensign tells me, but his Chief of Staff, a guy named Tenly, sure is. But I think the senator was amused. If anything, you probably gained some points with him."

"Good." Merikur swallowed the last of his coffee. "Well, I guess I'd better go and see him. What time are we scheduled to break orbit?"

Yamaguchi glanced at the watch strapped to her wrist. "About three standard hours from now. The senator's in a hurry."

Merikur stood. "That's understandable, I suppose. Thanks for the coffee, Marie."

"You're welcome, Anson. Come back any time." She said his name carefully as if it might break. "And Anson?"

Merikur paused by the door. "Yes?"

"Welcome aboard."

He nodded and disappeared around the corner. Yamaguchi leaned back and raised her coffee cup in salute. "To the Naval Appointments Board. I think the idiots finally got one right."

*   *   *

The wardroom was fairly large—Port Class Cruisers were large ships—and packed with people. Civilians talked to each other, officers came and went, and everyone shouted orders at the small army of aliens and enlisted people who actually did the work.

Remembering the attache case he'd left with Nolte, Merikur stopped a passing Cernian and said, "Excuse me. I left my attache case in my stateroom. Cabin four on B deck. Would you get it, please?"

"Of course, General. It would be a pleasure." The Cernian clapped his hands in a formal salute and disappeared into the crowd. Right at that moment a Chief Petty Officer noticed him, realized who he was, and bellowed, "Attention on deck!"

All the uniforms snapped to attention while the civilians looked around to see what the fuss was about. Merikur spoke. "I'm General Merikur. Would the most senior officer in this room please step forward?"

A harassed looking lieutenant commander stepped forward. From the red braid running over the lieutenant commander's right shoulder Merikur deduced he was one of Windsor's military aides. A rather recent one given the man's obvious confusion. Merikur sympathized.

"I think I'm senior at the moment, sir."

"Excellent. Your name?"

"Moskone, sir."

"Thank you, Commander Moskone."

Merikur turned to the now silent crowd. "From now on you will submit your needs to Commander Moskone. You will do this one at a time. He will prioritize your requests and assign people to carry them out. Please remember that this is a warship and not a cruise liner. Although the crew will do everything they can to ensure your comfort, military necessity may require them to return to their normal duties at any time. If this occurs please try to be understanding. In the meantime I see the wardroom bar is open. Perhaps those of you with less urgent requests would step over and have a drink on me. Thank you. Carry on."

As half the crowd headed for the bar, and the rest lined up to see Moskone, Merikur heard a voice at his elbow. "General Merikur?"

"Yes?" He turned to find a man in livery standing by his side. He wore a tight-fitting grey tunic with a high collar. He had nervous little eyes, a sizeable nose, and a forehead that looked like it must be perpetually wrinkled with worry. A large crest, Senator Windsor's no doubt, decorated his breast pocket. A vein throbbed in his right temple. Before the man could answer Merikur said, "Chief of Staff Tenly, right?"

"He's wired to the max," Merikur's AID volunteered. "Makes citizen Ritt look like a piker."

Tenly looked surprised, and disappointed. "That's correct, General, I . . ."

". . . Want to introduce me to the senator. Lead the way."

Obviously miffed, Tenly led him across the wardroom, the crowd parting before him. Merikur spotted Senator Windsor right away. The man had that special something which causes some people to stick out in a crowd.

Aside from that indefinable charisma, the senator was a handsome man with thick black hair, flashing brown eyes, and perfect teeth. If Windsor had any flaw at all it was his hawk-like nose, but even that worked to his advantage, granting him a slightly predatory air. He rose at Merikur's approach and stepped around Tenly to hold out his hand.

Forced aside, the Chief of Staff could only glower and watch the two men come together. "Senator Windsor . . . I'm General Merikur. It's an honor to serve under you, sir."

The senator's handshake was strong and firm. He nodded towards the other side of the room where Lieutenant Commander Moskone seemed to be bringing things under control. "You have a way with words, General. Perhaps you should give politics a try."

"And from what I hear you get things done, Senator. The military could use an officer like you."

Windsor laughed. "Point and counter point. Sit down, General. We have a great deal to discuss."

Merikur took a seat at what normally served as the wardroom table, and was now functioning as both desk and conference table for Windsor and his staff. Windsor gestured towards a tray.

Merikur shook his head. "Thanks, Senator, but I just had coffee with Captain Yamaguchi."

"Ah, yes. First a soldier must look to his weapons."

Windsor smiled, but Merikur got the point nonetheless. Windsor had raised the issue of Merikur's priorities and then put it aside. The message was clear. "I'm giving you this one but don't push your luck." Merikur decided to clear the air.

"Can we speak frankly, sir?"

"I sincerely hope so, General. A good working relationship is critical to our success. What's on your mind?"

"Simply this, Senator . . . Or should I say 'Governor'?"

"I won't be sworn in until we reach Harmony Cluster."

"Then for the moment I'll stick to 'Senator.' Ideally our relationship should be a simple one in which you give the orders and I follow them. And that's how I hope it will be. But I must warn you that under certain circumstances I have orders to act on my own."

Windsor nodded thoughtfully. "And those circumstances are?"

Merikur grinned. "Beats the hell out of me, sir. I'm to make sure you don't go 'too far.' What *that* means, the bastards wouldn't say."

Windsor threw his head back and laughed. "So if you're right they give you a medal, and if you're wrong they hang your ass! By God, General, we have something in common!"

Merikur smiled. The senator had all the gloss of a customized pistol and was just as dangerous. Merikur liked him. "It would seem so, sir."

Windsor slapped him on the shoulder. "Let's have an agreement, you and I. If you feel I'm heading in the wrong direction, you let me know. Then if we can't find a way to work things out . . . you'll do whatever you think is correct. Fair enough?"

"Fair enough, sir," Merikur answered, with unstated reservations.

"Good. What else is on your mind?"

"I'm told there's a possibility of conflict with Cernians."

"Excuse me." It was the Cernian servant with Merikur's attaché case. "Your case, sir."

"Ah, let's ask an expert about that. General Merikur, may I present my closest advisor, Eitor Senda."

Merikur felt the blood rush to his face. He'd sent Senator Windsor's closest advisor to bring his attache case! He started to speak but realized he didn't know a respectful form of address appropriate to aliens in general or Cernians in particular. As far as he knew the Cernian had no military rank, and he wasn't a citizen . . . so what was he?

Senda smiled and answered Merikur's unasked question. "My people do not use titles the way humans do, general. Please call me Eitor."

As the alien spoke Merikur was unable to spot any anger or resentment at his gaffe, but he apologized anyway.

"Think nothing of it," the Cernian replied easily. "I used to make the same mistake on Terra. All you generals look alike."

Merikur laughed and felt somewhat better. Another Cernian arrived and offered Senda a curiously-shaped metal device. Senda leaned on it and Merikur realized it was some sort of chair.

Noticing Merikur's curiosity Senda said, "On Cernia we use human furniture in our torture chambers."

The humans laughed and Windsor said, "Speaking of Cernia . . . why don't you give the general a quick briefing. I'm sure he'll sleep better."

"I have the most recent intelligence estimates on file," Merikur's AID volunteered. "Not that they'll do you much good unless you take the time to read them."

"Well," the alien said thoughtfully, "we Cernians are just part of a very complicated situation at the center of which is the Haiken Maru."

Like most naval officers, Merikur was familiar with the Haiken Maru Conglomerate. It had started as a simple shipping line, but it had grown over the years until it controlled entire systems, and its political influence reached deep into the Senate. In spite of strong evidence that the conglomerate was engaged in smuggling and unlawful commerce with pirates, navy ships still had orders to avoid undue "harassment" of Haiken Maru vessels.

"Like many other conglomerates," Senda continued, "the Haiken Maru has its own security forces."

"Which brings us to Harmony Cluster," Windsor added.

"Yes," Senda agreed patiently. "The Haiken Maru are quite strong within Harmony Cluster, and since they use a great deal of alien labor, they will probably resist the senator's reforms. The mining world called 'Teller' is a case in point. It seems the workers object to conditions there, and are fighting some sort of guerilla war."

"Which is where the Cernians come in," Windsor added helpfully.

The alien gave Windsor what might have been an annoyed look, although Merikur wasn't sufficiently familiar with Cernian facial expressions to be sure. "Yes, that is where we Cernians come in. The labor force on Teller is part Cernian."

"So Cernian forces might choose to intervene?"

Senda closed both eyes and opened them. The Cernian equivalent of a shrug. "Possibly. Like humans, various Cernians have various opinions. There should be more current information available when we reach the Cluster itself."

"Which isn't to say we won't have other problems," Windsor added cheerfully. "You know, pirates, crop failures, disease, that sort of thing."

"I can hardly wait," Merikur replied dryly.

"However," Windsor added with a smile, "there's something more pressing for us to worry about right now."

"There is?"

"Why, yes. I want you to marry my niece before we break orbit."

Chapter 3

The wedding was a brief and depressing affair. Bethany Windsor was beautiful, but her eyes were red from crying.

Merikur was grimly formal, replying to Captain Yamaguchi's questions with grunts of assent, flushing with embarrassment when asked to slip the ring onto her slim finger.

Even the ring was false, something Tenly supplied, and Bethany removed the second the ceremony was over.

Senator Windsor meanwhile looked on with cheerful enthusiasm, nodding as Yamaguchi read the traditional words, and slapping Senda on the back when it was all over. "Excellent, just excellent! All right you two, off to your stateroom, I'm sure you have lots to discuss!" The latter was delivered with a broad wink to Merikur.

Straining to maintain some semblance of dignity, Merikur ignored the wink, and extended an arm to his new wife. To his tremendous relief she took it.

35

They walked in silence until the stateroom hatch hissed closed behind them.

Bethany crossed the cabin and stood facing a bulkhead. Her head was bowed and her voice tight with emotion. "General, I wish to apologize for my earlier behavior. It was unforgivable. If I wanted privacy I should have closed the hatch. Can you accept my apology?"

She was so unhappy, so completely miserable, that Merikur wanted to comfort her. But all he could offer was a few inadequate words. "Of course. I can imagine how you feel, I'm . . ."

"Can you ?" She whirled to face him. "Can you imagine what it's like to have someone like Tenly show up at your home and tell you that your marriage had been dissolved? That the husband you love has been reassigned? That your father's brother is giving you to some general in return for services rendered? Can you really imagine what that's like? No? Well let me tell you something, General Merikur, it hurts so much that I'd just as soon be dead."

For a moment they stood there, she hysterical with grief, and he speechless from the utter injustice of it all. She'd been married? To another officer? Why hadn't Windsor told him?

Because Windsor didn't think it was important. After all, what were the wishes of two or three people when compared to the future of the whole human race? The senator's eyes were so full of his own vision he was blind to everything else.

But she didn't have to blame Anson Merikur. He didn't want the marriage any more than she did. He'd married her out of duty—under *threat*—goddamn it, the same reason she'd married him. The least she could do was not act as though he were an animal bent on dragging her off to bed against her will.

Merikur squared his shoulders and cleared his throat. "I'm sorry. Rest assured I have no intentions of . . . imposing myself upon you. I suggest that for the balance of the trip I sleep out here while you use the sleeping cabin. Please try to think of us as comrades in misery. If there's anything I can do to make your journey more comfortable, please call on me. Now, if you'll excuse me, I have work to do."

"No," said Bethany, looking down at her spread fingernails. "We have one more piece of mutual business."

"Excuse me?" said Merikur. He paused in the middle of a step toward the door and turned.

She ran her finger down the touch-sensitive closure beneath the left arm of her dress, then began to lift the garment's hem over her head. "We have to consummate the marriage," she said in a voice muffled slightly by the fabric.

"Don't be absurd!" Merikur snapped. He glanced reflexively over his shoulder to make sure the door was fully closed.

Beneath the dress was a body-stocking so sheer that only the fabric's slightly greater albedo permitted Merikur to distinguish it from his wife's bare, tawny flesh. Her breasts were too firm to need even minimal support. . . .

"Absurd, General?" she said coldly. She flung the dress into a corner, hooked her thumbs beneath the straps of the body-stocking, and took a deep breath. "What could be more absurd than to have my—let's

call it my life—" she looked up fiercely, meeting
Merikur's eyes for the first time since she'd made
her announcement, "yes, let's say my life destroyed,
by a political marriage. And have it benefit no one,
because I was too fastidious to make the marriage
legal."

Glaring at Merikur, she deliberately pulled the
body-stocking below the curve of her hips and then
began to step out of it, one shapely leg at a time.
"*That* would be absurd, would it not?"

Merikur nibbled his lower lip. "Ah," he said. "No
one needs to—"

And caught himself. Of course they would know,
the Kona Tatsu and their political masters. He and
Bethany might as well be the lead turn in a dock-side
floorshow. . . .

No. There were some things—

"Oh, come on, General," the woman said. A slick
gloss of indifference covered her expression and whatever her real emotions might me. "It needn't take
very long. Or are you—"

Bethany's eyes widened in real horror. "Unless
you . . . ? Oh, no, they *wouldn't* have married me to
a man who—"

"Nothing of the damned sort!" Merikur said in a
tone half-way between fury and disgust. He jerked
open the waistband of his uniform trousers a moment
before he realized that he should have taken off his
shoes first.

Damn the woman!

Halfway through the process that followed, Merikur
had the suspicion that his wife was no longer thinking only of the needs of the Pact.

And by the time the process was over, he rather regretted that it would be the only time that particular duty would be required of him.

From that point on Merikur immersed himself in his work. There was plenty to keep him busy from the moment the ship broke orbit until its arrival in Harmony Cluster.

First there was his AID to debrief, including a line-by-line reading of his voluminous official orders, and an endless series of intelligence reports on the Harmony Cluster. Lacking any sort of faster-than-ship communication, the material was probably outdated; but it did give him a base line against which to judge more current information when it became available.

Merikur also put himself through a number of computer-guided refresher courses on military strategy. Officer Training School was a long time ago, and besides, most of his training had been in tactics, not strategy.

Generals are supposed to plan overall strategy rather than tactics.

A lesson some senior officers never learn, to the detriment of their troops and the benefit of their enemies.

Merikur also formed an elite bodyguard for Windsor and his senior staff. It happened almost by accident and flowed from a desire to learn more about Cernians. "Know thy enemy" is an ancient military dictum and a good one. Merikur had it in mind when he invited Senda to the ship's gym. When the alien arrived Merikur was already there. "Hello, Eitor, how's it going?"

"Fine, General. Thank you for asking."

"Tell me something, Eitor, have you had any training in personal combat?"

"Yes," Senda replied, his entire body swiveling as he looked around the gym. "Why are we meeting here?"

Merikur smiled. He was dressed in marine camos. "Because if we fight in the wardroom it'll make a big mess."

Senda's grins were a bit disconcerting because the corners of his mouth turned down, instead of up, but it meant the same thing. "Fight? Why should we fight, General? Are we not allies?"

"Yes, Eitor we are—and that's one reason why we should fight. Try each other's mettle. How can we fight side by side if we don't know each other's strengths and weaknesses? And by your own admission, not all Cernians share your belief in the Pact. By fighting you, perhaps I'll learn something which will help me fight them."

"There is wisdom in what you say." As the Cernian spoke, he removed his jacket revealing a thick upper torso crisscrossed with ropy muscle. Merikur took one look and wondered if he'd made a serious mistake. "Will we use weapons or only our bodies?"

"I think our bodies will be sufficient, Eitor. I don't know about you, but I'd like to survive this match."

"Yes, it is the same with me, General. Please begin."

"No rules or anything?"

"Are there rules in war?"

"Not any more."

"Then rules would be superfluous, would they not?" And with that Senda attacked.

Merikur had assumed that while the alien might be stronger, a human would have the advantage of leverage due to his additional height, and greater mobility. Not so. Bending powerful legs, Senda launched himself into a forward roll and came out of it inches away from a surprised Merikur. The alien stuck his arms straight up and out. When he brought them together, they hit both sides of Merikur's head like sledgehammers.

Had Senda used his full strength Merikur would have died. As it was he fell to his knees, his head ringing like a bell

Merikur felt rather than saw the alien clasp both hands together and raise them into the air. Butting upwards, Merikur hit Senda low in the abdomen. The Cernian grunted and fell over backwards. Merikur stood, tried to follow up, but found himself too dizzy to move. He was forced to await the next attack. It was quick to come.

Stunned one moment, the alien was a blur of motion the next, rolling sideways toward Merikur and locking arms and legs around him. Merikur broke one leg free and brought his knee up towards Senda's genitals. When his knee arrived, the genitals were gone, retracted into the Cernian's body. For long moments he pounded again and again at the armored closure, as a red haze slowly built before his eyes.

Panting helplessly, he relaxed, and the air was squeezed from his body still locked in Senda's embrace. Then, breathless, he realized he had no means of signalling submission, decided what the hell, and bit into a fleshy ear.

Senda grunted in pain and brought both of his stumpy legs up and under Merikur's stomach. With a tremendous shove he launched Merikur towards the nearest bulkhead. The human hit with a loud thump and slid to the floor.

For awhile both sat there, Senda holding his ear, and Merikur, after re-learning the art of breathing, dividing his attention between head and stomach. Then Senda's mouth turned downwards in a grin. "Well human, what did you learn?"

Merikur thought for a moment. "Never try to knee a Cernian in the balls."

For awhile human and alien lapsed into chuckling quiescence. Then, laughing and slapping each other on the back, they stumbled off to get some first aid and a good stiff drink.

And later, after giving it some more thought, Merikur decided he'd learned something quite important from the encounter. He'd learned to respect stumpy Cernian bodies, and more importantly, the minds which inhabited them.

So, he thought to himself, what better way to foster equality than to integrate military units? You can't do something like that overnight of course, and he didn't have any Cernian troops to integrate with, still there might be a way to get started. Which is the way the Governor's Hundred came into being.

Merikur asked some questions and confirmed that yes, there was a small marine contingent aboard, and of course they'd be happy to do whatever he wanted.

Hey! Nothing like being top dog; if a junior officer

had offered the same idea he or she would have been roadblocked right away.

Having secured the necessary marines, Merikur needed some willing Cernians. He approached Eitor Senda and explained his idea. The alien was enthusiastic. Due to his controversial policies, Windsor would need a bodyguard—and what better way to demonstrate his belief in full equality? By placing his life in the hands of aliens, the senator would add to his credibility *and* his notoriety, both of which mean a great deal to any politician.

Windsor was also quick to lend his support to the idea. He loved the obvious political benefits, but he also took pleasure in Merikur's initiative and committment to alien equality. As Merikur left the wardroom, Windsor turned to Senda and said, "Could it be that we have here a general of more than military intelligence?"

With the help of their officers and noncoms, Merikur chose fifteen of the ship's forty marines while Senda rounded up an equal number of Cernians. It turned out that most of the 'servants' had served in the Cernian military, choosing to leave when their enlistments were up. They weren't in a hurry to put on uniforms again; but the offer of better pay and equal treatment was sufficient to generate fifteen volunteers.

Merikur made a mental note to recruit more when he reached Harmony Cluster. Under the cover of looking for new recruits, he could also sift the Cernians for spies and saboteurs. After all, what Windsor and Senda didn't know, wouldn't hurt them. But it could kill them.

Equality is one thing, stupidity is another, Merikur mused. It was curious that so many Cernian veterans had elected to settle within the Pact. Given Cernian status on this side, life must be pretty tough yonder.

When, on the first day of training, Merikur entered the gym he noticed that with two exceptions his volunteers had segregated themselves. The two exceptions, a marine and a Cernian, broke off their conversation and drifted back towards their respective groups.

For a moment Merikur considered making a speech. He could tell them the guard would be an integrated unit, that humans and Cernians were equal, that they should work together. But he quickly rejected the notion, knowing it would be a waste of energy. They'd have to find out for themselves just as he had. So he called them to attention, a concept familiar to the military of all races, and pointed out the two who'd been talking to each other. "You and you, front and center."

Both groaned internally as they broke ranks and marched towards the front. What the hell had they done? Stopping in front of Merikur they both came to attention, the Cernian veteran every bit as snappily as the marine.

The Cernian's version was similar to the marine's, except he crossed his forearms over his chest. Later Merikur would learn this was due to the design of Cernian battle harness. Crossed arms provided quick access to hand weapons and symbolized personal readiness.

"About face!"

Spinning around the two of them faced the rest of the troops. "Names!"

The Cernian spoke first. "Father, my name is Viko Keedor, father!" Merikur knew from talking to Senda that Cernian forces were originally organized along family lines. While this was no longer practical, the titles of "Father" and "Mother" were still used depending on the sex of the officer, and were roughly equivalent to "commander."

The marine was next. "Sir, my name is Manuel Costas, sir!"

Merikur nodded and turned to the troops. "Now listen up. You just met your officers. Who's got a coin?"

"Sir." Costas fished in a pants pocket and produced a coin. He tossed it to Merikur.

"Thanks. Heads it's Costas, tails it's Keedor."

Merikur flipped the coin and caught it. "Tails. Viko Keedor now holds the rank of captain in the Elite Guard. Manuel Costas is hereby promoted to lieutenant. Assuming they keep their new ranks, eventually these officers will recommend some of you for promotion. If I agree with their recommendations, those individuals will become NCO's. Until that time Captain Keedor and Lieutenant Costas may decide to appoint some of you as acting NCO's. All of you will obey their orders pursuant to the rules and regulations of Pact Military Forces. Copies of those rules and regulations will be made available. I recommend that those of you who haven't read them do so."

Merikur paused meaningfully. "This will be an elite unit entrusted with the lives of the governor

and his staff. You'll be rewarded if you perform well.
You'll also be punished if you screw up. If you screw
up though laziness, dishonesty, or the use of intoxi-
cating substances you'll wish your mothers had died
a virgin. Do you understand?"

Merikur heard a ragged collection of "Yes sirs."

"I can't hear you."

"The response was a ragged mix of "Yes sirs," and
"Yes fathers," but at least it was louder.

"That's better. Now pair off, one Cernian to one
human."

For a moment the two groups eyed each other in
consternation, surprised at Merikur's order, and unsure of what to do. Then, after moments of hesitation, Keedor and Costas took control. Keedor had a
voice like a Nugian swamp bull, and he used it to
good effect. "All right, you heard Father Merikur.
Pair off. One troll to one guwat."

It turned out later that "guwat," roughly translated,
meant "tall pile of feces," and was what Cernians
called humans in private.

There was complete silence for a moment as members of both races took this in and wondered how to
react. Then a marine laughed, a Cernian made a
strange coughing sound, and everyone else joined in.

Merikur let out a deep breath. Keedor's gamble
had paid off. It could've gone the other way.

Merikur addressed them again after they'd split up
into pairs. "It's important that you know each other.
So we're going to have a little get acquainted session.
The object of this exercise is to subdue your opponent. There is only one rule. If you put someone in
sick bay, you'll stay in the brig until they're released.

Your objective is to subdue your opponent, not kill him. Do you understand?"

"Yes sir!" Merikur noticed that the Cernians were now using the human response.

"All right. You may begin."

They moved with initial wariness, each waiting to see what the other would do, hoping for some kind of advantage. It was a Cernian who attacked first, launched herself into a forward roll like the one Senda had used against Merikur. Moments later another Cernian followed suit and before long the gym was full of thrashing bodies, grunts of pain, and occasional whoops of victory.

Merikur saw a pattern start to emerge. The Cernians were quite aggressive, using movements akin to gymnastics, while the humans were on the defensive at first, using a variety of styles that ranged from martial arts to street fighting. As they grew more accustomed to Cernian tactics, they counter-attacked.

Things were really starting to heat up when Merikur blew his whistle.

"All right. That's enough. Form up in alphabetical order."

As they sorted themselves into alphabetical order, Merikur noticed that some were hurt, but as far as he could tell, none seriously. For the most part the damage seemed limited to bumps, bruises and human pride. Some of both races were a little wobbly, but if he sent them to sick bay now he'd have to send their partners to the brig. Better to wait and let them drop by sick bay on their own—or tough it out if they chose.

When they had formed up Merikur stepped for-

ward. He swept them with what he hoped was a
steely gaze. "Now listen up. That was the only time
you'll ever fight each other outside of carefully designed drills. At least it had *better* be. I hope you
learned what the exercise was designed to teach.
This is an integrated unit. You will be treated as
equals and you deserve each other's respect. Anyone
who objects, please step forward now. You'll be released from the Hundred without dishonor. If you
stay, be prepared to fight and die with your brothers."

No one moved. Merikur smiled. "Welcome to the
Governor's Hundred."

As Merikur handed over the Hundred to Keedor
and Costas for calisthenics, Bethany Windsor watched
from the circular track above the gymnasium floor.
She usually ran five miles a day, although she found
the circular track incredibly boring.

She'd watched Merikur with an almost morbid
fascination. He was her husband after all, and a force
to be dealt with. Who was this man with the serious
eyes and white hair? She watched the way he commanded their attention, the obvious intelligence in
his eyes . . . the quiet strength of his body.

She caught herself. No damn it, no! How could
she?

With a little cry of pain, Bethany ran all the way to
the sleeping cabin and locked herself up inside.

Nola Rankoo sat on the veranda of her villa and
looked out over a portion of her property. On paper
it took up more than a hundred square miles of
prime agricultural land. In reality it was much larger,

including as it did a great deal of Augustine, capitol planet in the Harmony Cluster, and goodly portions of the Cluster as well. Not directly, since with the exception of her personal estate it all belonged to the company, but indirectly, because she was the third most powerful person in the Haiken Maru.

The prospect before her was indeed a beautiful sight. Starting at the edge of her veranda the Sweetberry vines grew in rippling purple rows for as far as the eye could see. The blossoms bathed her with perfume.

This was her favorite time of day, when the light lay soft on the land and the sun was about to set. It was a time to savor and enjoy. Rankoo smiled and sipped Sweetberry wine. And there was much to enjoy.

For the most part business was good. She had Victor Trent, the outgoing governor, to thank for that. Interested only in completing his term and returning to Terra, Trent had maintained a very low, if personally profitable, profile. As a result Rankoo had been free to run wild along with her profits.

Yes, things had gone very well indeed, with the possible exception of Teller. The human and Cernian workers there were a constant source of trouble. She'd asked Trent to send some marines, but he'd refused, citing the imminent arrival of a new governor. It was bullshit, of course, but on this one issue the old bastard had been adamant. Afraid of a bad report from his replacement, of course.

The new governor sounded as though he might be a problem. From all accounts he was a flaming liberal, spouting all sorts of garbage about giving the aliens equality as the only way of preserving the Pact.

The new governor might side with the very aliens she was trying to subdue. And then there was this general, what's his name, Merikur. What position would he take?

The tiny recording device had arrived by high-speed courier only hours before. Although she'd already listened to the message twice, she picked it up and gave a gentle squeeze. It began to play: "Senator Windsor will attempt to bring full equality to the Harmony Cluster. If he succeeds perhaps the Senate will follow."

Rankoo frowned as she squeezed the device off. Change usually brought with it an opportunity for profit. But this Windsor was a radical, and from the sound of it, a competent one at that. The combination could be very bad for business.

She heard a soft footstep behind her. "Yes?"

Coda's voice was hoarse and gravelly. 'It is time." He was a big man, layered with hard muscle, wearing only a genital pouch and a pair of sandals.

Rankoo nodded, swallowed the last of her wine and stood. She towered over Coda. Her body was slimmer than his but, thanks to DNA editing that had been necessary to survival on their planet of origin, equally muscular. She had wide shoulders, firm upthrust breasts, a narrow waist, and long muscular legs. Like Coda she'd been born and raised on the heavy gravity world known as "Lead." On Lead it takes a lot of strength just to get up and walk around, so Augustine's lighter gravity made them seem super human, a fact they'd used to good advantage.

Like Coda, Rankoo wore nothing but a G string and sandals. She saw and savored the hunger in his eyes. As usual she'd make him wait. His performance would improve accordingly. "I'm ready."

He nodded and together they walked down a short flight of stairs, along the side of the villa, and out beyond the barn. As they approached the holding pen she saw there were four Hornheads penned up inside. The beasts weighed close to half a ton, were covered with overlapping plates of green armor, and had mean dispositions.

Each was armed with three horns: a curving affair to each side, plus a lance-like growth which protruded from its forehead. All were razor sharp.

Rankoo's voice was calm and indifferent. "Four tonight?" In truth four was a lot.

But Coda liked to test his mate, assure himself of her strength and the status it conferred on him. His eyes were flat brown disks as he handed over the steel mesh gloves. "Yes. We're running low on meat."

Rankoo pulled on the gloves and entered the pen without comment. She stalked the largest Hornhead, choosing to ignore the others. It would take the most strength, so she would kill it first. Personal kills were something her mother had insisted on. *What your clan eats you must kill.* To do otherwise was to avoid responsibility and invite speculation on your fitness.

Some thought it an outdated hunting ethic, but it was one to which Rankoo chose to cling. For her, business was simply a complicated version of the hunt: the strong must kill, the weak must die.

The animal charged. She grabbed its two outside horns and leaned forward, feet skidding in the dirt, powerful legs pushing with all her might. Slowly, reluctantly, the beast came to a stop. Its three-pupiled eye regarded her with limitless hate, and its foul breath filled her nostrils. For a moment they stood motionless, each trying to best the other through sheer brute strength.

This was Coda's favorite part: Nola's naked strength against the brute force of the beast. He felt the familiar stirring between his legs and smiled. As usual she'd make him wait, but he agreed: it would be worth it.

Slowly, almost imperceptibly, she turned the beast's head. Then, with a mighty contraction of her shoulder muscles, she twisted it a half rotation to the right. There was a dull cracking sound; the animal fell dead at her feet.

The rest would be easy. As she grabbed the next set of horns and turned them, Rankoo was thinking of Senator Anthony Windsor.

Chapter 4

Things began to happen the moment the cigar-shaped ship dropped into orbit around Augustine. Shuttles came and went, staffs conferred, and all manner of problems were discovered and resolved. Windsor disappeared into a whirl of meetings, receptions and parties.

And of course so did Merikur. As senior officer, Harmony Cluster, he'd be at the center of military politics. Any officer desiring promotion or a new command would need his approval, so at any given moment there were hundreds of people clamoring for his attention. As a result, it was damn hard to do his real job. Inevitable it may have been, but he wasn't used to it, and he didn't like it.

Some officers love that kind of attention, basking in the warm glow of their own power, handing out decisions like precious gifts. Others, the kind who get things done, dread it.

In between meetings he managed to learn that at the moment thirty ships were under his command, along with 3,000 crew and support personnel and another 1,500 marines. With the exception of two new destroyers, the rest of his fleet was pretty old, dating all the way back to the days of expansion.

His single battleship was a good example. The *Nike* was 256 years old. In spite of her age, his staff assured him she was still quite serviceable. Too large for atmospheric landings, and lucky enough to have escaped major battles, *Nike* had had her weaponry updated from time to time, and structurally she was in better shape than many ships half her age.

Unfortunately the same couldn't be said for Merikur's 4,500 military personnel. Both his experienced eye and fleet records told him the same thing. Pact Command's forces in the Harmony Cluster were fat and lazy. The reason was obvious. His predecessor, Rear Admiral George Stender, was a crony of the outgoing governor's. They were in fact leaving for Earth aboard the same ship.

Like his boss, Stender was unaggressive and quite satisfied with the status quo. Consequently his term of office had seen a steady, and in Merikur's eyes treasonous, decline in battle readiness. They would ocasionally break orbit for an exercise or to chase a pirate who ventured too close to the main shipping lanes, but otherwise they just sat—by now it was about all they were good for.

To counter this, and break up the political groupings which flourished under Stender's command, Merikur ordered massive rotations. Every officer who'd served in a dirtside staff position for more than one local year was sent to a ship or other combat unit.

That freed up an equal number of officers to join his staff. These were often men and women Stender had banished from headquarters for political reasons, or people who just liked to fight. Either way, they were the kind of advisors Merikur wanted: people who knew the ships, the troops, and how to use them. True, some would be plain incompetents and psychological misfits, but he would weed those out soon enough.

Then Merikur began sifting through his officers for a Chief of Staff. Someone who could run the administrative end of things while he dealt with external military and political matters. It took some time, but after countless hours of reading personnel files, Merikur came up with the right man. The problem would lay in convincing Captain Wallace Von Oy to take the job. Von Oy demonstrated a pronounced aversion to things administrative.

In typical fashion, Merikur went to Von Oy instead of summoning the captain to his office. He did so for two reasons. First he wanted to pay Von Oy a compliment; second, he wanted to see the man on his own deck.

It would be a small deck, however, since Von Oy's ship, the M-2022, was modest.

It was, in fact, a tug. A tug which had been in orbit around Augustine for nine local months. Ever since Von Oy had drunk too much at Stender's military ball and suggested that the purpose of Pact military forces was to fight, rather than fuck.

As a full Navy captain, Von Oy rated a heavy cruiser at least, like the one he'd commanded until his unfortunate gaffe—and Stender reassigned him to a line officer's version of hell.

The M-2022 consisted of huge drives and very

little else. Not intended for atmospheric landings, the small ship had heat-release panels, antennas, and tractor beam projectors stuck out in whatever way was most convienent.

As Merikur's shuttle made lock-to-lock contact, Merikur wondered what he'd find aboard the tug. Just because Von Oy looked good on paper didn't mean he was. The captain might be floating in a lake of alcohol. . . . But even as the locks hissed open, Merikur's fears were put to rest.

Von Oy was there, along with his entire eight-person crew, rendering full honors to the cluster commander. As the sound of the pipes dwindled away, Von Oy snapped off a perfect salute. "On behalf of the ship and crew, welcome aboard sir."

Von Oy was of medium height; he had pale blonde hair and bright blue eyes. His uniform was perfect and his teeth flashed when he smiled. "If you'll follow me, we've laid on some refreshments."

As Merikur followed Von Oy to the mess, he saw gleaming electronics, fresh paint, and smiling faces. Whatever Von Oy's feelings, he hadn't let his imprisonment affect the ship. There wasn't a trace of self-pity in his tone or bearing.

Merikur liked that. It showed guts and maturity. "Here we are sir . . . small but cozy."

The rest of the crew disappeared as the two men took their seats, providing the appearance of privacy. On such a small ship there was no wardroom, and the captain's cabin would be little more than a closet. Privacy was almost impossible in theory and, if Merikur knew anything about small ships, absolutely impossible in reality. Whatever they said would be heard.

There was a pot of coffee and some cups in the middle of the table. Merikur helped himself. "You run a tight ship, Captain."

Von Oy smiled at the compliment. "I have an outstanding crew, sir." He meant what he said, but he was also aware that his crew was listening. Von Oy knew what many officers never learn: share the credit with your subordinates, and one day maybe they'll save your ass.

Merikur sipped his coffee. "As you know, Rear Admiral Stender's returning to Terra a few days from now."

Von Oy smiled sardonically. "A tremendous loss."

Merikur nodded, straight-faced. "Yes. And as the new commanding officer for Harmony Cluster I'm making a few changes. Much as I'd like to place officers of your experience and ability on *all* of my ships, it's a luxury I can't afford. So I came here to offer you a job."

Von Oy's eyes lit up. His old cruiser perhaps? Or maybe even the *Nike*? With Stender out of the picture anything was possible. . . .

"I'd like that sir. Which ship?"

Merikur said carefully, "I want you for my Chief of Staff."

There was a long silence while the light faded from Von Oy's eyes.

Merikur took another sip of coffee and smiled. "I know what you're thinking, Captain Von Oy. How useless desk jockeys are, and how much you want a ship. And that's exactly why I want you for my Chief of Staff. I want someone who's smart, wants to cut through the bullshit instead of making more—someone who know's what the Navy's for: fighting instead of fucking around."

Von Oy spluttered for a moment and wiped his mouth with the back of his hand. "You sure fight dirty sir. I like that. One desk jockey reporting for duty, sir."

Both men smiled at the sound of distant cheers and curses. Von Oy's crew had listened to the whole thing via an open intercom. The cheers were for a commander they held in obvious affection; the curses were the result of the natural pessimism with which they awaited his replacement.

As Merikur's shuttle touched down, his hover car swept around to meet him. His marine driver was a sergeant named Molly Knox. On his first day she'd shown up driving a black limo. "What the hell's this thing?" he'd asked.

"Your car, sir. Actually it's Admiral Stender's back-up limo, but he assigned it to you."

Merikur had nodded politely. "Very nice of the admiral. But it might get all dusty on field exercises. How 'bout something a little more utilitarian? Like a command car?"

And she'd found one. It was either new or freshly painted, mounted twin auto repulsors—and a whip antenna which flew his flag. Since it was a beautiful day, Sergeant Knox had retracted the roof. She cut the hover craft's power and dropped onto the hard surface of the tarmac as he stepped out of the shuttle. As he approached, she slid out of the driver's seat and snapped to attention.

Merikur returned her salute and smiled. "Good work, Sergeant Knox. I would've felt like a pleasure-planet pimp riding around in that other thing."

Knox was pretty in a slightly chubby way, and her green eyes twinkled as she spoke. "Thank you, sir. Where to?"

Merikur sighed. "HQ I suppose. I've got lots of bureaucratic crap to shovel."

"Yes sir."

As Merikur settled into the back seat Knox fed power to the fans lifting the car up and off the tarmac. Then she rotated the vehicle 180 degrees and skimmed over the ground towards the gate. The two sentries presented arms as the command car slid through and onto the open road.

Augustine was a beautiful planet. Merikur knew there were some slums southwest of Gloria, the capital city; but Troll Town wasn't visible at the moment, so everything looked pretty.

Low-lying villas hugged the land to either side of the highway, snuggled down into the cool embrace of formal gardens. Here and there, well-dressed humans relaxed on their verandas as servants brought out the noonday meal. Life was good—for the master class.

While Augustine had its wild and inhospitable latitudes both north and south, there was a wide temperate zone around the planet's equator, and that was very pleasant indeed. Much of it was given over to agriculture, especially Sweetberry vines, and they gave the land an orderly, cultivated look.

Unfortunately there were other less attractive uses of the land as well. The large areas owned or controlled by the Haiken Maru, for example. While Merikur hadn't been dirtside long enough to visit them, he'd seen the ugliness via holovids, and the images were still burned into his mind.

Machines the size of small towns inched across the planet's surface, consuming its flesh for markets light years away. When the strip mines were exhausted, huge ulcerous pits were left to scar the planet for thousands of years to come.

Merikur was a pragmatic man. He knew such mines were necessary, but also knew the resulting pits could be terraformed. But the Haiken Maru refused to do it. Their contract didn't call for them to do it, so why turn profits into scenery?

There was a buzzing in his ears. It was his AID. "I have a message from your other half."

"I wish you'd quit calling her that," Merikur subvocalized. "She's my wife in the legal sense only, and even if our relationship were deeper than that, she wouldn't appreciate being referred to as 'my other half.' "

"All *right* already. Excuse me for processing."

Merikur was surprised however. He hadn't talked to Bethany for days. He'd found it more comfortable to sleep in a room next to his office than to return to their temporary quarters. Somehow he always felt like an invader. "What's the message?"

"She'd like to meet you for lunch. With your permission I'll dump directions and the address into the car's computer."

"Go ahead." Merikur couldn't imagine why Beth

would suddenly request his presence at lunch; but
what the hell, anything was better than the pile of
work waiting at his office.

The mystery grew as Sergeant Knox followed the
AID's directions and steered the car away from the
city and towards the suburbs. Gradually businesses
grew almost nonexistent, villas were spaced further
and further apart, and the highway narrowed from
four lanes to two.

There was a hill ahead of them. Turning onto a side
road, they began to climb in ever smaller loops. The
views were marvelous. To the west lay Gloria, the
spires of the central business district glittering in
the sun, while all around suburbs gave way to lush
farmland.

Suddenly they rounded a corner and drove into a
paved courtyard. There was another vehicle, a civilian roadster, and beyond that a sprawling villa.

As Knox cut power and put the car down a human
servant hurried out to greet them. In spite of his
white house coat, Merikur recognized him immediately: Kevin Matsumoto a member of the Elite
Guard. Merikur started to say something but a tiny
shake of Matsumoto's head stopped him.

Matsumoto had read somewhere that Orientals were
once considered inscrutable; he was doing his best to
live up to that reputation. Apparently there was more
to this than met the eye.

"Right this way sir. Sergeant Knox, if you'll wait
here for a moment, someone will be along with
refreshments." Knox looked to Merikur for instructions.

Merikur shrugged. "Beats me, Sergeant. If I'm not
back in an hour hose the place down with the twin

.50's and send for reinforcements. In the meantime, have a good lunch."

Knox laughed. "Yes sir!"

Merikur followed Matsumoto through a well-kept garden and into the villa. Inside everything was cool stucco and comfortable furniture. Vases of fresh flowers complimented the nicely executed landscapes which decorated the walls.

Stepping out onto the veranda, Merikur was greeted by a Cernian, also a member of the Elite Guard, and Bethany, stunning in slacks and a loose blouse. God, she was beautiful. She smiled, and despite himself his pulse began to quicken. "Welcome home, General. Can you join me for lunch?"

For a moment he stood there like a foolish schoolboy filled with confusing thoughts and emotions. Finally he managed to smile and stutter a reply. "Thank you, Bethany. I'd enjoy that."

Was that relief in her eyes? He thought so but couldn't be sure. Moments later he found himself seated at a linen-covered table, sipping cool wine, and enjoying the sound of her voice. Another servant materialized, a Cernian, and after some brief instructions from Bethany disappeared into the kitchen. "I wasn't sure if you'd come, so lunch won't be ready for a few minutes."

Merikur smiled, searching her face for signs of the grief and anger which he'd always seen there before. He thought he detected a reserve, a barrier deep in her eyes, but all other signs of her previous distress had disappeared. "That's fine. It feels good to get away from the office. This villa is absolutely beautiful. Whose is it?"

Bethany smiled. "Ours if you want it. We've got to live somewhere and I thought you might like something a little more elaborate than the room next to your office."

The room next to his office? How did she know about that? "It's wonderful,'" he said looking around an awe. "Can I, we, afford it?"

She laughed. "You really don't know, do you? As it happens, cluster commanders rate pretty good quarters —and while you obviously haven't given it any thought, your wife is quite wealthy."

Merikur hadn't thought about it, but he realized she was right. His new rank plus allowances meant he was quite well off. And while of course she was wealthy, he hadn't considered that either. . . .

He laughed self-consciously. "I'm afraid you're right. The, ah, the new job keeps me pretty busy."

Suddenly anxious not to break the mood he said, "The villa is absolutely wonderful. How did you find it?"

She leaned over to pour him some more wine, and he caught the scent of her, the faintest hint of feminine muskiness mixed with some subtle perfume. The effect brought catnip to his mind. He found his eyes drawn down the curve of her cheek to the fullness of her lips

"It was quite easy actually. When the new governor is your uncle, and the planet's ranking military officer is your husband, real estate agents line up to assist you."

He laughed and took a sip of wine.

"Anson?"

Merikur mentally sat up and took notice. To the

best of his recollection this was the first time she'd ever used his first name. Up till now she'd always called him "General."

Looking at her he didn't care what she called him. Bethany was so beautiful it hurt.

"Yes?"

"I'm sorry. I know this hasn't been easy for you. Please accept my apologies for the things I've said. It's not your fault Spencer and I were separated. She looked at her fingers "Damn, it seems like I'm always apologizing, and then doing something stupid to apologize for."

"Not at all," Merikur replied. "You and your . . . ex-husband were separated against your wills. That's a fact and it's better to discuss it than pretend it doesn't exist."

"Really?" Her brown eyes flicked across his face as if searching for reassurance.

"Really. Perhaps we could be friends, you and I."

"Oh, Anson I'd hoped you might feel that way. It's so much better than enemies, isn't it? And I'll try to hold up my end. I'm a pretty good businesswoman, really I am, and that's what we have isn't it? A partnership. And if you want someone on the side, well, why not? My father always had a mistress or two . . . and my mother was absolutely notorious."

She was so eager, and so sincere he could do little more than smile and nod. A mistress, by God. He didn't want a mistress . . . he wasn't quite sure when it had happened, but he wanted her. But divorced or not the memory of her ex-husband was powerful enough to reach across the light years and hold her captive.

Merikur forced a smile. "I'm kind of busy right now, but if I need a mistress, I'll let you know. Maybe you'd be kind enough to pick one out for me?"

Bethany laughed, obviously relieved. "Of course! It's the least I could do! Ah, here's our lunch."

It was soon apparent that Bethany would be a valuable ally.

For one thing she paid attention to things he tended to ignore. This became painfully apparent when he asked about the two members of the Governor's Hundred lurking about the premises.

She looked surprised. "You don't know? Of course you don't. You're a prime target for assassination, silly. By killing you, my uncle's enemies make him more vulnerable. I pointed that out to Eitor, and he sent the guards over right away."

"I suppose," Merikur agreed doubtfully. "But why waste the guards? A squad of marines would do just as well."

Bethany shook her head sadly. "Not so. If you have a squad of marines hanging around it looks like you're scared. Then they really come after you."

"Or you," Merikur said suddenly concerned. "They might try to hurt you to get at me."

"Or my uncle," Bethany agreed gently. "That's how these things work."

Merikur suddenly found himself plunged into a world he didn't understand. Invisible enemies, plot and counterplot, suspicion and deception. Bethany had been raised in an atmosphere of Senatorial intrigue, so it was second nature to her, but Merikur

had always met his enemies head on with repulsors
blazing. . . .

They talked the afternoon away, some of it business, some of it not.

By the time the shadows grew long, they were
ready to watch the sun plunge down beyond the far
horizon as friends.

Chapter 5

Stepping out of the limo, Merikur and Bethany nodded to some functionaries, and started up the wide flight of stairs toward the governor's mansion. Tomorrow it would be Windsor's, but tonight it still belonged to Governor Trent, and he was throwing himself a going-away party. Bethany's hand felt light on his arm, and in spite of the fact that she wasn't really his, Merikur felt proud to be with her.

The crowd parted to let them through as they moved up the stairs. Officers moved to get out of Merikur's way, women craned their necks to see him—and everyone stared at Beth.

She wore a gown of shimmering pink and blue. It seemed to shift with the light, almost transparent one moment, and completely opaque the next.

To Merikur's amazement Bethany seemed to know everyone, calling them by name, and whispering little asides in his ear. "That's Captain Asta's wife, she wants him transferred dirtside to spend more time with her, but he doesn't want to go. Can't say as I blame him. Oh, and that man over there, the one with the white goatee. That's Citizen Solakof. Very big in planetary politics. Wants to meet you in the worst way. Be careful though. He uses a lot of alien labor in his sweatshops. Uh oh, there's one to watch, Nola Rankoo and her husband Coda. She runs the Haiken Maru hereabouts."

Merikur had a quick glimpse of a woman who towered above the crowd. With her was a beefy-looking man who looked ready to burst out of his evening clothes. As the couple disappeared inside they reminded Merikur of his security problems.

It was Trent's party, so Windsor and his staff had no control over the guest list. In addition to which, the former governor was far from cooperative. Calling their precautions "hysterical," he'd refused their requests for a routine security sweep of the mansion, and only grudgingly allowed the guards access to the grounds.

All Merikur could do was beef up security and hope for the best. A destroyer sat in geosynchronous orbit over the mansion, aerospace fighters skimmed the edge of space, and attack helicopters patrolled a few hundred feet up.

Marines were scattered around the grounds with orders to keep a low profile. Another fifty or so were inside. They were disguised as servants, and while they'd be handy in a brawl, they wouldn't be much help if someone pulled a weapon. Since Marines aren't trained for security work, they were unarmed. The last thing Merikur wanted was some Marine with a repulsor, hosing down half the guest list to nail a possible assassin.

And then there was the Governor's Hundred. Unlike the regular marines, they *were* trained for this sort of situation and were heavily armed. Six wore identical gray suits and would stay close to Windsor at all times. Besides screening the senator with their bodies, Merikur hoped they'd intimidate any would-be assassins as well. If not, the rest of the unit would be nearby, disguised as servants and guests.

As they stepped through huge double doors, Merikur knew hidden scanners were sweeping over him and locating the hand gun concealed under his dress tunic. A fraction of a second later they would scan his retinas and cross-check the electronic code provided by his AID. Anyone who failed these checks would be arrested whether Trent liked it or not. It wasn't perfect, but without Trent's cooperation it was the best he could do.

"General Anson Merikur, and his wife, Bethany Windsor-Merikur, Baroness of Skeed." As he finished the announcement, Trent's majordomo brought his ceremonial staff down with a heavy thud.

As they descended a short flight of stairs into the main ballroom, Merikur pretended to smile and talked from the side of his mouth. "Baroness of Skeed? You're a baroness?"

"Of course. I thought you knew. These days it's just an honorary title, but good for thirty thousand credits a year nonetheless."

Realizing all over again that he knew very little about his new wife, Merikur looked out at the ballroom, and was amazed by the spectacle of it all. Hundreds of people and no small number of aliens filled the room. Brightly-colored gowns fought to capture his eye, a hundred perfumes assailed his nostrils, and the hum of conversation filled his ears.

As usual he wanted to run. As a junior officer he *had* run, making his appearance, then slipping away. Now the golden comets on his shoulders weighed a ton apiece and held him in place.

Long slim fingers suddenly squeezed his while warm lips brushed his right ear. "Relax, Anson. Just remember, you scare them more than they scare you."

She knew! She cared! The thought warmed him through and through but was soon lost in the crush.

"General Merikur, I'd like you to meet so and so." "I suppose I shouldn't ask, General, but all the girls want to know, why is your hair white?" "No offense, General, but this alien equality stuff is rubbish. I trust you believe in keeping the trolls in their place?" "General, it's my pleasure to introduce Nola Rankoo, and her husband Coda."

The crowd faded into the background as Merikur gave Nola Rankoo his full attention.

It would have been hard not to. The woman was huge. A full foot taller than Merikur. The hair coiled on top of her head added to the impression of height; her red evening gown consisted of more skin than cloth, revealing large sections of her muscular body. There was no artifice about her. She was exactly what she seemed.

A powerful and dangerous woman.

And not just because of her size. Even greater danger lay in her eyes. She was an enemy, and they both knew it. Her hand closed around his with bone-crushing strength. "Welcome to Augustine, General. I've heard so much about you."

Merikur tried to ignore the pain. She wanted him

to withdraw, to admit his weakness, but his pride wouldn't allow it.

Forcing a smile he said, "All good, I trust. My, that's a beautiful necklace. May I see it?"

Placing his right boot on her left foot, he stepped forward while shifting all his weight to that foot. His left hand went up to touch her heavy necklace. With one movement of his hand he could choke her with it. He saw her wince.

Rankoo let go of his hand and he took a step back. Coda moved in but stopped when his wife held up a hand.

"As you were, Coda. The general and I were just getting acquainted. It's been a pleasure, general. I hope you'll live long enough to have dinner with us sometime."

"I'm impressed," Bethany said as Rankoo and Coda moved away. "You certainly have a way with women."

Merikur responded absently as his mind ran through the possibilities implied by her expressed "hope." Was it a manipulative threat intended to bring him into line? A promise? Or a mere empty boast? Though she might be arrogant enough to telegraph a punch, Nola Rankoo didn't strike him as someone who made empty boasts.

Be conservative then. Attempted manipulation could be ignored, so assume the implied threat was real; when and where would it happen? He'd have to assume the attempt could come at any moment— and clearly the governor's enemies wouldn't try to kill his general without trying for the man himself. He turned to Bethany. "Let's find your uncle. I think he's in danger."

Bethany's eyes widened, but she nodded silently and followed as he started pushing his way through the crowd towards the long buffet table. He caught a glimpse of Windsor every now and then. He was standing at the far end of the buffet table next to Trent. Eitor Senda was by his side. They were surrounded by a large group of people. Merikur and Bethany were only halfway down the length of the buffet table when his AID buzzed him. "Hey, your generalship . . . somebody's pumping a pulsed signal through here. The source is within a hundred feet."

"Did it just start?"

"Yup."

Straight-arming an elderly woman, Merikur charged forward. "Senator, hit the deck!"

But he was too late. Everything shifted into slow motion. As Merikur went for his gun, he saw a Cernian servant plunge both hands into a cake, and pull out a pistol. Off to his right another Cernian ripped the back off an upholstered chair and pulled out an auto repulsor. A Dreed reached under a table and grabbed a needle gun taped there days before. Merikur sensed rather than saw that others were doing likewise all around the ballroom.

Whap! Whap! Whap! Glass beads began to fly in every direction. Women screamed, but no louder than some of the gorgeously attired military personnel of both sexes. Merikur watched in horror as a line of miniature explosions ran the length of the buffet line, promiscuously throwing up geysers of food and gobbets of living flesh, not stopping until it reached Governor Trent, the man who had made it all possible. Trent was dead before the first piece of him hit the floor. Two guards died shielding Windsor before Senda threw him down and covered the senator's body with his own.

Tenly disappeared under the buffet table. Unarmed marines charged the aliens with their bare hands and died in bloody heaps.

Glass balls and needles cut through the crowd. The needles were almost silent but the *whaps!* of hypersonic glass beads merged with *whumps!* of flesh exploding on impact. The assassins carved bloody trails through the packed bodies as they sprayed the room with lethal projectiles.

Pulling his handgun free of his tunic, Merikur brought it up and fired. His shots punched a Cernian backwards to slide across the buffet table and fall off the other side.

Bethany! He whirled ready to throw her down, but found she was covering his back, her small purse gun spitting death. Beyond her a Dreed grew a third eye and fell backwards into a pile of screaming men and women. There was a *lot* he didn't know about his new wife!

Merikur picked another target and squeezed the trigger. Whap! Whap! Whap! A sloppy job. His projectiles blew the Cernian's right arm to pulp before crossing his chest and putting him down. And what would Warrant Nister have had to say about that? Neat meant 'fast,' and speed counted. . . .

It took a few seconds for the Governor's Hundred to pick their targets. Then it was all over. When the firing stopped there was a moment's silence then moans and hysterical laughter.

In the distance Windsor was swearing and pushing

Senda out of the way while members of the Elite
Guard formed a circle around him. Tenly had emerged
from under the table and was doing his best to get in
everyone's way.

Turning, Merikur saw Bethany was untouched and
already helping the wounded.

Merikur scanned the room as troops flooded in
through open doors and windows. Movement caught
his eye as Nola Rankoo and her husband stood. They'd
been concealed behind the bar, the room's heaviest
piece of furniture, and therefore the most projectile
proof. There wasn't a mark on them. Meeting his
gaze Rankoo nodded and smiled. Then, stepping
delicately over and around the bodies, she and Coda
left the ballroom.

He knew to a certainty that Rankoo had planned
the whole thing. He couldn't prove it. But as Merikur
looked out over the bloody ball room, he swore an
oath that Nola Rankoo would pay.

Two days later later the wounded were on the way
to recovery, the worst of the shock was over, and the
ballroom floor was cleansed of blood. Trent's wife had
departed for Earth with an attentive Admiral Stender
by her side and her husband's body, or most of it,
stored in the ship's hold.

Members of the Hundred were buried as they'd
lived, side by side. Mixed among the human and
Cernian guards were the sixteen marines who had
attacked the assassins with their bare hands and posthumously earned a place in their ranks. On Merikur's
orders, all were buried with full honors in a section
of the military grave yard that had been reserved for

the Hundred alone. Some of the living marines were dubious about having their comrades interred with aliens, but the honor of it overcame their reservations.

And with the perversity of soldiers everywhere, applications for the Guard doubled, and then tripled within a few days. Members of all races represented on the planet were rushing to join up.

The public swearing-in was cancelled due to Governor Trent's death. Instead, there was a quiet ceremony witnessed by only a few. As Windsor raised his right hand and swore to defend Harmony Cluster from all enemies foreign and domestic, it occured to Merikur that they had plenty of both.

Windsor and the senior members of his staff met in a conference room just off his spacious office.

Governor Trent had spared no expense to make the room both comfortable and attractive. Light poured in from a series of large rectangular windows. A long black conference table of highly polished native stone ran the length of the room. Upholstered chairs surrounded it and added to the atmosphere of elegant comfort. Gray drapes with burgandy trim covered the walls and also served to conceal a holo tank.

Governor Windsor was seated at the head of the table, with Senda on his right and Tenly on his left. Also present were Merikur, Captain Von Oy, and Lieutenant Commander Moskone.

As usual, Windsor looked quite dashing with his quick smile and flashing eyes. A small bandage over his left eye gave him a slightly piratical air. In spite of Merikur's strenuous objections, Windsor insisted on working in the planet's spire-like administration building. "I appreciate your concern for my safety, General, but government is two-thirds smoke and one-third accomplishment. This office has symbolic value. By staying here I tell both friends and enemies alike that I'm not afraid."

He grinned, "Even though I am."

Merikur knew there was truth in what Windsor said, but also harbored a strong suspicion that the new governor liked the trappings of office and was loath to give them up. In any case, Windsor's decision was final. Merikur beefed up security and hoped for the best.

Again.

Windsor opened the meeting.

"Thank you for coming. I know how busy you've been since the assassination attempt. I'd especially like to praise Eitor Senda for a smooth transition of power under trying circumstances, and General Merikur for the military's heroic efforts, including his own. It gives me great pleasure to announce that, along with a detailed report of what's happened here, I've sent Pact Command my recommendation that General Merikur receive the Medal of Valor." Every decade or so, someone among the billion-plus members of Pact Military forces received that medal. Usually posthumously.

Merikur blushed at the general applause and mumbled something about his people. His comments were generally ignored; cluster commanders who behaved like line marines were something special, it seemed.

"All right," Windsor said as the applause died down, "we have a great deal to discuss. If successful the attack would have eliminated Governor Trent, myself, and all my senior staff. It's likely that a good deal of time would have elapsed before another governor arrived. During that time the cluster would be highly vulnerable, both to internal and external opportunists.

Everyone nodded. Windsor was right—and he was in charge. He sipped water before going on, "That much is fairly obvious. What's not so obvious is that even if the plan failed it would still succeed in another way."

He glanced at each of his subordinates in turn. "I refer of course to the exclusive use of alien assassins. Its purpose was to feed existing racism—while also acting to discredit me. Those who wish to may now conclude that I was not only *wrong* to advocate human-alien equality—but criminally stupid as well. Their motto will be that the only good alien is a dead alien."

"Or one who is working in a mine," Senda added calmly.

"Exactly," Windsor agreed, steepling his fingers. "However there are some bright spots in all this darkness. For one thing, the loyalty of the Governor's Hundred does much to prove that some aliens *can* be trusted, not to mention Eitor's willingness to sacrifice himself for me.

"By the way, Eitor, next time you save my life, try to do it a little less enthusiastically." Windsor's hand went up to the bandage on his forehead.

Senda grinned his upside down grin. "Well Governor, as you humans would say, robust fecal matter."

Windsor laughed. "Sometimes I think we're a bad influence on you." Turning to the others he said,

"Ever since we landed, Eitor has been pouring over
the cluster files. I've asked him to report on potential flash points. Eitor?"

"Thank you, Governor. As one would expect, Harmony Cluster has its share of problems. A major crop
failure on Siskens II, a pirate raid on Asteroid 568BX,
and the makings of a nice little civil insurrection on
Little Mektor, just to mention a few. One way or
another we will have to deal with all of them. But
our most pressing problem by far is Teller."

Getting up from his odd-looking Cernian chair,
Senda aimed a small remote at a wall and pressed a
button. There was the hum of a hidden motor; the
gray curtain slid aside to reveal a large holo tank.

"Although far from perfect, our intelligence on
Teller is fairly accurate, and there's little doubt that a
major crisis is in the making."

"Yes," Windsor agreed. "And how we deal with
the situation on Teller may very well determine the
success or failure of this entire administration."

Senda waited through the interruption with characteristic patience. Merikur knew the Cernian well
enough by now to detect a trace of annoyance in the
set of his shoulders and the look in his eyes. When
Windsor was finished the alien continued. "As some
of you know, Teller is a mining planet in one of the
cluster's major systems."

Senda pressed another button. A planet popped
into existence in the middle of the holo tank and
started to slowly turn. There wasn't anything especially remarkable about it: some good-sized mountain
ranges, lots of cloud cover and one small ocean.

"The planet is closer to Cern normal than Earth

normal, but is habitable by both races, and members of both species have lived on it for some time. Teller belongs to the Haiken Maru by right of occupation, in accordance with Pact law." The planet shimmered and disappeared, being replaced by a small city of pre-cast concrete buildings, shanties, and encroaching jungle.

"This is the planet's largest town, a charming little place called 'Port City.' As we speak, it's under virtual siege by the rebels. More on them in a moment." The city vanished and a three-dimensional organization chart appeared to replace it. Merikur saw a vertical looking structure headed by a general manager, a member of department heads, sector chiefs and other functionaries.

"Planetary government could better be described as 'planetary management,' and is exclusively comprised of Haiken Maru professionals from off planet. They run the planet to maximize profit and minimize expense. If they generate sufficient profit, they are promoted off planet. Otherwise they stay—or are sent to even worse posts. As a result their policies have been less than enlightened."

The holo shimmered and coalesced into a shot of ragged looking Cernians trudging towards the gaping mouth of a mine. In the background a Haiken Maru overseer could be seen, repulsor rifle dangling from a sling, lounging against a small hut.

"Cernians and humans, whose grandparents came to the planet as contract labor, now work in a state of virtual slavery."

"But slavery's illegal," Lieutenant Commander Moskone objected. "Surely Governor Trent would have done something."

Senda blinked both eyes in a Cernian shrug. "You are correct, Commander, slavery is illegal. Note the qualifier 'virtually.' The workers must pay the Haiken Maru for their food, for their quarters, for their medical care, for . . . everything. If a worker were extremely frugal, and extremely lucky, he or she might work their way out of debt in fifteen or twenty years. But how would they get off planet? The Haiken Maru controls everything, including the cost of transportation aboard their ships. Thus the only option for someone who manages to pay off the debt is to work as a miner for the Haiken Maru—under the same conditions as before. And as for the former governor, his representative on Teller returned to Augustine some seven months ago for medical treatment. And was never replaced."

"Which brings us to the rebels," Tenly said impatiently. "Let's get on with it."

But Senda wouldn't be hurried. "All in due time. First it is necessary to understand why the Haiken Maru brought Cernians and humans to Teller in the first place. As I said earlier, the ancestors of both groups were originally brought to Teller as contract labor. The Cernians to work the mines, and the humans to work the farms. And they weren't chosen casually. The Haiken Maru put considerable time and thought into the matter." The holo changed to show shots of Cernia.

"Cernia has a very red sun, plus large areas of triple-canopy forest. As a result, members of my race cannot tolerate direct sunlight for extended periods of time. We evolved on the forest floor, developing our green skin color as protective coloration. Due to the low light levels found there we also have excellent night vision. That, plus our short height and low incidence of claustrophobia accounts for our selection as miners." The holo shimmered, giving way to shots of emaciated-looking humans tilling fields with hand tools.

"We Cernians are vegetarians, but since we cannot work in the open the Haiken Maru brought in humans to grow our food. Humans have always been good at agriculture and can tolerate a great deal of direct sunlight. During the early times the humans were better paid and better treated than the Cernians, but that advantage has slowly slipped away; today farm humans are no better off than Cernian miners."

"Haiken Maru management regards both groups as inferior, claiming they have become so mutated and inbred that they are little better than animals." He paused. "This claim is absurd. Both groups have more than adequately large gene pools."

"Plus there's strong evidence that outside genes are sometimes added to the local pool of both species," Merikur put in dryly.

Senda's lips turned downwards. "General Merikur is correct. There is evidence of traffic between the government of Cernia and the Cernian miners. There also seems to be considerable commerce between pirates and human farmers."

"All of which brings us to the rebellion," Tenly added impatiently.

"As you wish," Senda replied patiently. "Actually the rebels are nothing new. For a long time, members of both races have escaped into the jungle. Although 'escape' doesn't accurately describe the transition from one kind of hell to another."

The holo changed to a point of view shot as the camera walked down a jungle trail. Vegetation pushed in from both sides, strange sounds came from all around, and the sun was a dim presence far above.

"The hostile environment is partly due to Teller's ecosystem which has its share of unfriendly animal and plant life. Far worse however are some off-world life-forms imported by the Haiken Maru. This is a good example."

The jungle trail dissolved into a shot of an innocent-looking, broad-leafed plant. "This is called 'Nakada,' which in the language of my people means 'painful death.' Brief contact with this plant makes us very ill, and prolonged exposure is fatal. The Haiken Maru imported this plant from Cernia and used aerial seeding to spread it across the surface of Teller."

The picture changed once more. This time it showed a large snake. "As those of you born and raised on Terra may already know, this is a fer-de-lance, a rather large and venomous reptile harmful to both races, but lethal to humans. These are examples only. The Haiken Maru have imported other hostile life-forms as well. In spite of that the rebels are not only surviving, they are by all accounts flourishing."

Senda pushed a button. The holo disappeared and the gray curtain slid closed. "I mention this for three reasons. It tells you the Haiken Maru are ruthless. It tells you the rebels are tough. And it tells you we are in deep fecal matter. Making the whole thing worse is the fact that over the last few years the rebels have received outside help."

Senda raised his eyebrows in a gesture equivalent to that of a human pursing his lips as he considered how to proceed. "It is no secret that the Cernian government is split into two factions. On one side are those who desire independence from the Pact and feel war is inevitable; on the other side are those —like myself—who favor membership in the Pact, if that membership can be obtained as full and equal partners."

For a moment there was silence in the room. Everyone knew what Senda had left unsaid. The truth was that while the Cernian Confederation would be a tough nut to crack, the central fleet would eventually win, and Cernia would be reduced to glazed rock. Weakened though it was, the Pact was still stronger than the Confederation. This more than anything else accounted for Senda's devotion to Windsor. It was Senda himself who broke the silence.

"There is little doubt that those who favor Cernian independence have smuggled arms, ammunition, and other supplies to their countrymen on Teller. Haiken Maru security forces simply aren't numerous enough to stop them, and General Merikur's predecessor made no effort to do so. In addition I suspect that a Cernian insurgency expert known as 'Jomu' has been sent to Teller. His leadership, plus the smuggled arms, have apparently tipped the balance in favor of the rebels. Jomu belongs to that fraction of our government which believes war is inevitable. It is their desire to recognize Teller as an independent state preparatory to annexing it to the Cernian Confederation. Once they secure a base on Teller, they believe their forces can withstand not only Cluster Command, but units from the central fleet as well. And even if they're wrong, Teller could still be useful as a bargaining chip in future negotiations."

"But," Senda added with one of his upside down grins, "we Cernians are not the only problem on Teller. As General Merikur once pointed out to me, some humans never give up, and the farmers of Teller are a case in point. It seems the human rebels managed to hijack a ground shipment of rare ores a year ago, and have since used it to buy arms from the pirates. They too are harassing Haiken Maru operations and laying siege to settlements. As a matter of fact the two groups seem to have entered into an uneasy alliance. Between them they've managed to slow production to a crawl. As I mentioned earlier, Port City is under siege, and contact with outlying mining and agricultural stations is via armed convoy, since aircraft are vulnerable to ground fire."

Senda smiled around the room. "To sum up, things have reached a critical stage on Teller, and we need to respond. Governor?"

As Senda took his seat Windsor stood. "Thank you, Eitor. You've done an outstanding job of pulling it all together. There's only one factor left to discuss, and that's the Haiken Maru."

He picked up a bound document and held it out for them to see. "I received this a few hours ago. You're all welcome to read it, but I'll give you an executive summary. The Haiken Maru are demanding that I send in the marines and restore peace to Teller."

Lieutenant Commander Moskone frowned. "Assuming we restored peace, and from what Eitor says it wouldn't be easy, we'd be supporting the moral equivalent of slavery."

"And almost guaranteeing war with Cernia," Von Oy added thoughtfully.

"The law is the law," Tenly countered. "It's our job to enforce it, not to make it. And if Cernia wants war we'll give it to them. Sorry Eitor . . . but that's how I feel."

Windsor nodded gravely and smiled. "You all have valid points. I must confess that I don't see an answer yet. He turned to Senda. "Eitor, I want you and Anson to leave for Teller as soon as possible. Try to find a solution everyone can live with. Anson, I can't put Eitor in charge because most humans wouldn't accept him, but I want you to follow his advice on political matters. Is that clear?"

"Yes, sir."

"Excellent. I'd go myself if I could. But unfortunately we've got other problems as well. They'll keep Captain Von Oy and myself occupied for some time. As soon as we put some of them to rest, I'll drop into Teller for a visit."

Merikur cleared his throat. "Sir?"

"Yes, Anson?"

"Who signed the communication from the Haiken Maru?"

"One Nola Rankoo."

"She tried to kill you, sir."

Windsor nodded. "She tried to kill all of us, but we don't have any proof. Or did your interrogation turn up something new?"

Two aliens had survived the ballroom massacre with only minor wounds. Merikur's intelligence people had debriefed them extensively—and gotten nothing.

It wasn't that the aliens were taciturn; on the contrary, they babbled everything they knew—but what they knew was worthless.

One prisoner had been a mercenary pure and simple; the other was a political crazy who spouted endless drivel. Neither knew who'd organized or paid for the assassination attempt. Both believed no humans were involved. Nola Rankoo and her agents had hidden their tracks well.

"Nothing new, sir," Merikur replied. "I'm afraid that's a dead end."

Windsor rocked back and forth on his feet. "That's too bad. I'd love to nail her hide to the wall. What will you do with the two assassins?"

Merikur looked Windsor in the eye. "Bury them."

Chapter 6

Merikur headed for Teller with 1,000 of his 1,500 marines and seven of his thirty ships. He had left the remainder under the command of Captain Von Oy, who would need them to keep a damper on the rest of the cluster while Merikur was gone.

Merikur was using Commander Yamaguchi's cruiser, *Resplendent*, as his flag ship. He also had two transports, two destroyers, a destroyer escort and a scout. They were two hours out of Augustine when he put the scout to use. Lieutenant Commander Moskone took two steps into Yamaguchi's day cabin, snapped to attention, and rapped out, "Lieutenant Commander Moskone reporting as ordered, sir!"

Merikur smiled. "Cut the crap, Paul, and have a seat. Coffee's over there."

Once Moskone was settled in with a cup of coffee, Merikur got down to business. "Paul, I've got a little chore I'd like you to handle." Merikur tapped a sealed document case with his right index finger. "I want you to take this to Admiral Oriana at Scorpion Base. It contains a report on what's happened so far, and a request for a thousand marines. From what we've heard about Teller I think we're gonna need 'em."

Moskone raised an eyebrow. "Whatever you say, sir, but why not dump it in a message torp?"

Merikur shook his head. "Because the Haiken Maru have an extremely effective intelligence network. If we send the message by conventional means, chances are they'll intercept it. That's why I waited till now. No one will know you're heading for Sector HQ. Take the scout. Just make damned sure nobody sees that report except Oriana. Agreed?"

Moskone gulped his coffee. "Agreed, sir. I'll have a drink at the officer club for you."

Merikur nodded. "Make it a double."

An hour later the small scout broke formation and headed for Sector Headquarters. Merikur watched it go via the ship's plotting tank. The scout was a tiny spark of red light as it swung away from the rest of the fleet and picked up speed. "Good luck, Paul," Merikur thought. "We're all going to need it."

A few minutes later Merikur headed for his cabin, the same stateroom he'd shared with Bethany on the uncomfortable trip out. At least he'd have it to himself this time.

The door slid open to reveal an enormous pile of baggage. Merikur stepped through the hatch and looked around. "Bethany, what the hell are you doing here?"

Bethany stepped out of the sleeping cabin. "Why Anson, is that any way to talk to your devoted wife?"

God, she was beautiful. She didn't even have to

work at it; she just was. He struggled to put a frown on his face. "I thought we agreed that you'd stay on Augustine . . . How did you get aboard anyhow?"

Bethany smiled. "I changed my mind. As for getting aboard, that was easy. I just told the officer on duty that you wanted me here." She paused for a second. "You *do* want me here, don't you?"

Merikur searched her face for some sign of sarcasm and saw none. His reply seemed to come without volition. "Of course I do. Welcome aboard. The sleeping cabin is all yours."

For a moment he thought she might—hoped she might . . . but instead she smiled and said, "I'll get my luggage out of your way in the next hour or two."

The trip to Teller was uneventful and quite pleasant. There were regular workouts with Eitor in the gym, and instead of dreading his stateroom as he had on the way out, Merikur looked forward to going there.

It was a haven, a hideaway from the pressures of his job where he and Bethany spent long hours together. They talked about everything, their childhoods, their likes and dislikes, everything.

Everything but her previous marriage. The trip was over all too soon.

The fleet dropped out of hyperdrive a safe distance off planet and blasted in towards Teller. A quick check revealed nothing but an old freighter and a few satellites in orbit. Nevertheless Merikur ordered the single destroyer escort and a destroyer to patrol a half light out.

If anything came his way he wanted to know about

it. In the meantime the cruiser and the remaining destroyer would provide protection for the two transports.

There were two ways he could arrive. The friendly way, "Hello, just dropped in to see if I could help," and the threatening way, "Hello, I just landed with a thousand marines. Now whose ass am I gonna kick first?" It took Merikur about ten seconds to decide on the second approach.

Like everyone else, Artha Nugumbe ran out into the street when the first sonic booms began to roll across the sky. At first she was scared. Who was it? Friend or foe? But her fears disappeared as a low-flying LCS (Landing Craft Shuttle) did a slow roll revealing its Pact design.

So the new Governor had enough balls to send in the marines. Good. Maybe there was hope after all.

She went back inside and began to summarize her reports. Maybe someone would read them for a change.

On the other side of Port City, Arthur Treeling felt his erection disappear. Climbing off the frightened farm girl he rushed to a window and threw it open. A sonic boom rolled across the town and shattered a window across the way.

Goddamn them! He'd been begging them to come for months, and now that he didn't need them, the stupid bastards were here, showing off, and destroying company property. He'd have someone's ass! The Haiken Maru was a force to be reckoned with, and Arthur Treeling was Haiken Maru's general manager on Teller, by God!

The girl had curled into a fetal ball on his bed, clenched around her tears. Treeling ignored her as he struggled to get his clothes on. A quick check in the mirror and he was gone.

The girl waited for awhile, her pulse pounding, making sure he wouldn't return. Then she unwound, swung long shapely legs over the edge of the bed, and stood. She listened for a moment. Nothing. Bending over she found the ragged dress he'd ripped off her half an hour earlier. Next to it was a pathetic looking purse fashioned from a grain bag.

Reaching inside, she withdrew a small camera and a memory matrix. Still nude in case he returned, she stepped into his office and went straight to his desk. Slipping the memory matrix into the appropriate slot in his computer terminal, she used his personal code to gain entry, and ordered a full data dump.

She smiled. The code was easy. The horny bastard didn't have enough brains to memorize it, so he'd kept it on a scrap of paper. She'd seen him refer to it earlier in the day.

While the computer whirred she sorted out the documents on top of Treeling's desk and taped their contents. Horsehide would be pleased.

Deep in Teller's verdant jungle a Cernian named Jomu looked up in eager anticipation. Maybe they were early. But instead of a Cernian lander he saw an olive-drab LCS flash by. A fraction of a second later his troops launched three missiles.

But this was no Haiken Maru security flier. The shuttle was a hardcore military ship designed to take a lot of punishment and dish out even more.

All three missiles were blown out of the sky. Seconds later a second LCS passed over and dumped a thousand anti-personnel bomblets into the area. They were still shredding the jungle when a third ship roared over and hosed the area with repulsors.

When it was all over, and Jomu emerged from his bunker, he found half his force dead. The balance of power had suddenly shifted. With characteristic calm he cut a transceiver loose from its dead operator and began to give orders.

Merikur's gig landed with the second wave. It takes a lot of LCS's to land a thousand marines, so he'd crammed ten in with him. As they jumped out the main hatch and headed for the jungle, a cheerful sergeant yelled, "Thanks for the lift sir. It's nice to arrive in style for once!" Then he was gone.

Soon the radio reports began to flood in. No opposition on the ground as yet. Elements of C company were approaching the edge of town. Three ground to air missiles had been launched and destroyed. The launching area had been sanitized. Elsewhere an LCS was missing and presumed lost. A search was underway. Meanwhile Senda's LCS had landed safely and the Cernian had disappeared into the jungle. Merikur didn't like it, but Senda had insisted.

There was coded radio traffic on freq's four, nine, and twenty-six. Some rebel, some Haiken Maru. Merikur gave orders to jam it all. Two Cernian-made courier missiles were launched from the jungle and destroyed in space. Three unidentified surveillance satellites were also destroyed. Merikur allowed the reports to wash over him as they flowed in, absorbing content, but not interfering unless someone screwed up. A good general knows when to sit down and shut up.

Two hours later C company linked up with D company to secure the city. For the moment, anyway. Merikur knew he couldn't hold Port City against a serious assault, and had no intention of attempting to do so. By nightfall C and D companies would pull back and join the defensive perimeter his engineers were throwing up.

The city would be lousy with spies, hidden weapons, and god knows what else. Besides, it belonged to the Haiken Maru, and he disliked the idea of defending it. Much better to build a base on neutral ground and see where things went.

Climbing into his troop carrier Merikur headed for town. His staff, consisting of a major, a lieutenant, and six members of the Elite Guard did likewise.

Molly Knox was at the controls, and she avoided all roads and paths whenever possible, skimming over virgin jungle instead. SOP for a landing like this. Roads, paths, and clearings are all natural spots for booby traps and ambushes. That's why they'd hold back on the hover craft and wheeled vehicles until the area could be checked out. As it was they came into town low and fast, jinking in case of snipers. There weren't any.

Port City wasn't much to look at. Most of the buildings were vaugely white and had the look of prefab warehouses and processing plants. Stuck in and around them were dorm-style buildings for lower ranking personnel linked by a system of makeshift walls and barricades. Crooked, unplanned streets meandered here and there, dead ending or continuing according to whim and necessity.

A perimeter of blackened ground surrounded the city, the ruins of buildings sticking up here and there, sacrificed to create a free-fire zone. It seemed the rebels came damned close sometimes.

Choosing an asymmetrical central square as her landing place, Knox put the carrier down with a solid thump. From what Merikur could see through a narrow view port, the city's nicer dwellings seemed to front on the square. The hatch opened with a loud whine, allowing hot, humid air to flood in. The air brought with it the faint stench of rotting vegetation laced with the more powerful odor of backed-up sewers.

Within minutes, the previously empty square was full of people all vying for attention. Merikur wore no badges of rank, but the troop carrier and the attitude of his staff made it obvious who he was. His bodyguards jumped out and took up positions all around the carrier. Their eyes scanned surrounding roofs and windows, weapons ready.

Meanwhile Knox kept a close eye on all her detectors. She planned to haul ass at the first sign of trouble.

Gesturing towards the outside Merikur said, "Sort 'em out, Major. Local officials first and then the rest."

Major Fouts was a taciturn woman with muscles on her muscles, a broad flat face, and a pug nose. Dark crescents had already formed under her arms and sweat ran down her neck. She nodded, jumped to the ground, and waded into the crowd.

Merikur wanted to get out and walk around but resisted the impulse to do so. Walking around alone in an unsecured area is one more thing generals shouldn't do. Not unless they want to provide snipers with some target practice. Besides, the carrier had better communications than a marine could carry on his back and was armored should someone dump a few tons of HE (High Explosive) into the area. It made sense to hide like a rabbit, but he still didn't like it.

Fouts returned a few minutes later with a tall black woman. "General, this is Artha Nugumbe. She's the assistant port administrator. I've also got a guy named Treeling out there. Says he's general manager for the Haiken Maru. What shall I do with him?"

The way she said it Merikur got the feeling Fouts would be delighted if the answer were, "Put one through the back of his skull."

"Let him rot, Major. I'll see Administrator Nugumbe first. Have a seat, Administrator. Sorry we don't have any refreshments to offer."

Nugumbe wore a loose blouse, some shorts, and a pair of sandals. She had a high forehead, quick brown eyes, and a nice smile. Merikur liked her at first glance.

Nugumbe smiled. "Just seeing your troops is refreshing enough, General. For months I begged Admiral Stender to send some but he didn't even reply."

Merikur wondered if the good Admiral had even seen the requests. They could've been intercepted.

Though from what he'd learned about Stender, the admiral didn't need help to convince him to avoid his duty.

"Well I'm glad somebody's happy to see us," Merikur replied. "I get the feeling there's some folks in the jungle who feel otherwise."

Nugumbe nodded soberly. "Closer than that I'm afraid, General. The rebels have spies everywhere, as does the Haiken Maru. As do I, for that matter. It's a very complicated place to live. May I ask what you intend to do?"

"Sort it all out," Merikur replied wryly. "Let's start with you. I take it you were left holding the bag when the Cluster representative returned to Augustine for medical treatment?"

"That's about the size of it," she agreed. "I'm afraid I haven't done a very good job of holding things together. The rebels have slowed production to a crawl, the Haiken Maru are more repressive than ever, and I hear rumors about ships landing in the bush."

Merikur shook his head. "It's hardly your fault. No one gave you the authority or tools to get the job done. Who controls Port City?"

"I'm supposed to, but in truth the Haiken Maru security forces do."

Merikur nodded. "I want you to take control. Weed out as many spies, rebel sympathizers and unreliables as you can. If necessary I'll assign marines to replace them. Remember though . . . I plan to withdraw towards evening. So don't bite off more than you can chew." Lieutenant!"

"Sir!" Second Lieutenant Fhad was about twenty-years old, as green as grass, and eager to make his mark. He practically quivered at the vehicle's hatch.

"Take a squad and accompany Administrator Nugumbe. Follow her orders. If Haiken Maru security people get in your way, arrest 'em."

"Sir!" Fhad's eyes were shiny with eagerness as he and a squad of marines followed Nugumbe away. God help any security people who looked crosswise at them.

Nugumbe was barely gone when Major Fouts reappeared with a natty looking man in tow. He had long, lank hair which swished around his shoulders as he moved, oily good looks, and clothes a good deal too fashionable for Teller.

"This is the one I told you about. Says he's general manager for the Haiken Maru." A broad grin slid across Fout's homely face. "Says he'll have you broken to private if you don't see him now."

"Well, I guess I'd better see him then, hadn't I? A pay cut's the last thing I need. Have a seat, Manager Treeling."

Merikur felt a buzz in his ear. "This one's wired and armed," his AID cautioned. "Be careful. Maybe you're expendable but I'm not."

Treeling eyed a fold-down seat disdainfully, brushed it off, and seated himself. He did his best to look cold and imperial. "Enjoy yourself while you can, General, because when your commanding officer hears what you've done here, you'll be lucky to come out a private."

"Oh, really," Merikur said lazily. "And just what have I done?"

Treeling puffed out his chest. "Reckless endangerment of Teller's civilian population for one. I refer of course to the aircraft which buzzed Port City at supersonic speeds. Why, I can't imagine."

"To scare the hell out of everyone," Merikur answered calmly. "Nothing like a little show of force to tighten a few sphincters. I'm surprised however. I thought the Haiken Maru wanted us to control the rebels. Have things changed?"

"Well, no," Treeling replied, suddenly crafty. "It's just that Teller's law-abiding citizens deserve more respect."

Merikur raised an eyebrow in mock astonishment. "Law-abiding citizens? And who might they be? According to my information rebels are in control of the countryside, alien and pirate ships come and go as they please, and the Haiken Maru exploits its workers under conditions of virtual slavery. Where are these law-abiding citizens hiding? Bring 'em out. I'd like to meet 'em."

Things were becoming distinctly uncomfortable inside the carrier, and Treeling had a sudden desire to be elsewhere. He tried to muster some righteous indignation nonetheless. "I don't know what you've heard, but I assure you that our workers are well-treated and well-paid. As for the rest, my company can hardly be held responsible for the government's incompetence."

Merikur nodded thoughtfully. "Now there we agree. The previous government was lax in carrying out its responsibilities on Teller. That has changed, as my presence testifies. With that in mind, perhaps we can pool our resources to resolve the present difficulties."

Treeling managed an ingratiating smile. "Of course. I hope you'll forgive my earlier comments, but things have been somewhat tense around here. Tell me, how many marines did you bring?"

"Enough to do the job," Merikur lied. "Provided of course that I have the Haiken Maru's full cooperation."

"Oh yes," Treeling said eagerly. "You can be assured of that. How can I help?" If Merikur were suddenly coming around . . . Well, in the long run if he couldn't get him cashiered perhaps he could have him killed; in the short run maybe he'd better cooperate.

"The loan of some ground vehicles would be a good start," Merikur answered thoughtfully. "We've got our own of course, but there never seems to be enough to go around."

"I'll have some assigned to you right away. Just give me a call if there's anything else I can do." He got up and moved towards the hatch.

Merikur nodded amicably. "I'll do that."

Treeling waved and was gone. Merikur gave him a moment to clear the area and said, "Major Fouts!"

Like magic she appeared in the hatch. "Sir?"

"Have that one watched."

"Yes sir."

Treeling didn't feel safe until he was half a mile away. He hadn't risen to his present rank without being a pretty good judge of character, and Merikur scared hell out of him. Most generals were mere functionaries who wore the uniform but didn't like to get it dirty. This guy was different. He had orders to pacify the planet and intended to do so.

Would do so if he had enough marines; and while that would have been good a few months earlier, it would be a disaster now. The Haiken Maru would be on the wrong side of the fence, Nola Rankoo would

be very unhappy, and Treeling would wind up sucking vacuum as a one-man asteroid. The thought made
him sweat. So did Merikur have enough marines to
do the job or not?

Treeling rushed to his office and activated his com
unit. A distant part of his mind noticed the girl had
left. No problem. There were lots more where she'd
come from. He spent the next two hours talking with
as many of his subordinates as possible. He couldn't
talk with all of them because the rebels had blown
up quite a few of his relay stations, and someone, the
navy most likely, was jamming his satellite communications.

Nevertheless, Treeling soon had an accurate picture of Merikur's force, including how many marines
he had on the ground, and how many ships he had in
orbit. It all added up to around a thousand marines,
two thousand max, and that wasn't enough to bring
the rebels under control.

His security people swore it would take forty thousand or more.

Treeling gave a sigh of relief and leaned back in
his chair. He'd made the right choice after all. Soon
he'd be promoted.

Treeling picked up his handset and called a nearby
farm to send a girl over to help him celebrate.

"So," Lieutenant Commander Moskone said, as he
placed the sealed container on Admiral Oriana's desk,
"the general ordered me to deliver this to you
personally."

"And you have son, you have," Oriana said agreeably. "I'll read it immediately. Meanwhile you must

be ready for a little rest and relaxation. Why don't you head on over to the O club and have a drink on me?"

"Why thank you sir," Moskone replied happily. "I'd like that." He stood to attention and snapped off a smart salute. "By your leave sir."

Oriana returned the salute with a casual wave. "Carry on."

As soon as Moskone was gone Oriana opened the case and withdrew the document. It was short and to the point. Someone had made an attempt on Windsor's life, all hell was about to break loose on a mining planet called Teller, and Merikur wanted another thousand marines to deal with it.

The admiral shook his head sadly. Merikur meant well, but he was obviously caught up in forces beyond his understanding.

Oriana heard the door open behind him. "He's gone. You can come out now. You'll want to see this."

Oriana turned his chair slightly and handed Merikur's report to Nola Rankoo.

Chapter 7

Three days after landing on Teller, Merikur did something generals shouldn't do. With Nugumbe's help and Treeling's acquiescence, he had gained control of Port City and the surrounding area. He'd also established a strong base just outside town. The rebels had attacked it twice, though not in strength, and were driven off both times. In spite of that, they still controlled most of the countryside while his own forces were forted up.

Mining Station 458 was a case in point.

Weeks before the Cernian rebels had used their knowledge of mining to tunnel their way into the compound. Deciding the eight-person Haiken Maru security team was unworthy of their efforts, the rebels waited for an even better target, and got one when Merikur sent twelve marines to reinforce the station. The rebels attacked it that night and wiped it out.

The attack had come about dusk. By prearranged signal the workers left the compound through holes cut in the fence. Seconds after the last one left, a

103

computer-controlled mortar barrage marched across the compound. Seconds later, both the security personnel and the marines were behind their weapons waiting for the attack. Unfortunately they were looking in the wrong direction; the rebels came boiling up out of the ground behind them.

Merikur could imagine their terror as enemy troops appeared out of nowhere.

The screams as the butchery began.

He could still hear the calm voice of Staff Sergeant Higgins on the radio. "Blue dog to base. We have fifty, repeat fifty hostiles inside our perimeter. Entry made via existing tunnels. Repeat, entry made via existing tunnels. Request air strike on our position. Repeat, request air strike on our position. And base, after you kill these bastards, be sure to have a beer for us. Blue dog out."

His throat tight with emotion, Merikur ordered an air strike on Mining Station 458. Twelve minutes and thirty-eight seconds later two LCS's screamed out of the sunset and slagged the entire area.

Everything died. Cernians, humans, the six-legged lizards which infested the compound, everything.

And now Merikur felt a need to see it. To try and pull some kind of meaning from it. He could have, and should have called for Sergeant Knox and his troop carrier. But he was tired of bodyguards, tired of sixteen-hour days, and tired of being a general. He slipped out and fired up the aircar Treeling had placed at his disposal.

It was a fancy model and came to life with a pleasing hum. Merikur closed the canopy over his head, settled back into the comfort of the genuine Nek-hide seats, and lifted off.

As the ground dropped away he saw a tiny figure run out of the command center and look up. He thought it might be Major Fouts, but he couldn't be sure. Whoever it was ran towards the parking area where his troop carrier waited. Merikur grinned sourly.

Banking right he headed out over virgin jungle. By the time the troop carrier lifted he'd be long gone. Station 458 was about a hundred miles away; at two hundred miles an hour he'd be there in no time at all.

"Time to earn your keep," Merikur told his AID. "Give this heap the coordinates for Mining Station 458."

There was a momentary pause before the AID answered. "The coordinates have been transmitted and checked. Should we be traveling alone?"

Merikur groaned. "Not you too. Aren't you getting just a little paranoid for a fancy computer?"

"I'm *not* a computer, fancy or otherwise," the device replied resentfully. "However there's some truth in what you say. Lately I have been oddly concerned with my own continuance."

"Terrific," Merikur replied. "Well, do me a favor and worry quietly."

Reaching down, he flipped a series of switches and pushed a button. An indicator light went from red to blue as the autopilot kicked in and Merikur removed his hands from the controls.

Leaning back in his seat, Merikur watched the jungle canopy flash below as the aircar chased its own shadow across the land. Every now and then he'd pass over a dark canyon and catch the glint of water twinkling far below. To either side, vast flocks of green bi-winged birds rose to circle above the jungle. As one flock took to the air, another settled into the treetops.

Were they taking turns eating insects Merikur couldn't see? Or just having fun? There was no way to tell.

For a time his anger and guilt abated as Merikur lost himself in the warmth of the sun and the almost hypnotic beauty of the jungle below. "Hey, your generalship, according to my calculations the remains of Station 458 are a few miles ahead, and this crate hasn't slowed down. I suggest you check the autopilot."

His AID was getting paranoid again.

He reached down, flicked three switches into the "off" position, and hit a button. The indicator light stayed blue. Now *he* was concerned.

Merikur ran through the sequence again. Still no result. The autopilot was locked on. The aircar would fly until it ran out of fuel and crashed into whatever happened to be below. He glanced at the fuel gauge. Three quarters full. The aircar would travel another two thousand miles before going down.

A rock began to grow in his gut. A hundred miles of jungle was one thing, a long walk but possible, two-thousand miles was damned unlikely. He ran through the switches one more time. Still no reaction. He turned the radio on. Dead. No static, no indicator light. His lips made a straight line. This was no accident. Someone had sabotaged the car. He pulled his sidearm. "Can you reach base from here?"

"Affirmative," his AID replied. "But are you sure you want me to? Whoever sabotaged the aircar is waiting for you to crash. If I send a signal to base, they'll know you're alive and send someone to finish the job."

The AID was right. Although the part about being alive was subject to change during the crash.

"Good point. Well here goes nothing."

Merikur climbed into the back seat, strapped himself in, and aimed his handgun at the control panel. He fired three times. Exploding glass beads chewed their way through the panel and the wiring behind.

The engine died, the nose dropped, and the aircar screamed towards the ground. In the few available seconds Merikur thought about Bethany and wondered how she'd feel if he died. Would she care? Or would she rejoice in her new-found freedom? She was up there somewhere, beyond the blue sky, safe in orbit. God, she was beautiful.

And then he hit.

Strangely enough it was the jungle which saved him. Any other surface would have flattened the aircar, and him with it. But the triple canopy jungle had just enough give, just enough resiliency, to cushion the crash.

That didn't make it a pleasant experience.

The aircar hit the tree tops and bounced like a flat stone skipping on a pond. It fell again. This time the car crashed down through the treetops to hit the second layer of jungle growth.

Merikur was smashed back and forth against his restraints as the world outside the canopy whirled and skidded. Then the bottom of his stomach dropped out as the aircar fell another thirty feet into the lowest layer of vegetation.

A tree trunk was waiting a fraction of a second later. He blacked out.

"Wake up, your generalship. I can read your vital signs so I know you aren't dead. You're just screwing off. Laying down on the job when you should be up and at it. Come on, dumb shit, you just made a huge hole in the jungle. In a few minutes everything for miles around is going to come looking for you. Animals, rebels—you name it."

"Dumb shit?" Merikur sat up, or tried to. The restraints held him down. "Who the hell are you calling a dumb shit?"

"Ooops. Sorry. I got carried away. But you should get the hell out of here nonetheless."

"Roger." Merikur hit the quick release on his harness and felt it fall away. He moved and the car moved with him. He paused and looked out through the shattered canopy. No wonder the car swayed. It was fifty or sixty feet off the ground, resting in a cradle of vines and branches.

Moving with great care, he managed to crawl forward. Opening the console which separated the two front seats he gave a sigh of relief. The standard survival kit was still there. Either they hadn't expected him to survive the crash, or they hadn't thought to remove it. Either way it improved his chances.

Slipping his arms through the straps, he heaved the small pack onto his back. Now he had to work his way out of the car. Slowly, planning each move before he made it, Merikur climbed up and out.

Grabbing a thick vine he heaved himself up and away. Looking back, he saw how crumpled the car was. He'd been very, very lucky.

It took Merikur a full half hour to work his way to the ground via the network of trees, larger plants, and interlocking vines. Once a branch broke, and dropped him into a network of vines, and twice he almost fell, but managed to catch himself.

He descended through a land of perpetual twilight.

Sunlight was a rare and precious commodity on the jungle floor, much sought after, and rarely found. Where it touched there was life, and where it couldn't reach, death held sway.

But death was a transitional state. As plants died they quickly decomposed to feed the living and were therefore born again. Merikur felt a sense of awe as he looked upwards. The forest was so huge and so complicated that it dwarfed the races who fought over it. Humid warmth closed in around him and he wondered why Teller had no sentient species of its own, when other, seemingly less hospitable planets did.

"If it isn't too much trouble, you might get your butt in gear," the AID said sarcastically. "I have six, maybe seven unknowns headed our way. Body mass and infrared patterns are a ninety-percent match with Cernian body type."

"How long?"

"Five minutes max."

Merikur looked around for a place to hide. The trees were a natural, but he wasn't agile enough to get up there and find a place to hide in the allotted time. There were probably some hidey-holes in and around the huge tree trunks too; but once again, there wasn't enough time.

So, following as best he could the ancient military dictum that the best defense is a good offense, Merikur laid an ambush. Pulling his sidearm, he jumped into a hollow formed by two huge roots. He placed his weapon in his lap and reached out to pull a double armful of dead leaves over him. They smelled musty.

He lay back and closed his fingers around the coolness of the pistol grip. As ambushes went, it wasn't much—but it'd have to do.

As the sounds of the jungle closed in around him, Merikur told himself it was no big deal. He'd faced worse odds in simulation and come out alive.

Suddenly he remembered his last run at Sector HQ and the burning pain between his shoulder blades. The APE's had fried him that time. He forced himself to lie perfectly still and listen.

"One minute."

He knew no one else could hear, but it seemed as though the AID was shouting.

He heard them. Feet scuffling through dry leaves, an unintelligible murmur of conversation, and the clink of metal on metal. For a moment he considered remaining where he was. Maybe they'd miss him, walk right on by, and he'd be O.K.

"And maybe they brought you a picnic lunch too," he thought as he sat up and opened fire.

Mother Mista had been leading her family for a year now, and even though she was jungle wise, she'd never been ambushed before. The Haiken Maru security forces had no taste for the jungle and were too few in number to wage true counter-insurgency warfare. As a result, the Cernian rebels were used to one-sided situations in which they attacked convoys and mining stations but themselves only faced defensive fire. Jomu and the other leaders had tried to train them in every aspect of jungle combat, but without the leavening of personal experience, the training could only be partly effective.

So as Mother Mista approached the crash site her weapon was slung across her back, her eyes were on the crumpled shape of the aircar far above, and her mind was working out the problem of climbing up to it.

She never saw the shape that came up out of the forest floor, or felt the small explosion which blew half her chest away, or understood why she died.

The radio operator went next: Merikur had identified him by his long whip antenna, and put him down before he could even think about calling for help. They'd been bunched up, the fools, so he had an accurate count; two down, four to go.

He caught the third rebel with two rounds in the abdomen and felt something whip by his head. Whap! Whap! Whap!

Glass beads hit the tree trunk behind him, severing one of the tree's major arteries. Green coolant gushed out to soak his right leg. High above, an entire section of leaves over-heated in the direct sunlight and died.

Back on the forest floor number four screamed as her jaw disappeared. The screaming stopped as another bead went through her visor and finished exploding between her eyes.

Merikur threw himself to the right. A stream of

glass ripped past into the tree, blasting away huge chunks of the soft porous wood and cutting through its digestive system.

White sap spurted out to soak the jungle floor. Just below the surface, dormant seeds sensed the presence of food and opened themselves to take it in.

The last two had made it to cover and had plenty of time to get their weapons ready.

Merikur rolled over a plant with a single white blossom and came up running. He screamed. A Cernian fell for it; she stuck her head up and he blew it off.

Then searing pain ripped across the front of his right thigh. As he fell, the open wound came into contact with his coolant-soaked pant leg and laced his body with agony.

He awoke to a sharp pain that verged on agony shooting up his right leg. There was also a deep throbbing background of general pain, but it was the leg which demanded his attention.

So did his AID, which, he now realized, had been maintaining a steady drum beat of "wake up, wake up, wake up . . ." Realizing that Merikur was again aware; "Well it's about time," the AID said. "I suggest you get up before the jungle recycles your ass."

Startled at the effort required, Merikur opened his eyes. Only the tiniest bit of sunlight filtered down through the array of foliage. Night was coming. He had to get moving, find shelter, fix food, before the murk was transformed to utter blackness. The necessities of survival spurred him into a sitting position.

Looking down at his major source of pain, he froze

in horror. His AID had been speaking literally. A long brown tendril had snaked its way up through the jungle floor to plant its head in the open wound. The vine jerked spasmodically.

It was eating him!

He saw the swaying tips of other tendrils all around, twitching as they pushed their way a little closer to a meal. Reaching down, Merikur's hand found the handle of his combat knife. He slashed through the first tendril and saw the rest quiver in sympathy. A single organism then.

Favoring his right leg, Merikur stood and limped out of the feeding circle.

Then he saw the five mounds. The surviving Cernian had scraped out shallow graves for his comrades. All were encased in networks of pulsating vines as their bodies were broken down and consumed by the voracious jungle. "He buried them and left," his AID said. "You looked dead, so he assumed that you were. Luckily you didn't rate a burial."

Merikur looked around. "My handgun?"

"Beats me," the AID replied, "but chances are he took it with him."

"Terrific."

"Things could be worse," the AID commented cheerfully. "You still have me."

"Great," Merikur replied. "If I see a rebel, I'll throw you at him."

He knew of course that the AID was worth far more than his weapon. Before he had boarded for the passage from Augustine, the AID had downloaded every recorded datum about Teller, its ecosystems and geography. On top of which its sensors consistently warned him of trouble long before trouble arrived.

Merikur looked around but saw no sign of either his weapon or those carried by the rebels. Well, at least he still had the survival kit on his back and the combat knife in his hand. They'd have to do.

Limping a little, he set out through the trees to put some distance between himself and the crash site. As soon as the surviving rebel reached camp and reported to someone with a triple-digit I.Q., they'd come looking for him in a big way.

As day faded into night Merikur limped east, away from Port City. With luck they'd concentrate the search in the wrong direction. Soon he was tripping over tree roots and falling into hollows. The third time it happened he decided to hell with it.

He'd gone as far as he could. It was time to rest and make repairs.

Merikur shrugged out of the survival kit, pulled it around, and opened it. It contained a little bit of everything.

After some fumbling he found a small flash and turned it on. Holding it with his teeth, he used his hands to pull his pant leg away from the wound. Where he expected to see an open wound there was a greenish scab. "What the hell?"

"Problems?" the AID asked. While the AID had a variety of sensors it had nothing equivalent to direct sight and couldn't see Merikur's leg.

Merikur described the scab to his mechanical side-kick. "Don't worry about it," the AID told him. "The coolant from that particular tree has an astringent effect. The Haiken Maru even harvests some of the stuff and sells it off planet. Not much of a market but every credit counts. Even though it hurt, it did you a world of good."

"Easy for you to say," Merikur replied caustically, "since you never feel pain." There was silence for a moment as Merikur put a bandage on his wound. When the AID replied there was a hint of sadness in his words.

"What you say is true . . . but I never experience pleasure either."

Merikur considered that as he popped a pain pill and returned the first-aid kit to the pack. "That's only partly true. While you can't experience physical pleasure, nothing stops you from enjoying the other kinds."

"What other kinds?"

Merikur rummaged around for something which didn't require water. There wasn't any near at hand and he wasn't about to go looking. He found a high-energy ration bar. "The cerebral pleasures."

"For example?"

Merikur took a bite. The ration bar was chewy and slightly sweet. "For example, the way you feel when I ignore your advice and wind up in trouble as a result."

"Like taking the aircar and traveling alone?"

Merikur grimaced. "Yes, like taking the aircar and traveling alone."

"Oh," the AID said. Then after a moment's thought it added, "You know, you're right! That does feel good! Thanks."

Combat knife in his right hand, Merikur curled up in a ball and awkwardly pulled dead leaves over himself, more for insulation than camouflage. "You're welcome. Okay, sleepless wonder, you have the perimeter watch. If anything approaches I want to know about it."

"No problem. Good night."

"Good night," Merikur replied, and in spite of mysterious noises all around him, fell quickly asleep.

Merikur awoke to the sound of distant thunder. For a moment that was the only sound that disturbed the jungle's early morning silence; the next it was filled with the sound of rain against a billion leaves.

Within minutes it had dripped, gurgled, and sloshed all around him, collected in the bottom of his hollow and drove him out. Small, eel-like creatures oozed out of the mud to flop and slither as the rain turned the hollow into a temporary pond. When the rain stopped, and the pond was absorbed into the earth, they would go with it, estivating until the next downpour.

"Good thing I'm water proof," his AID said.

By now Merikur was soaked to the skin. "Yes," he replied dryly. "Thank God for that." Spotting a huge plant with broad leaves he squished his way over and stood in front of it. "If I take shelter will it eat me?"

"Nope. Go for it."

Merikur stepped under the plant's leaves and out of the rain. He looked around. "Which way is home?"

The quickness of the answer told him the AID had already considered the matter. "You have two choices. You can head west on foot, which will improve your chances of going undetected, or you can head north. If you head north you'll hit a mining road about

thirty miles from here. Both the Haiken Maru and
the rebels use the road, so the chances of discovery
rise dramatically. On the other hand, the chances of
hitching a ride into Port City also rise dramatically,
which would cut five or six days off the trip."

Merikur considered his alternatives. The safer route
was a *lot* safer. He'd be damned hard to find in the
middle of all that jungle. But there was the time
factor to consider. He needed to get back as soon as
possible. God knows what might happen in his absence. Someone had arranged for him to die. Who?

The rebels were an obvious choice, but the aircar
had been supplied by the Haiken Maru, so they
were suspect too. But why would they want him
dead when he was ostensibly there to protect company interests?

There were too many questions and too few answers; but one thing was clear. If someone wanted
him out of the way time was of the essence; he'd go
for the road, and rely on his skill and good luck to
get him through.

And while luck was a problematic factor, his skills
were not inconsiderable. Like all officers, Merikur
had been through an extensive survival course at the
Academy and numerous refreshers since graduation.

One of the things they'd taught him was to
improvise.

Merikur used his combat knife to lop some leaves
off the plant, piling them at his feet. Cutting some
lengths of mono-filament line from the reel in his
survival kit, he overlapped the leaves like the shin-
gles on a shake roof, then tied them together to

make a crude rain cape. A conical leaf hat completed his new outfit.

He stepped out into the rain. His rain gear leaked a little, but it was much better than nothing at all.

So far so good. Glancing around he saw a thicket of eight-foot sticks topped by frothy purplish foliage. Stepping close to the thicket so the AID could use all its sensors Merikur asked, "How 'bout this one?"

The AID was silent for a moment before replying. "I suggest you throw something at it first."

Kicking into the forest detritus, Merikur found a rock. He pried it up and saw all sorts of little things go skittering in every direction. But he wasn't that hungry. Not yet. Checking to make sure none had adhered to the underside of the rock, he chucked it into the thicket.

To his amazement one of the rigid sticks suddenly collapsed into a seven-foot snake. Coiling in on itself, a deadly looking head emerged from a collar of purplish skin and darted this way and that, seeking either food or foe—or both. Seeing neither through its single, apparently nearsighted eye, it slithered away.

Merikur watched it go and shook his head in amazement. "Good suggestion."

Stepping up to the thicket he selected a sturdy looking shaft and cut it off near the ground. He trimmed the foliage and tied his combat knife to one end with some more mono-filament. A spear, as any caveman can tell you, beats the hell out of a knife. Why stick something from up close and intimate when you can do it from six or seven feet away? Not to mention the additional leverage a spear provides.

Deciding to delay breakfast until the rain had stopped, Merikur glanced at his compass and headed north. Within a single rotation of the planet, he'd been reduced from a general with starships at his command, to a lonely, leaf-clad spear chucker. He'd had better days.

Chapter 8

As Jomu allowed his gaze to drift down across the computer screen, his mouth turned upwards in disapproval. All the reports agreed. Things weren't going well. Yes, his forces continued to control the countryside; yes, there was less and less money flowing into Haiken Maru coffers—but there was a long list of reverses as well.

The marines were in control of Port City; their firebase on the outskirts of town was too strong for his forces; and their leader was unusually competent for a human.

Making matters even worse was news of a mysterious Cernian who, if rumor could be believed, served as an advisor to the new governor, and who had disappeared into the jungle. Who was he? And more importantly, *where* was he and what was he doing?

If the stranger were part of the Cernian faction favoring a hard line with the Pact—Jomu's faction—he would have come announced. Was he instead soliciting Pact support among the miners? If so he might just get it.

Some Cernians continued to cling to the foolish hope that humans would change their ways and allow Cernia full membership in the Pact. Jomu coughed a laugh. That would be the day.

Well, time would tell. In spite of the marines, Teller was almost in the rebels grasp. In a few more days, a week at most, Jomu's fingers would close on the planet and never let go.

Jomu heard a floor board creak as Varek shifted his weight from one foot to the other. He'd been standing at attention in Jomu's makeshift office for half a zek now and should be quite penitent. Jomu found it useful to keep his subordinates waiting.

Especially when they'd performed as poorly as Varek had. The idiot had walked away from a dead— he'd *better* have been dead!—human officer without even searching the body.

A heavily armed patrol was already on its way to the ambush site. Who knew what data or device the human might have had about his person?

Raising his eyes from the computer screen, Jomu looked at Varek as if viewing a guwat. In truth, Varek wasn't a bad looking specimen. His homemade combat harness gleamed with polish, and his body was broad and muscular. At the moment his eyes were focused respectfully on Jomu's right ear; only equals engaged in mutual eye-to-eye contact.

"So," Jomu began. "A moron stands before me. Or is it a coward who runs from dead humans?"

"Yes, father, I mean no, father," Varek stammered, his leathery features wrinkled with misery. "I am a fool, but no coward."

For a moment Jomu said nothing, allowing the

silence to build. Then, "I agree. You are a fool but no coward. Therefore you may live. But you are hereby stripped of all status. In addition to any other duties you may be judged competent to perform you will make yourself available for all extra-labor details for a period of one year. Return to your unit."

"Yes, father. Thank you, father." Varek did a smart about-face and marched towards the door. A year of K.P. was a lot less punishment than he had feared.

As Varek left, a com tech entered. She was no escapee from a mining camp but a Cernian regular smuggled in three months before. She was extremely competent. The fact that she was also quite attractive was an added bonus. She snapped to attention.

Jomu waved a hand. "Save it for the troops, Jund. What have you got?" He expected a smile but didn't get one. Bad news then.

"The patrol reported in a few bix ago, father. They found the aircar and the graves. But no sign of a human body."

Jomu's massive fist crashed down so hard the computer console jumped. "He's still alive! Alert all units. I want this human *found*, and I want him found *now*."

The rain had stopped, and from the level of ambient light Merikur guessed that the sun was at zenith. But Merikur had a problem. The river was full and fast, running up to the edge of its banks, where it lapped at Merikur's boots. Wavelets splashed his toes occasionally as if inviting him to jump in so that it could sweep him away. Since he had to get across, that left the log.

Months before, a raging storm had caused the
river to flood, undermining a huge tree and causing
it to keel over. The trunk now formed an impromptu
bridge across the river. The only such bridge he'd
been able to find in a five-mile section of river bank.
It stretched before him like a shining path to Hell.

Spray leaped up to make its smooth surface even
slicker, and the log dipped a little ways out, allowing
the river to roll over the top. But it was either the
log or what might turn out to be a long, long detour.

First however he took the spear apart and restored
the combat knife to its sheath. Otherwise he'd lose it
if he fell in. He checked to make sure the survival kit
was securely fastened to his back.

For a moment he debated whether to walk or
crawl. Both had advantages. In the end he decided
to walk and drop to his knees if it became necessary.
Using the roots as a staircase he made his way up and
onto the log.

Gingerly, Merikur moved out onto its smooth surface. He slid his left foot forward, then his right. So
far so good.

The river leaped, jumped and chuckled at his feet,
daring him to move forward, laughing at his caution.
Using his staff as a counterbalance, Merikur ignored
the river's insinuating laughter and concentrated on
the stretch ahead.

It was the bad section, where the tree trunk
swooped down towards the river, and water rolled
over the top. Bit by bit, Merikur eased down the
incline. The water had little force where it sloshed
across the top, so the main danger lay in slipping.

Edging his way through the water, Merikur started

up the opposite slope. By climbing sideways, and using the non-skid surface of his combat boots, Merikur made his way up the slope. First a third of the way, then halfway, then almost there.

That's when the two person hovercraft roared around the bend and came straight at him.

It had not occurred to Merikur, until he flipped over backwards and was immediately sucked under, that his entry into the river would be a voluntary act.

The first sensation was shock as the cold water closed around him. Then he felt fear as the river dragged him down, bouncing him along the bottom. What saved him was training; suddenly he was a cadet standing at the edge of the computer-controlled river which flowed through the Academy's huge campus, shivering in the morning chill. In front of him the river was smooth and calm, but just a few hundred yards downstream white water gleamed and churned its way through artificial rapids, smoothing out again further on down. Each cadet would have to jump in and make it through those rapids.

He remembered Nidifer's sadistic grin. Nidifer was more machine than man, one of the few survivors of the famous Ferro Drop. Five thousand marines had fallen through Ferro's noxious atmosphere to fight in the crystalline forests below. Less than a hundred survived. Those who did were the toughest, meanest, and luckiest people alive.

A fact Nidifer never let them forget. As if his face wasn't reminder enough. The single glaring eye, the gouged-out face, the rasping voice, all were constant reminders that this man had been through hell and fought his way out.

So when Nidifer spoke it was with the voice of authority. "You cretins will be glad to hear that this course has only killed five cadets so far."

He held up a gleaming pincer to still any objection. "Yes, I realize this course it too easy, but so far Academy Command has ignored my requests to make it more challenging." His expression brightened.

"You *could* kill yourself by forgetting these simple rules however: One. Do not fight the river. Two. Hit the boulders with your feet instead of your head. Three. Work your way to the side where the current is weaker. Four. Don't panic. Think instead. Questions, ladies and gentlemen?"

Nidifer's single eye swept their naked ranks like a laser. "No? Then how about you, Cadet Merikur? Since shit floats, you shouldn't have any trouble at all."

The river pushed Merikur up, gave him one quick gulp of air, and then jerked him back down. Twisting and turning he managed to bring his feet around and point them down-river.

He hit the first boulder. His boots felt as if they weighed a ton apiece, but they helped absorb the shock. Flexing his knees with each impact, he bounced off two more rocks before the current brought him back to the surface. Gulping air, he saw the hovercraft waiting down river.

This time he ducked under the surface on purpose.

The rapids were past now, but the river had narrowed slightly as it passed through a huge rock formation, and that made the water move even faster. Feeling the main current to his left Merikur slid into it and was pulled quickly downstream.

His lungs began to burn, demanding that he open his mouth and take the river in. To hell with the hovercraft. He had to breathe. Fighting his way to the surface, Merikur took a deep, gasping breath.

The river had tired of its human toy and tossed him aside. The current disappeared; and he was swimming in a side eddy. Something bumped him from behind. Turning he saw he'd been pushed into an alcove of rock carved by a million years of running water.

There was a roar over and above the roar of the river. Kicking with his feet he pushed himself back into the alcove just as the hovercraft slid into view.

It held two Cernians. Both were scanning the surface of the river looking for him. Keeping low Merikur ducked behind a spur of rock. They searched the area for ten minutes, coming within twenty feet of him on one occasion, before finally giving up and heading down river.

Heaving a sigh of relief Merikur swam along the rock face until it gave way to a small gravelly beach. Gratefully he crawled out and lay shivering on the warm rocks.

"Well, it was probably the longest river crossing in the history of the corps, but you finally made it. Congratulations."

Merikur would have pulled the AID off his belt and smashed it with a rock, but he didn't have the strength. He ignored the device and crawled into the jungle for a rest.

It took him three days to cover the thirty miles from the crash site to the dirt road. It wasn't much fun. Once in a while he found a game trail going vaguely north and could follow it for a while, but most of the time he wasn't that lucky and had to make his own way through the jungle maze.

There were countless streams and rivers to cross, torrential storms to wait out, and swamps to circumnavigate. He had close calls with specimens of a hundred nasty life-forms, some native to Teller, and some brought in by the Haiken Maru to make the jungle even more unpleasant. The latter were an unnecessary expenditure of effort, in Merikur's opinion.

The least difficult to deal with were the broadleafed Cernian Nakada plants. Though not fatal to humans, contact with the plants could produce some very unpleasant symptoms, and Merikur had enough problems already.

Of more concern were the Terran fer-de-lance, the Noolu night cat, and the Corvall death disk. The latter had an uncanny ability to masquerade as a giant leaf.

From its perch twenty or thirty feet up, the death disk would watch a path below, waiting for something to pass by. Spotting a target, the disk would spin down from above to slap itself across nose and mouth, a thousand little suckers holding it firmly in place. As its prey slowly suffocated, the creature started to feed, sucking its victim's bodily fluids until it had transformed itself into a green ball. Sated, it would release its grip, and roll away from the now desiccated corpse to digest its meal. Three months later it had shrunk to a disk once more and had begun the long torturous journey up into the trees.

The first attack had come with mind-numbing swiftness. Only the disk's poor luck saved Merikur. The creature slapped itself across his nose and eyes, missing his mouth. Merikur gripped an edge and ripped the death disk off before it could lock itself in place. Throwing it down, he impaled it with his spear.

After that, Merikur constructed a wicker-work mask that fit over his head. Without knowing it he had reinvented the masks worn by Corvall's primitive bipeds. It was damned uncomfortable but worth it.

With the mask on the death disks were more annoyance than danger. They'd come spinning down and slap themselves across the wickerwork; then he'd peel them off and spear them. After a while it became fairly routine.

Nonetheless it felt damned good to see the road and take off the mask.

The road wasn't much to look at. An unpaved two-lane affair, it was rough and followed the meandering path of a large river through the jungle. The shoulder was scorched where a flame thrower had been used to clear the vegetation.

The jungle wanted the road back. In the fullness of time, the jungle would get it.

Merikur had a sudden appreciation of what the Haiken Maru security forces were up against when they tried to move convoys down roads like this. Every curve could conceal an ambush. Every square foot of road could hide a mine.

He made a mental note. Treeling had been after him to provide his convoys with marine escorts. No damned way.

Merikur carved out a place for himself just inside

the edge of the jungle and sat down to think. His
problems were far from over. According to his AID,
both the Haiken Maru and rebels used the road. The
Haiken Maru during the day, when they stood a
better chance against attack, and the rebels at night,
when they were less likely to be detected.

The rebels were clearly his enemies, but since the
Haiken Maru could have sabotaged his aircar, he
couldn't assume they were friends. That ruled out
anything like stepping out onto the road and flagging
down the next vehicle. "I say old chap, how 'bout a
lift to town?"

Merikur smiled at the thought. No, it would have
to be something unexpected, something sneaky. The
only problem was he couldn't think of anything unexpected or sneaky.

Morning slipped into afternoon as Merikur waited
and tried to come up with a plan. As the hours
passed he thought of all sorts of possibilities. He
could use a power cutter to fall a huge tree across the
road, and then, when a vehicle was forced to stop,
use a repulsor rifle to pick off the machine's occu-
pants as they stepped out to investigate.

Unfortunately he didn't have a power cutter, or a
repulsor; and even if he had, the tree would stop
only wheeled traffic. Ground-effect vehicles would
go up and over.

Of course he could use his AID to contact base,
but the reasons to avoid that were as good as they
had been when his car went down. He was still
sitting, munching on a ration bar, when the first
vehicle went by.

It was headed east, the opposite direction from

where he wanted to go, and was buttoned up tight. Thick armor protected both sides, a wire cutter was welded to the front bumper, and the vehicle bristled with auto repulsors.

There was a trailer hooked on behind which was loaded with boxes of something and covered with a tarp. Both vehicles were of Pact manufacture but there was no way to tell who was at the wheel. The rebels had captured plenty of Haiken Maru equipment. Not an easy nut to crack even with a squad of marines.

"Give up?" It was his AID.

"Yeah," Merikur replied sourly. "I give up. So smart ass, what's the answer?"

"I wondered if you'd ever ask," the AID replied smugly. "The answer is to wait for a west-bound vehicle, find a place where it has to slow down, and climb aboard. As you do, I'll transmit something unintelligible to their comset, and divert their attention."

Merikur considered his AID's proposal as he chewed the last mouthful of ration bar. It sure beat the hell out of sitting on his ass in the jungle. Merikur tucked the ration bar wrapper into his pack, squirmed into the shoulder straps, and stood. "Looks like you're finally earning your keep," Merikur said looking up and down the road. "I'll head west looking for a good spot while you make sure no one catches me in the open."

"Yes sir, your generalship sir, don't worry about a thing."

There was a spring in Merikur's step as he set out. He imagined himself finding the perfect spot just around the next bend. Hours later he'd gone around lots of bends without finding the right spot.

Someone had done a nice job of laying the road out. Still, there were bound to be a few bad spots and he'd find them. In the meantime it was getting dark and he was tired.

Retreating into the jungle he found a protected hollow, pulled the tab on the last of his dinners, and waited for it to heat up. Stew again. Not as good as the ration bars, but a lot better than nothing.

He had just finished when the AID spoke in his ear. "Something coming . . . a lot of something . . . a convoy, from the sound of it."

A few seconds later and Merikur too could hear the rumble of powerful engines and the squeal of metal on ungreased metal. Tracks then, a heavy crawler pulling ore cars towards Port City. They sure had guts running a convoy at night. They'd be damned lucky if the rebels didn't cut them up.

Merikur squirmed his way forward into a place where he could watch. The last of the light was fading fast, but he could still see the big square-nosed tractor as it rounded the bend. There was a train of open ore cars behind. In spite of the heat, all the hatches were closed.

Inside the tractor was loud music with a pounding beat. After all, noise had kept the boogey man away for thousands of years, maybe it would work one more time. Indicator lights glowed their various colors, and the air smelled of stale sweat. The crew weren't friends, so there wasn't much conversation.

Their sensors probed the darkness while their repulsors swung back and forth in sweaty hands. If they made it, each would collect a fat night-run bonus. If they didn't, Treeling would shake his head sadly and delete the shipment from his desk comp.

Outside Merikur froze and prayed his infrared signature would pass as a warm rock. The sound of the tractor's engine and the squeal of its tracks became a roar as the train passed by him. Damn. An opportunity missed. Well, at least the road was well traveled. Tomorrow he'd find the perfect spot.

He was up early the next morning, walking west with the sun behind him. It threw a long shadow up the road. He hadn't gone very far at all when the AID yelled in his ear. "Aircraft! Hit the deck!"

Merikur did as he was told, diving for the ditch at the side of the road. Seconds later the aircar screamed over and buffeted him with its slipstream. He rolled over on his back as it roared away and swore. It was a marine scout car!

"It's one of ours," he said. "Try and reach it!"

"I'm trying," the AID replied, "but our ships are using some sort of a computer-controlled jamming program. Designated frequencies open up on a computer-controlled rotating basis and I can't keep up with them."

Merikur stood and dusted himself off. "Damn."

There was silence for a moment and then the AID said, "I'm sorry. Maybe the pilot would have seen you if only I hadn't told you to hit the deck." The AID actually sounded contrite.

"It's OK," Merikur replied. "We all make mistakes." He stepped onto the road and headed west.

*   *   *

It was ten minutes before the AID spoke again. "If I feel pleasure when I'm right, then maybe I feel pain when I'm wrong."

"Seems logical," Merikur agreed. "How do you feel right now?"

"Pretty bad."

"Join the club. It's all part of being sentient."

"Am I? Sentient, I mean?"

Merikur thought about that for a moment. "I don't know what the scientific types would say, but it seems to me that you think, therefore you are."

"Descartes."

"You've got it, pal."

There was silence for a moment and then the AID spoke once more. "Thanks, Anson."

"No problem. Besides, maybe they'd have blown me in half before they got around to checking my ID."

Half an hour later, Merikur found the perfect location. The road had started up towards the crest of a low hill. He chose that point to roll a number of largish rocks onto the road. The vehicles would simply surmount them or push them aside, but it would take a moment, and that would be his chance. The exact placement of the rocks was dictated by a fortuitous branch overhanging the road that was just wide enough for Merikur to lie on. True they might spot him, but his chances were pretty good if he limited his ambition to an ore car. Passenger vehicles obviously wouldn't work; people tend to notice when generals land in their back seats out of nowhere.

After positioning himself on his strategic branch

there was nothing to do but wait. Four hours later his throat was parched, his muscles were stiff, and the back of his neck was sunburned. Gritting his teeth, Merikur took a break. After stretching himself, rubbing some ointment on his neck, and sipping some purified water, he felt better.

Nothing had passed by while he was gone. He took his place once again. The sun hammered him as the minutes slipped slowly by. Eventually he fell into an uneasy sleep, counting on the AID to awaken him if something came his way.

It did. "Company's coming, sleepy head."

Merikur's eyes snapped open. A few moments later he heard the rumble of powerful engines and felt the branch vibrate. Still, it seemed like an eternity before the huge, blunt-nosed tractor rolled beneath him, enveloped in a great cloud of dust.

There were six ore cars. He'd try for the last of them.

Just as he'd hoped, the boulders momentarily slowed the train. He watched as the fourth car, then the fifth car, and finally the sixth rolled under his position.

Merikur took a deep breath and rolled off the branch. At that same instant, his AID flooded the crawler's radios and intercom with high-gain electronic gabble.

Both the driver and the guards were too busy grabbing for earplugs to notice a body fall into the last ore car with an additional puff of dust. The ten-foot fall knocked the wind out of Merikur's lungs and left him gasping for breath.

Then he started to sneeze. The noise concerned

him at first, but after he managed to bring the sneezing under control, he realized the tractor was so loud he could sing "All Hail the Pact" without being heard. All he had to do was keep his head down and hope they didn't conduct routine inspections of each car.

Given the possibility that rebels were lurking behind every bush, he didn't think they would.

Satisfied that he was temporarily safe, Merikur scooped out a shallow place in the loose ore, lay back and watched the sky. Clouds formed fantastic shapes as they marched across the sky. On one occasion he saw a lazy contrail arc its way towards the east as an LCS passed high above. It served to remind him of all the things he should be doing but wasn't.

He mentally urged the tractor to greater speed; and as he did, it topped a hill and started down the long slope to Port City.

Major Fouts was in a bad spot. Colonel Henderson, in charge of Merikur's marine component, had taken a sniper's round between the eyes. That left Fouts in command, faced with an endless list of military problems.

Which were nothing, however, compared to the political problem created by Merikur's own disappearance. He'd been gone five days now and was probably dead. By all rights she should call off the search and carry on as best she could.

But how to tell the general's wife? Especially when she wouldn't listen? Bethany Windsor Merikur was sitting opposite Fouts skimming the day's intelligence summaries for signs that her husband was still alive, just as she'd done for days. Since the day of Merikur's disappearance in fact.

Over everyone's objections, the general's wife had commandeered an LCS to conduct her own air search. Failing in that, she'd moved into HQ and transformed Fout's life into a living hell. The continuation of the search was moving from pointless to absurd, but who was going to tell the lady to sit down and shut up?

Certainly not a major like Fouts, who had every intention of making colonel someday.

Thunder crashed outside the troop carrier. Rain began to fall, a few heavy drops followed by a roar beating the roof in a quick rhythm.

Fouts cleared her throat.

Bethany looked up, still beautiful, but haggard in the glare of the lum-lights, her eyes rimmed with red and her skin an unhealthy gray. She'd been sleeping less than the three or four hours a day that Fouts had managed to catch.

She met Fouts' gaze with an intensity that froze the marine's words in her throat. "I know what you're going to say, Major, but my husband is alive."

There was a sudden gabble of voices just outside and the scrape of boots on metal steps. Fouts turned and gaped at the apparition which filled the hatch.

General Merikur.

Dirty, wet, and a few pounds lighter, but the general nonetheless.

He grinned. "Major, I'd listen to what my wife has to say if I were you. She tells me she's always right."

Chapter 9

Merikur looked around as people filed in and found seats. The bunker was quite posh as such things go, boasting a board floor, folding chairs, and a conference table made of ammo cases. The table was covered with maps, printouts, used meal paks and stray pieces of clothing.

A portable com board and tac tank combination took up the far wall, while the others were of raw earth covered with plastic. Cables snaked this way and that and a haze of blue smoke misted the air. All of Merikur's key people were present including Major Fouts, five or six other senior officers, Senda, Administrator Nugumbe, and Bethany.

Bethany had steadfastly refused to return to orbit— and in all truth, he didn't want her to go. A marine patrol had stopped the ore train about twenty miles outside Port City for a routine contraband inspection. Instead of contraband they found one tired general.

From there it was a short ride to the firebase and

his personal troop carrier. The sound of Bethany's voice as she told Fouts he was alive, and the look on her face as he stepped through the hatch, were memories he'd always cherish. Minutes later, she'd been coldly furious in reaction to the days of fear he'd put her through . . . but even that meant Bethany cared.

There was a great deal Merikur wanted to talk to her about; but as usual, their personal relationship was taking a back seat to military and political necessity.

Everyone was seated and looking expectantly in his direction. Merikur cleared his throat. "Welcome, everyone. I understand there's coffee and carbos on the way. When they come please help yourselves. First let me apologize for causing you so much trouble. I know many of you were involved in the search." Merikur looked at Bethany as he spoke. She smiled.

There were general sounds of dissent as people said things like, "It was no trouble at all," and "Good to have you back, sir."

Merikur smiled. "Thanks, but let's cut the bull. I screwed-up. I promise I won't commit that particular screw-up again. As for other possible screw-ups, well, you'll just have to take your chances."

There was general laughter, with perhaps a tinge of relief in some voices.

"Now, as most of you know, I'm not the only one who's spent the last few days in the jungle. Eitor Senda, Governor Windsor's chief political advisor, and mine as well, has just returned from parts unknown. I think you'll be interested in what he has to say. Eitor?"

Senda stood and made his way to the front of the

room. "Thank you, General. Although it's true that I spent a few days in the jungle . . . I suspect they were much more pleasant than yours. I would like to join the rest of your staff in welcoming you back."

There was general applause. When it died down Senda spoke. His face was quite serious and Merikur could see tension in the set of his shoulders. "I am sorry to say that the news I bring is . . . not good. Taking advantage of an intelligence network created by associates of mine on Cernia, I have made contact with some of the rebel leaders. What they told me was quite disturbing.

"It is important to understand that while Jomu is the overall rebel leader, there are seven Cernian sub-leaders, plus two human leaders as well. And while Jomu favors Cernian independence and control of Teller, some of his sub-leaders feel his ambitions are unrealistic. They would prefer membership in the Pact as full and equal partners."

Senda paused and looked around the room. "Governor Windsor agrees with them, and so do I. In spite of my presence here, I too am a loyal Cernian. As such, I know the price of Cernian independence is war, a war Cernia could not survive. And there are other things at stake. We came here to translate the Governor's belief in sentient equality into reality. Then, with Teller as an example, perhaps even greater achievements would be possible."

Now the weight of Senda's shame dragged his eyes to his feet and his voice dropped to a monotone. "Now all of that is threatened. I thought the Haiken Maru and their policies of alien exploitation would be our biggest problem. Being as ethnocentric as any human, I assumed Cernians were operating on a higher moral plane."

Senda paused; when he continued, there was tremendous sadness in his voice. "And then I learned the Cernian War Faction has joined forces with the Haiken Maru to take over Teller."

There was an audible gasp as people looked at each other in stunned amazement. Merikur knew how they felt. Senda had explained it to him hours before and he still couldn't believe it. Why would Cernia join forces with the hated Haiken Maru? And for that matter, why would the Haiken Maru cooperate with Cernia? He listened along with everyone else as the alien looked up and resumed his explanation.

"I see you are surprised. Well, so was I. But surprising though it is, this alliance makes sense when you realize that our two races have as many similarities as differences. For example, both the human and Cernian races are quite pragmatic. Bigotry is part of Haiken Maru corporate culture. But even more important is the concept of profit, and when faced with continued financial loss, the company took the most profitable way out, even if that meant dealing with the trolls."

Heads nodded around the table. *That* was Haiken Maru, all right.

"Meanwhile the Cernian war faction hated humans —but was under increasing fire from its opposition. Alliance with the Haiken Maru meant an opportunity to build support through an easy victory on Teller. Both sides were motivated to seek some sort of accommodation.

"And that is exactly what they have done."

Senda blinked both eyes in a Cernian shrug. "The agreement brings honor to no one. On the human side, the Haiken Maru has agreed to cede control of Teller to Cernia. In addition, the Haiken Maru has agreed to pay off its human and Cernian workers and provide them with transportation off planet. In return, Cernia will allow the Haiken Maru to exploit the planet's resources in whatever way the conglomerate chooses, and will help them to bring in new workers. The new workers will be drawn from a race called the Mak. They will be exploited in the same way that Cernians were in the past."

Anger seeped into Senda's leathery features as he spoke. "In other words ladies and gentlemen, one subjugated race will be substituted for another. I speak for Governor Windsor when I tell you this is *not* acceptable. We did not come here to foster merely human-Cernian equality, we came here to start a movement towards the equality of *all* races, and I swear to you on the blood of my family's mother that is what we will do!

"I apologize for the excessive emotional content of my words. Thank you." With that Senda returned to his Cernian chair.

Merikur stood and nodded towards Senda. "Thanks Eitor, and no apologies are necessary; I suspect we all feel the same way.

He cleared his throat. "Based on Eitor's information it seems likely that there's some sort of Cernian fleet headed this way. It's interesting to note that in spite of that possibility, the rebel attacks have continued unabated. In fact computer analysis indicates a slight increase in overall activity. This runs counter to what we would expect. Why suffer more casualties when there's help on the way? The fact that they continue to do so suggests the possibility that top rebel leadership are unaware of the Cernian-Haiken Maru agreement. I remind you that Eitor's rebel contacts don't necessarily confide in Jomu. There may be a schism there which we can exploit.

"In any case, based on their agreement with Haiken Maru, the Cernian fleet will expect an unopposed landing. They'll be wrong. With your help I intend to throw a little surprise party in their honor. You're all invited."

There was laughter—some of it nervous—around the table.

Merikur's eyes swept the room as the laughter died away. "First however, we must gain complete control of this planet. If we try to fight rebels and an invasion force at the same time, we'll lose. It's as simple as that. So we must defeat the rebels, and do it in record time. We don't know when the fleet will arrive, but it's liable to be very soon indeed."

Merikur smiled. "While wandering around out in the jungle I had plenty of time to think. About jungle warfare, among other things. Military history is full of jungle campaigns and they all have things in common. They're miserable, nasty, and long. Even if we wanted to fight one, we don't have enough time.

He smiled tightly. "So I've devised an alternative. Like most plans this one isn't perfect, and requires some luck, but I believe it's our only chance of controlling Teller before the Cernian fleet arrives. Major Fouts will provide a unit briefing in two hours. Thanks for your attention."

* * *

Merikur stood on a hill top one day later and watched Operation Boomerang get underway. The focal point of the operation was an enormous supply convoy which was supposed to resupply fifteen Haiken Maru mining stations.

Merikur had put the convoy together with Treeling's reluctant help. After all, the Haiken Maru manager knew the Cernian fleet was on the way, and knew that afterwards he'd be allowed to transport supplies wherever he wanted to.

Unless, of course, something happened to tip the scales the other way.

So, unwilling to commit himself to the Haiken Maru-Cernian alliance prior to the fleet's arrival, Treeling was forced to go along. Merikur made the process as uncomfortable as possible.

Citing Treeling's earlier demands for help, Merikur had his marines strip the Haiken Maru warehouses of all supplies and load them aboard the convoy. He also took almost all of the troops guarding Port City and assigned them to guard the convoy.

The convoy was an awesome sight as it rolled out of Port City's main gates and headed into the jungle. As he swept his imager across the scene, Merikur counted fifty huge tractors, each pulling five or six cars full of supplies. Armored weapons carriers rolled along on both sides, loaded with marines armed to the teeth. Scout cars ranged ahead dashing here and there while armed aircars skimmed the tree tops. Hundreds of feet above them, a full wing of LCS's screamed across the sky, throwing delta-shaped shadows across the land below.

A huge cloud of dust had risen to hang over the scene. Merikur could hear the radios in his troop carrier crackling with traffic. He smiled.

It was one of the most impressive and absurd sights he'd ever seen. But it was just the sort of approach the rebels would expect. Brawn instead of brains. And Merikur hoped to use their expectations against them.

Jomu certainly knew the convoy was coming. After all, it had been loaded right in front of all the rebel spies and informants. The orders assigning most of Port City's troops to the convoy were posted on walls. Then, just to make sure the rebels had enough time to react, Merikur had given them the better part of a day to talk the whole thing over. It was the perfect opportunity for the rebels to take and secure Port City while Merikur's forces were running all around the countryside.

There was no question in Merikur's mind that Port City, if garrisoned by troops as good as Jomu's rebel army, could hold against any possible marine counterattack.

Then Merikur would play his hole card and hope for the best. If it worked he'd have control of the planet. If it didn't he'd be dead.

"But," he thought grimly, "so will they."

Jomu handed his imager to Horsehide and said, "See for yourself. The idiots have stripped the city of marines."

Horsehide was tall and lean. He had bright brown eyes, high, flat cheekbones, and a nose hooked like a hawk's. Long black hair hung down below his shoulders in the fashion of his ancestors, but there was nothing ancient about the repulsors he wore, or the ventilated armor that clad his muscular body. He was the more powerful and popular of the two human leaders, and therefore, the one summoned for a conference.

Jomu watched him refocus the imager and aim it at the convoy. The tall human looked for a long time before handing the glasses back with a shake of his head. "I don't like it, Jomu. It just doesn't fit. Maybe it's a trap."

Jomu blinked both his eyes. "How? Your own people swept the city. Outside of civilians and one company of marines, there's nobody there. If Merikur had a larger force of marines hidden in Port City you would have found them. In addition, my scouts have a rough head count on the marines assigned to the convoy, plus the marines holding the firebase. It adds up to the right number—eight hundred, give or take."

"If they land more from orbit after we're committed?"

Jomu's mouth quirked down. "Then we eat them alive. We'll have Port City's fixed defenses and enough troops to man them properly. They can't break through the perimeter any more than we could—until the fools stripped it to protect their convoy."

Horsehide looked out at the huge dust cloud and frowned. Everything Jomu said made sense. Still he couldn't shake the empty feeling in his gut. If there were an honorable way out. . .

But there wasn't.

"All right Jomu, we're in. What's the plan?"

*   *   *

Nugumbe guided her ground car through Port City's main gates and waved to the bored looking sentry.

She smiled. If Merikur's plan worked he wouldn't be bored for long.

The streets seemed empty without the usual marine and Haiken Maru patrols. Shops were closing early, restaurants went without patrons.

Valuables were disappearing into the ground.

As usual, all sorts of rumors were making the rounds, some of which were quite true. No one spared so much as a glance when Nugumbe slid her car into the usual place under the fourplex and got out.

After assuring herself that no one was looking, Nugumbe walked around and opened the largest of the car's three storage compartments. "It's all clear, General. You can come out now."

Merikur groaned as he unwound his long legs and scrambled out. "No offense, but that was the pits."

"Well," Nugumbe said primly, "most people like riding in my luggage compartment. Here, let me give you a hand with that luggage."

Bending over, she grabbed one of the two packs Merikur had brought along with him. It weighed a ton. She put it back down.

"On second thought maybe you'd like to handle it yourself."

"No problem." Merikur picked up the first pack and another just like it without apparent effort. "Where to? It feels a little exposed out here."

"Right this way." Nugumbe palmed the lock and motioned him inside. Stepping through the door,

Merikur rediscovered air conditioning. Cool air bathed him from head to toe as he put the packs down and looked around.

Elsewhere Nugumbe's quarters would have been average at best, but on Teller they were the height of luxury. Sun streamed in through a large window, splashy paintings decorated the walls, and comfortable furniture invited him to sit down.

"Very nice," Merikur remarked, walking over to draw curtains across the window. "I like your taste."

"Thank you," Nugumbe replied, obviously pleased. "Can I get you something to eat? Or show you the rest of the place?"

Merikur's answer was delayed by the thump of distant gunfire and the wail of an emergency klaxon. The rebel attack had begun. Merikur smiled. "How 'bout the bedroom? I could use a little nap."

Fouts swore under her breath. The whole damned thing went against all her training and instincts. She hadn't joined the marines to *lose*.

She'd said as much to Merikur. "About my orders sir, isn't there some other way to get the job done?"

Merikur had looked up from the tac tank and raised an eyebrow. "Are you questioning my orders, Major?"

"No sir. I'll back you a hundred percent. It's just that, well I don't know what's going on."

Merikur slapped her on the back. "Don't take it so hard, Major. Outside of Eitor, I haven't told anyone else either. What if you were captured? What you don't know you can't tell. Just fall back and make it look good."

Fouts' mouth made a straight hard line. "Yes sir. But to make it look good we've got to fight, and that means casualties. I don't like throwing away lives for a plan I don't understand."

Suddenly Merikur's eyes were rock hard and his voice like steel. "End of discussion, Major. You have your orders. Follow them."

Fouts was jerked back into the present as the com tech spoke. "It's C Company, Major. They're taking heavy casualties near the main gate."

Fouts gritted her teeth. "Well tell them to keep fighting, goddamn it. That's what marines are for."

"There are only a few of them, Father, but they will not give up," the runner said, still panting from his dash through the streets. Jomu waited patiently while the young Cernian gulped down more oxygen and spoke again.

"And that is not all, Father; the citizens are shooting at us from the roof tops and ambushing us in side streets. Father Lata requests instructions."

Jomu did his best not to smile. "Tell Father Lata to kill them."

The runner looked at him in astonishment. "There is no other message, Father?"

"No," Jomu replied. "There is no other message."

Merikur lay down but found he couldn't sleep. The sound of gunfire made that impossible. Outside his people were fighting and dying. He told himself any other plan would have caused even greater casualties . . . but then Major Fouts would appear, asking if there wasn't some better way.

*　　*　　*

The fighting finally stopped around midnight. Merikur prayed the casualties were light. He wondered what Bethany was doing. He'd considered sending her up to Yamaguchi's ship, but with a Cernian fleet on the way, they'd decided she was just as safe on the ground. When he finally drifted off to sleep her face filled his dreams.

The rebels were in complete control of Port City by the time the sun rose the next morning. Jomu had placed his command post in the main square, the city's defenses were ready for a counter attack, and the process of rounding up all Haiken Maru personnel was well underway.

Jomu knew that the convoy had returned during the night, and unable to enter the city, had entered the marine firebase.

He smiled. It was too little, too late. There were close to two-thousand rebels inside Port City, almost his entire force; more than enough to stop the marines.

Yes, their ships were still in orbit and could turn Port City into molten slag if they chose; but he didn't think they had the stomach for it, not with the Haiken Maru prisoners he had, and not until they'd tried everything else.

When the support elements arrived from Cernia, the human navy would have its hands full.

Jomu heard a loud explosion as an empty building half a block away blew up. Klaxons went off, nervous rebels started firing in every direction, and Jomu ran outside.

He was back ten minutes later. A single missile

perhaps, or some fool playing with a grenade. It made little difference.

At Jomu's desk sat a human who wore a Marine dress uniform, complete to the holstered pistol. In his left hand was something that looked like a radio handset, and the pleasant smile with which he greeted Jomu was belied by the tension obvious in every line of his seated body.

The intruder's thick white hair and the comets on his shoulderboards left no doubt of his identity.

"I've been expecting to see you, General Merikur," Jomu said. Fairly sure he could shoot Merikur before the human drew his own repulsor; fairly sure that a solution so simple would turn out to have been simply wrong. "At a time more of my choosing, I must admit."

"Please," Merikur said with a sincerity underlined by what was surely a quaver in his voice. "If neither of us acts hastily, there needn't be a problem."

If he was so afraid of surrendering, why had he—

"I'm here to take your surrender, Commander Jomu."

"*What?*" It was only the movement of Merikur's hand that froze Jomu's instinctive reaction to draw and end this absurd exchange.

Merikur's left hand. If what he held was a—

"I have two companions with me," Merikur continued, nodding toward the canvas divider separating Jomu's cot from the working area of his tent. "I'm going to have them come out now, very slowly."

Merikur rose to his feet as he spoke, a careful, supple motion like that of a cat facing danger. The canvas was pushed aside by a human being propelled by the Cernian behind him with a hand over his mouth.

"I had to hold—" the Cernian said, releasing the human—Manager Treeling, and again Jomu's mind twitched toward his pistol, because if ever a man deserved to die it was that—

"Merikur!" Treeling snarled. "When this is over—"

"Jomu!" blurted Eitor Senda, Jomu's brother.

"Eitor!" Jomu said in equal amazement. Nausea gripped him. "I know we didn't agree, but to think a member of Nest Senda is a traitor. . ."

The Cernian whom Merikur knew only as the governor's political advisor stepped forward, brushing Treeling aside as easily as he'd held the administrator a moment before. "Jomu," he said, then caught himself. Jomu had seen the formal challenge on the tip of his brother's tongue.

"Jomu," Eitor resumed in a controlled voice. "Later we will discuss treachery and the Nest. For now— listen to General Merikur."

"Killing me won't affect the struggle," Jomu said. "Not now. It's over for you and—"

"This is a deadman switch," Merikur said, waggling the object in his left hand. "It's coupled to the 20-megaton warhead buried in the center of the Plaza." He gestured with a nod.

"*What*?" said Treeling, turning back to Merikur with a look of absolute fury.

"If I release the switch," Merikur continued, noticeably calmer now that he'd gotten past the initial contact, "Port City is gone. A crater. And all the rebel forces you were able to concentrate for this assault. Gone. For good. Your rebellion is gone."

"You won't do that!" Jomu snapped.

"You can't do that!" Treeling cried. He balled a fist; Senda gripped the manager from behind.

"Commander Jomu," Merikur said steadily, "I win either way. You surrender and accept my proposals for restructuring Teller's administration—"

"You have no authority!" Treeling began, until the pressure of Eitor's hands on his wrists reminded him of the situation.

"—which I believe I can convince you are in your interests also," Merikur continued. "Or you shoot me, the warhead goes off, and Pact forces put down the scattered remnants of your rebellion. Only a handful of my troops will be in the blast radius."

"Merikur!" Treeling blurted, so amazed that the personal implications of the threat had apparently escaped him. "If you *dare* destroy Haiken Maru property, you and your Governor Windsor are *dead!*"

"This is a whole *city* full of your people!" Jomu said. "You won't dare—"

"Haiken Maru's people," Senda said quietly. "Believe him, brother."

"I can't believe him," Jomu said. He began to turn deliberately toward the tent flap.

"I was afraid you'd say that," said Merikur. He drew and fired.

The speed of the motion shocked Jomu even more than the slap of the repulsor. Jomu had been very optimistic when he thought he could draw and shoot before the intruder reacted. . . .

Treeling's head exploded upward as the colloid of his brain tried to follow the path of the hypersonic glass bead slapping through it. Blood and brains thumped the tent roof violently.

The bead's impact drew Treeling's expression into a perfect blank. His body began to crumple as the guard whirled into Jomu's tent shouting, "Father!" His rifle was caught in the canvas, but—

"No!" Jomu cried, grabbing the guard with both hands. "No, everything's all right. Go back to your post."

"Father?"

Jomu thrust the guard gently back through the flap. "It's all right," he repeated, wondering if it was. . . . Wondering if *anything* was right anymore.

Merikur laid his pistol on the desk instead of reholstering it. "The warhead is real too," he said. "And the switch." He blinked his left eye. Part of Treeling was dripping down that side of his face.

Eitor turned his back to mop at his own face. "We've been through Treeling's records," he said in a rigidly emotionless voice. "Ten regiments of Cernian regulars are on their way to Teller now."

"*Now?*" Jomu repeated with emphasis. He straightened. "Then detonate your warhead, General. The liberation of the planet is assured anyway."

"Not liberation, brother," Eitor said, facing around to meet Jomu's eyes. "They're coming in Haiken Maru ships. The War Party has made a deal with Haiken Maru."

"Impossible!" Jomu snapped.

"Read Treeling's records," Merikur said. "It's all there." He smiled, an expression very like that he wore as he shot the Haiken Maru administrator. "A profitable arrangement benefitting everyone—except the Mak slaves that would be brought in to replace the Cernians now in the mines."

"Brother Jomu," Eitor said, "I am not a traitor. Not to Cernia; not any group on Cernia that the Nest Senda could support and retain its honor."

Jomu Senda rubbed his knuckles together fiercely. "I didn't . . ." he began, staring at his scarred, powerful hands.

He looked up; met his brother's eyes, met Merikur's. "I haven't spent two years out—" he gestured crisply, dismissively "—out there so that Cernians could rule as many slaves as the Haiken Maru does."

Jomu shook himself before continuing. "General Merikur," he said, "for now we'll declare a cease fire. If the records are as you claim, you'll have my surrender. On the honor of Nest Senda."

Jomu bowed deeply to Eitor before adding, "And since my brother vouches for you, there can be no doubt of what the records will show."

As the brothers clasped arms, Merikur felt a soft buzz in his ear. It was his AID. "You may feel suicidal but I don't. With your permission, I'll summon the weapons techs to defuse that bomb."

Merikur looked down at the black box in his hand. Suddenly the pack weighed a thousand pounds. "Yes," he said, "I think that's a very good idea indeed."

Three hours later the bomb was defused, a bilateral cease fire was in effect, and Jomu was Merikur's guest at the firebase. Wary negotiations had begun, and all parties were seated around the cluttered table in Merikur's bunker.

Present were Merikur, Eitor, Jomu, Nugumbe, Horsehide, Fouts and lesser functionaries from both sides. A mixed meal of human and Cernian food had been served and eaten. Now there was little left except a litter of empty plates and dirty utensils. The humans enjoyed a final cup of coffee while the Cernians sipped cool fruit juice from tall glasses.

"They lied to me," Jomu said sadly. "They knew what I would say about any kind of agreement with the Haiken Maru, and because of that, they misled me into thinking a Cernian fleet was on the way. And it would have worked, too. Once the Haiken Maru ships dropped out of orbit, there would not be much I could do."

Jomu looked from Eitor to Merikur. "But even that I could forgive. I am a soldier, and as you humans say, 'war makes strange bed fellows. . . .' But the enslavement of the Mak, that is something else again."

"Exactly," Eitor agreed. "I have collaborated with the humans in order to end slavery, not extend it."

Jomu took a thoughtful sip. Like all Cernians he preferred drinking through a straw. Doing so simulated drinking from the stem of the Lekuna, or 'sweet water' plant native to Cernia. "This Governor Windsor . . . he's serious about alien-human equality?"

"My presence as his representative would suggest that he is," Eitor said with a smile.

Horsehide's bright brown eyes flashed as they moved from Eitor to Merikur. Glass beads had left new scars on the ceramic surface of his body armor. They reminded Merikur of the price Company C had paid to make this conversation possible. Only twelve had survived. "So," Horsehide said, "does the governor's belief in alien-human equality go so far as to permit a coalition government?"

"If it is consistent with and true to the laws of the Pact, then he does," Merikur responded.

Both Jomu and Horsehide were visibly surprised. They looked at each other and then back. "Then let's talk," Jomu said.

And talk they did. Through the afternoon and far into the night. Form of government, laws, worker compensation and much, much more. Most issues weren't resolved, simply identified and put aside for further discussion.

But by the time the sun rose, one important decision had been reached. The marines and rebels would merge forces and meet whatever came as a single force. When the Haiken Maru fleet orbited, every effort would be made to negotiate. With all the workers free citizens of Teller and a coalition government in the offing, perhaps the Cernian war party would reconsider and abandon their plans. This was the option most favored by all concerned. But if the Cernians refused to listen and began to land troops—

Then the combined human and rebel forces would engage them.

The prospect troubled Jomu, for as a Cernian regular it not only went against his training, it made him a traitor as well. Yet to free Cernians by enslaving another race, that too was wrong, and a perversion of his mission. Well, he could always suicide later.

He remembered the wrinkled face of Mother Mafa, the ancient instructor of military ethics at the Cernian military institute. She'd never lectured them like their other instructors. Mother Mafa told stories instead. Stories of ancient wars and battles described so clearly that he could still feel and taste them. And when her students were completely enthralled, lost in the middle of some ancient conflict, the main characters would be confronted with an ethical dilemma. Through gentle questioning Mother Mafa would bring the main issues to light, encourage her students to discuss them, and when all sides had been presented, she'd finish the story.

Sometimes the students and the ancient characters resolved the problem the same way, though that was unusual. But in neither case Mother Mak did pass judgment. She said that while hindsight might be perfect, it wasn't fair. Not unless the people looking back were doing so under the same pressures and conditions as those being judged.

But she said something else as well, something which applied to Jomu's present situation, something which no other instructor had ever said.

She said the purpose of the military was to fight, but to do so within the framework of civilian law, because to do otherwise would lead to the destruction of that which they'd set out to defend. Jomu was on Teller to help free Cernians enslaved there. If that meant killing the slave masters, then so be it. But to free Cernians by enslaving others, that was a violation of legal purpose . . . and would make him just as guilty as the Haiken Maru.

Jomu remembered Mother Mak's wrinkled face, the way she'd smile when he got something right, and her voice as she said, "Not bad, little father. Keep it up and someday I will tell a story about you."

Jomu smiled to himself. Maybe she would. He wondered what she'd think of it.

*   *   *

The few days were busy for all concerned. The Haiken Maru fleet could arrive at any time, so a sense of urgency prevailed. To have any chance at success the defense had to be as organized as possible, yet there wasn't enough time to effectively combine forces. With the exception of some liaison personnel, the troops weren't integrated.

But they were deployed under a unified command structure with a single plan of battle. Merikur was in command, with Jomu as his XO, (Executive Officer), and with Fouts and Horsehide as battalion commanders. Though invited to join, the other human leader—a rebel named Travis—declined. Even though she'd been a slave herself, Travis wasn't about to fight side by side with trolls.

Slowly at first, and then with increasing speed, orders were given and troops began to move. It takes months to really combine diverse military units into a single entity. In this case the members of those units belonged to different races, spoke different languages, and had different training. Although the Cernian upper classes spoke Pact Standard—and did so better than most humans—the lower classes did not. Add to that the fact that most of the rebels, Cernian and human, had no formal military training, and there was a tremendous potential for disaster.

Merikur left the internal structure of the units alone. If the Cernian rebels wound up fighting their own kind, they'd be confused enough without humans to contend with as well. And, since the rebels were used to jungle warfare and his marines weren't, Merikur used each differently.

The marines were placed in and around Port City where they could use their heavy weapons in a head-on clash with Cernian regulars, while the rebels were hidden in the surrounding jungle, ready to ambush and harass the enemy flanks.

Important mining stations and farms were defended in a similar manner: marines manned the outposts' heavy weapons, while a mixture of human and Cernian rebels lurked in the surrounding jungle.

If an outpost was overwhelmed, the surviving marines would use rebel tunnels to escape and fade into the jungle. Then, as soon as the Cernians were settled in, the rebels would touch off the demolition charges the marines had left behind. Meanwhile, other rebels would lead the surviving marines to prearranged staging areas where they could be reformed into larger units and resupplied.

So while he would have preferred more time to prepare, Merikur felt fairly good about their overall readiness and thought his combined ground forces had a chance of winning.

The situation in space was another matter. After giving it a lot of thought he'd arrived at a difficult decision. He sent for Fouts.

She showed up about fifteen minutes later. There were dark circles under her eyes. She'd been working around the clock. Fouts sighed as she dropped into a chair and put her boots up on an empty rations box. "That feels good. By the way General, it's good to have you back."

She grinned. "I never realized generals did any work until you disappeared."

Merikur laughed. "Thank you, Major. It's good to

be back. And my compliments on the way you held everything together. It was an outstanding job under difficult circumstances. Unfortunately our difficulties aren't over . . . which brings me to the matter of our ships."

Merikur sat on the edge of the makeshift conference table. "I've decided to send most of them back to Harmony. As you know, we're facing Haiken Maru ships loaded with Cernian troops. Ships which are almost certain to get hit if a fight develops. After which the conglomerate will swear it was an unprovoked attack on unarmed transports carrying contract laborers or some other crap like that. We might prove otherwise, but we'd be old and gray by then, and I don't think it's worth it."

Fouts frowned. "But what if they use their ships against us on the ground?"

It was a good question, and one Merikur had wrestled with for some time. If they wanted to the ships could sit in orbit and pound them into molten slush. He gave her the same answer he'd given himself and prayed he was right.

"It's possible, but it would destroy a lot of company property, and I doubt they'll do that. No, the decision point is here on the ground, and that's where we'll fight."

Fouts slipped behind her professional mask. She thought, "Yes, sir, you're completely out of your mind sir, but I'll do anything you say sir." She said, "Yes, sir. Is there anything else, sir?"

Sensing her unhappiness Merikur smiled, not because Fouts was funny, but because she was so transparent. "Yes. Round up my wife, and make arrangements for her to go aboard Captain Yamaguchi's ship. Tell her I'll see her back on Harmony."

"Yes, sir." Fouts got to her feet, popped him a perfect salute, and disappeared.

Merikur went to work on the task he hated most, logistics. For the next few hours he scanned computer screens, matched needs to supplies, and dealt with constant interruptions.

Outside, shuttles came and went in a constant non-stop roar of sound. Before the fleet could leave, tons of supplies and ammo must be landed, stored, and dispersed. Bethany would be on one of those shuttles. He'd miss her, but he'd also feel better knowing she was on Harmony, and out of harm's way.

Eventually he was finished. He killed the terminal, stood, and stretched. Then he strapped on his sidearm, grabbed his hat, and made his way out of the bunker. After the constant roar of the shuttles it seemed strangely silent outside. Stars twinkled overhead and night sounds crowded in around the base. Low laughter came from the other side of a troop carrier as Sergeant Wilker cracked one of his jokes, a com set burped static, and a distant caw announced a jungle bird's hunt.

Walking carefully, Merikur found his way between the prefab shelters, sandbagged weapons emplacements, and parked vehicles to where the dark bulk of his gig loomed. It crouched on stumpy landing jacks like a huge bug. The shuttle creaked slightly as ceramic-coated metal contracted in the cool air. With the exception of a single destroyer on picket duty a few lights out, the gig was his entire fleet. The thought brought a smile to his lips.

"Halt! Oh—sorry sir, I didn't realize it was you."
The sentry stepped forward, separating herself from
the darker shadow cast by the gig.

"No problem, Private. How's that ankle doing?"
Private Slocum had sprained her ankle during the
original landing, and he'd noticed it on a sick call
muster.

Slocum was surprised and pleased. "Just fine, sir."

Merikur palmed the entry lock. "Glad to hear it,
Private. Don't let anyone sneak up on us tonight. I
need some rest."

"I won't, sir," Slocum replied, meaning it.

The hatch hissed open and Merikur stepped inside. He waited while the outer hatch closed and the
inner hatch opened. The lights were dim and he left
them that way. Hundreds of tiny red, green, and
amber eyes stared at him from their various electronic lairs.

Stripping off his uniform he stepped into the tiny
fresher and sighed as the warm water hit his bare
skin. He stood there for a long time, allowing the
water to massage the tension from his muscles and
mind. He finally turned it off and triggered the hot
air blower. Once he was dry, Merikur stepped out of
the fresher and into the narrow corridor.

He padded his way aft, palmed the hatch, and
stepped into the darkness of his cabin. Before he
realized he was not alone he knew who was with
him. The soft scent of Bethany's perfume floated up
around him. He sat down on the bed and two arms
came out of the darkness to encircle his waist. The
arms urged him down and back. He started to speak,
but soft warm lips covered his, and conversation died

aborning. Slowly, and with exquisite tenderness, their bodies met and became one.

Meanwhile in the darkness of the hall, Merikur's AID lay amongst the dirty laundry, and wondered what sleep was like. It seemed less than attractive. What if they never turned you on again? The AID gave the electronic equivalent of a sigh.

Chapter 10

Merikur awoke to an incessant buzzing. He burrowed under his blankets but it didn't go away. Giving up he slapped the com set's "on" switch, and said, "You'd better have one helluva good reason for waking me up."

Eitor Senda sounded amused. "Would a battle fleet dropping into orbit around Teller constitute sufficient reason?"

"Yes," Merikur replied, suddenly upright. "I'll be right there." He hit the "off" switch and started to climb out of bed.

"You'll be right where?" Bethany reached up to pull him down beside her. Her eyes were sleepy, her hair was a mess, and she looked absolutely beautiful.

Merikur kissed her forehead. "I have to go to work. The Haiken Maru fleet just popped into orbit with a few thousand Cernian troops aboard."

She smiled. "How rude. One should always call before dropping in for a visit."

"He nuzzled her neck. "Really? You didn't call last night."

She bit his shoulder. "Are you sorry?"

"Sorry? I'll show you sorry."

"Oh really? What about the Cernians?"

"Cernians. Oh yeah the Cernians." Merikur rolled out of bed and rummaged for a fresh uniform. "I'm not complaining mind you . . . but how *did* you wind up in my bed? I thought you were safely stowed with Yamaguchi aboard the *Bremerton*."

Bethany sat up. "I was. But I changed my mind and hopped a shuttle back."

"You do that a lot."

"What?"

"Change your mind."

She smiled. "Like changing my mind about you, for example?"

"Yes."

"I was right though."

Merikur finished tying his bootlaces and stood. "Right about what?"

"You did want to get me into bed."

Leaning over he kissed her lips. "Yup. You were right about that. Now get up and get dressed. I want you in the bunker ASAP. Things may get real hairy around here."

Stepping into the corridor Merikur stopped to retrieve his sidearm and AID. As he buckled them on his AID said, "Good morning, sleepy head. I hope all that reproductive activity hasn't tired you out."

Suddenly Merikur realized he'd left the AID well within broadcast range of his implant. "My advice to you is to shut up," Merikur snarled. "Unless you'd like to be reprogrammed."

"Well ex*cuse* me," the AID replied. "By the way . . . I'm picking up some interesting radio traffic."

"So give," Merikur said, returning the sentry's salute, and heading for the bunker. He was careful to maintain a brisk but normal pace. The reading of commanding officers is something of an art form, and the slightest frown can start rumors racing through any military base. "I just saw the old man, he sure looked worried, I'll bet there's some heavy shit coming our way."

So Merikur didn't run, smiled at everyone he met, and generally used body language to lie like hell.

Meanwhile his AID was reporting on radio traffic. "Your picket ship reports nine Haiken Maru hulls in orbit around Teller, and here's a surprise, there's also four warships with a 99 percent match to Pact design. Wait a minute . . . yes they're identifying themselves as navy ships . . . and requesting an audience with you."

Merikur's mind began to spin. Why was the navy providing the Haiken Maru fleet with an escort? Especially when the fleet was loaded with troops bent on invading a Pact planet? He felt a sudden emptiness in the pit of his stomach. Something was very, very wrong.

That impression was reinforced when he entered the bunker and saw Eitor's face. The Cernian wore an upwards scowl. "You heard?"

Merikur nodded. "If you mean the naval escort, yes." He turned towards the cluster of uniforms against the far wall. "Major Fouts."

"Yes, sir." Fouts separated herself from the others.

"Put out orders that no one fires without my permission. Marine or rebel. One mistake and we're all in deep trouble. Understood?"

"Yes, sir." Fouts turned to a com tech as Merikur stepped over to the tac tank. At the moment the holo projection showed Teller as a transparent globe. Grid lines matched latitude and longitude. At a flip of a switch the tac tech could alter the projection to a topographical map, a geological survey grid, or any of a dozen other possibilities.

For the moment however Merikur was more interested in the space around the planet than the globe itself. The Haiken Maru ships were bright blue deltas spaced 40° apart in equatorial orbit. The Pact vessels were red dots: two destroyers, a cruiser, and a battleship according to the numeric codes associated with each. By assuming higher orbits than the Haiken Maru fleet they had placed themselves between the merchant vessels and any threat from space. Any hope that the navy vessels were a coincidence rather than an escort was destroyed by that positioning.

Merikur swore softly and turned to Fouts.

"All right, Major. What are they saying?"

Fouts consulted the printout in her hand. "The Haiken Maru vessels request permission to land shuttles, sir. There's a Commander Moskone aboard the battleship asking to see you."

"Tell the Haiken Maru vessels permission denied. Tell Commander Moskone to come on down. My compliments to the senior officer aboard the battlewagon, and all the usual niceties. You know, does he or she need anything, and all that sort of stuff."

"Yes, sir."

As Fouts relayed the orders, Merikur poured himself a cup of coffee and tried to think. He'd been mentally prepared for all sorts of things. If the Haiken Maru fleet had dropped out of orbit with weapons blazing, he'd have known what to do. But this was completely unexpected. The Haiken Maru fleet was brazenly requesting permission to land, a naval escort was protecting them, and he was standing around looking stupid.

And why Moskone? The battleship rated a vice admiral. Where the hell was he or she in all this? Maybe the admiral was a disinterested observer and happy to stay that way. There was no way to tell. All he could do was hope for the best.

"Major Fouts."

"Sir?"

"Contact Commander Jomu and Commander Horsehide. Bring them up to speed. And Fouts . . ."

"Sir?"

"Make sure they know I denied the Haiken Maru ships permission to land."

"Yes, sir. I'll tell them."

Merikur knew Fouts understood. The rebels had communications equipment of their own. By now they had pieced the situation together and smelled a rat. They'd be more upset about the naval escort than he was. One wrong move and the coalition would come apart, and if it did, his marines would be caught between the Cernians in orbit and the rebels on the ground.

He'd already risked his life to prevent that.

A nervous hour passed. The Haiken Maru ships were kept under careful observation. They had acknowledged Merikur's orders and made no attempt to launch shuttles.

Merikur didn't trust them. They were waiting for something, Moskone's visit most likely . . . and that meant they knew what the naval officer was going to say. It also meant Moskone's message would favor them and their objectives.

Merikur had harbored a secret hope that Treeling's files were wrong, that Oriana had granted the request for more marines and chosen to load them aboard a fleet of Haiken Maru ships. It was still possible of course, but damned unlikely. The tone would be different. He'd be swamped with bored naval officers asking where to dump the grunts, grunts fighting for the best LZ's, and a vice admiral who had nothing better to do than throw his or her weight around.

Moskone was coming down with some sort of message instead. It couldn't be good.

Merikur did his best to smile reassuringly when Beth entered the bunker. She saw right through it.

She smiled in return, and left him alone, knowing it was the best way to help.

Moskone arrived a few minutes later. As usual, the young officer looked like a recruiting poster come to life. His fatigues were carefully creased, his boots were only slightly dulled by dust, and his expression was jovial. "Good to see you sir. Eitor . . . good to see you . . . and it's always a pleasure to see you, Baroness."

Merikur frowned. Trust Moskone to remember Bethany's title. He did his best to appear bored. "So Paul . . . nice of you to drop in. I assume those navy ships are loaded with marines?"

Moskone smiled and dropped into a chair without

invitation. "I'm sorry to say they aren't, sir . . . but I'm sure you'll approve. Admiral Oriana sent you this." Moskone opened a thin briefcase, withdrew an envelope, and handed it to Merikur.

As Merikur accepted the envelope, he noticed Oriana's seal. Whatever the envelope contained had been witnessed and made part of official naval records. Merikur felt the emptiness in his stomach grow a bit larger. Sliding a finger along under the flap Merikur broke the admiral's seal and withdrew the letter. It was on official stationery.

It was about what he'd expected. About as bad.

Dear Anson,

> *Hope this finds you happy and well. Sorry to hear about the difficulties out there. I'd like to help, but I'm a bit short on marines myself. However, since the rebels are largely Cernian, the Cernian government has agreed to send some troops to your aid, and the Haiken Maru has agreed to transport them. Apparently the Cernian government is afraid the rebels will give them a bad name or something. (Send a troll to fight a troll, I always say.)*
>
> *In any case, it solves your problem, and that's all I care about. So allow the trolls to land and bring their unruly relatives under control. Hang onto the planet though, we may need it later! Once the Haiken Maru ships reach Teller, the battle group has orders to return here.*
>
> *My compliments regarding Commander Moskone.*

He seems just the sort of young officer to have around.

Best always,
Ori

A number of things became suddenly clear. Oriana had set him up: Merikur was to let the Cernians land but retain control of Teller. And that was clearly impossible once the Cernians landed. How could Oriana be so stupid?

But Oriana wasn't stupid; which implied he'd sold out to the Haiken Maru. The letter would allow Oriana to blame alien treachery and Merikur's incompetence for the loss of Teller. . . .

Merikur could imagine Oriana shaking his head sadly and looking around at a board of inquiry. "Like Governor Windsor, I thought the aliens could be trusted. And Merikur, well he seemed a steady fellow. Unfortunately appearances can be deceptive. In spite of my orders to the contrary, he handed control of the planet over to the Cernians. I accept full responsibility, of course."

But he wouldn't have to accept full responsibility. Oriana's fellow officers would decide in his favor. After all, it wasn't his fault—just his bad luck—that treacherous aliens and an incompetent subordinate had joined forces to lose a planet. Besides, Teller, was a hellhole. If the trolls wanted it so bad, let 'em have it. . . .

Shaking with contained rage, Merikur handed the letter to Eitor. The Cernian read it and scowled as he handed it back. He started to say something, but glanced at Moskone, and gave a slight shake of his head.

Suddenly Merikur realized the alien was right. The last lines of the letter should have tipped him off. "My compliments regarding Commander Moskone. He seems just the sort of young officer to have around."

Yeah, if you like spies. Oriana had thought of everything. The letter would set things in motion, Merikur would commit professional suicide, and Moskone would be there to witness the whole thing. Perhaps Moskone was part of the plan, or maybe he'd allowed himself to be used.

As if to drive the point home Merikur's AID spoke softly in his ear. "Moskone's AID is recording up and down all spectrums and transmitting in bursts. Giving me a headache."

"Naturally," Merikur thought. "Admiral Oriana wants a full record of the proceedings. Well fine. We'll give him what he wants." He forced a smile. "Well Paul, it's good to have you back. I wish you could stay, but I'm afraid that's impossible."

Moskone was visibly surprised. "Impossible, sir? But the admiral told me . . . that is . . . he wanted me to stay and help."

Merikur nodded sympathetically. "That's what I like about Admiral Oriana, he's so thoughtful. However I want to send him a message. Things have changed here, rather dramatically in fact, and I'm sure the admiral would value your impressions. He speaks very highly of you."

Moskone was suddenly alert. "Changed, sir? In what way?"

Merikur waved Oriana's letter. "Are you familiar with the admiral's orders?"

"Well, I haven't seen them," Moskone replied cautiously, "but the admiral was kind enough to brief me before I left."

Merikur smiled understandingly. "Good. Then you're aware that he sent the Cernian regulars to assist me. And a helluva good idea too. I wish all our senior officers had a tenth of Oriana's guts. But as I said earlier, things have changed. The rebels have been pacified, they're participating in planetary government, and I have control of the planet. All of which means we won't need any assistance from Cernia. I'm embarrassed, of course to have asked for help and then turn it away. But after the admiral reads my report, I'm sure he'll understand. So why don't you and Major Fouts grab a cup of coffee while I draft a letter to Admiral Oriana?"

Fouts looked surprised. Moskone stood, his face full of doubt. "But sir . . . I don't think you should . . ."

"What?" Merikur asked with one eyebrow raised. "Surely you aren't questioning my orders?"

"Well, no sir, but I . . ."

"Dismissed, Commander. I'm sorry if I seem abrupt . . . but I'm a busy man. I have a planet to run, you see."

"Yes, sir." Looking around the bunker for help and finding none, a confused Moskone followed Fouts up the ramp and towards the surface.

Merikur scowled after him. "Asshole." He said it softly so only Eitor could hear him. Spy or not, asshole or not, you don't criticize your officers in front of the lower ranks.

"A true guwat," Eitor agreed cheerfully. "But you handled him admirably. I only wish the governor had been here to see it."

"I'll be glad to tell him about it," Bethany added as she joined them. "You were superb, Anson. I haven't read the letter . . . but I can guess what's in it. Your strategy should neutralize Oriana."

Merikur shrugged. "I'm arguably guilty of insubordination. But if we win Oriana won't dare make an issue of it. If we lose . . . well, we'd better win, hadn't we?" His real fear had been that the Pact ships would try to enforce Oriana's will.

Eitor said thoughtfully: "But the Cernians may land anyway." Then he continued more cheerfully: "But if they do we will, as you humans put it, 'kick their posteriors.'"

Merikur laughed. "That's how we put it, all right. Well, one thing at a time. First I'll write a letter to Oriana."

Stepping up to a small remote, Merikur punched in his code, and dictated a letter to Admiral Oriana.

Dear Admiral Oriana,

I can't tell you how much I appreciate your help. But as Commander Moskone will explain, I already control Teller, and won't need the Cernian troops. With that in mind I'll release and thank them on your behalf. Again, thanks for your timely support, and my apologies for all the trouble.

I agree with your estimation of Commander Moskone's abilities, and am transferring him to

*your command, hoping you'll be able to provide
him with the opportunities he so richly deserves.*

"Like a one way trip to the frontier," Merikur
thought grimly. He signed the document, *General
Anson Merikur*, stored it, and printed out a copy for
Moskone. Then he placed the printout in an envelope, sent it to Moskone via runner, and heaved a
sigh of relief.

He wouldn't have to look at Moskone again.

Half an hour later Moskone's shuttle lifted towards
a cloudy sky. Merikur wasn't there to see it. He was
deep in the bunker instead, talking with Jomu and
Horsehide, and finalizing his plans.

Shortly thereafter all his troops, both marine and
rebel, went on a higher state of alert. Merikur's gig
lifted and headed for a protected landing zone deep
in the mountains. The marines around Port City dug
their foxholes a little deeper, the rebels in the surrounding jungle drew already sharp blades across
stones one last time, and Merikur's remaining destroyer was ready to run.

Then the waiting began. Fouts' com techs tried to
contact the Haiken Maru ships but received no answer. Apparently they were waiting to hear what
Moskone had to say before talking with Merikur.

And there was lots of coded radio traffic between
the battlewagon and the largest Haiken Maru ship.
Action speaks louder than words. When the battleship broke orbit and headed out system, Merikur
had his answer.

The Cernians had decided to stay.

Shortly thereafter the battleship's escorts broke orbit as well, and two hours after that, all four warships disappeared into hyperspace.

But the Haiken Maru ships stayed, loaded with Cernian troops, circling Teller like vultures over a corpse.

"Well, it looks like phase two of their plan is going into effect," Eitor said grimly. "The navy has discharged its duty and left. Whatever happens after they leave isn't their fault."

"I'm afraid you're right," Merikur agreed. "The other shoe should drop any moment now." Both laughed as Fouts called across the room. "It's the Haiken Maru sir, apologizing for their late response, and asking for you."

Merikur looked at Eitor and then Bethany. Both smiled and did their best to look optimistic. Merikur smiled in return. "Well, here goes nothing." He stepped in front of the com unit and nodded to Fouts. "Put them through, Major."

There was a large screen in front of him. It swirled with color and locked up into a picture.

Nola Rankoo. The same long hair, worn in a braid this time and draped over her left shoulder, the same penetrating eyes, and the same thin lips. She spit the words out one at a time. "Greetings, General. We meet again."

"So it would seem," Merikur replied evenly. "What can I do for you?"

Rankoo smiled slowly. "Very little. There are however some things I can do for you."

"Such as?"

"Help you bring the rebels under control. My

ships carry a thousand Cernian troops. With their help we can control the rebels and put the mines back into operation."

Merikur feigned surprise. "I'm surprised Commander Moskone didn't tell you. The rebels are no longer rebels. They're now part of a coalition government which rules Teller. I hope you'll thank the Cernians on my behalf . . . and take them home. I'm sure Governor Windsor will draft a letter of thanks and send it through proper diplomatic channels. Meanwhile, I deeply regret that I must deny you permission to land."

Rankoo's lips became a hard thin line. "Since entering orbit I've received numerous reports that the rebels are holding Port City and numerous other key areas. You may regard this as acceptable; but I don't, and I plan to do something about it. The Haiken Maru and the Cernian government have reached an agreement under which the Cernians will assume responsibility for planetary security while we continue to operate our mines. I remind you that Teller belongs to the Haiken Maru."

Merikur said evenly, "And I remind you that the Haiken Maru operates under Pact law. Pact law requires senate approval for transfers of planetary ownership. You cannot *give* a Pact planet to Cernia. You don't have the right. Nor can you legally land troops. Any such attempt will be met with force."

Rankoo sneered. "Then prepare to die, little man. My troops are on the way."

Chapter 11

The screen had no sooner faded to black than reports began rolling in. "One, two, make that three ships launching shuttles, sir." Another voice, "Two ships have entered descending orbit, sir . . . it appears they intend to land." And the first voice again, "Two ships headed out system, sir. They're a lot faster than they should be . . . and it looks like they're overtaking our tin can."

Merikur absorbed the incoming data and began to issue orders. "I want projected landing zones on the shuttles ASAP. Ditto the two ships. Warn the destroyer. Two ships in pursuit. Speed suggests warships rather than merchant vessels."

"Acknowledged, sir."

"Good. Now send the tin can this message: 'Governor Windsor. Rebel problem solved. Coalition government in place. Corruption in high places. Under attack by combined Haiken Maru and Cernian forces. Intend to win. Please send ships along with a case of champagne.' Signed, 'Merikur.' As soon as they acknowledge tell 'em to jump."

The com tech grinned. "Yes, sir!" Merikur's message would soon spread and do more for morale than a hundred pep talks.

But Merikur was worried. Days would pass before a relief force *could* arrive—assuming other pressures, political or military, permitted the governor to send one.

In the meantime Merikur's forces were badly outnumbered. Rankoo claimed only a thousand troops, but the size of her ships suggested a much larger force, probably five to six thousand. That meant his three thousand rebels and marines could be outnumbered two to one. Not very good odds. And the Cernians weren't amateurs either. They were well trained and led by officers like Jomu. Victory wouldn't come easily, if at all.

Eitor Senda appeared by his side. "I was on the radio with my brother. The Cernian commander, a crusty old war monger called Unolo, ordered him to attack your forces."

"And what did your brother say?"

Eitor smiled. "First he told Unolo what he thought of the war party's treachery, and then he told the old geezer to sit on his own swagger stick."

Merikur laughed.

"Excuse me, sir," interrupted one of the com techs.

"Yes corporal?"

"Our tin can just destroyed one of the pursuing vessels and jumped for Augustine. The commanding officer sent you this just prior to the jump."

The tech handed Merikur a short printout. It said, "Sorry sir, but I just couldn't resist," signed, *Captain Siskens*.

Merikur tried to frown. There were a number of junior officers around. "Siskens had no right to take unnecessary chances. When this is over I'll have a word with him." *And buy him a drink*. But Merikur didn't say that out loud.

Shortly thereafter the flow of incoming reports grew from a trickle to a stream and then a flood of information. As it washed over and around him, Merikur became a machine. Absorbing data, sorting it, searching for patterns and opportunities. Some of his decisions were based on accepted military tactics and others were little more than educated guesses. Some of his decisions would be wrong as a result— but that very randomness explained why computers hadn't replaced but could only advise human generals.

Though better equipped to manipulate facts, computers can't deal with emotion, and emotion is an important part of war. Without emotions like love, hate, and fear, war wouldn't exist. Perhaps two robot armies, each led by computers, could wage the perfect scientific war. But without emotions, why *would* they? So as long as soldiers can feel, generals will be required to do likewise.

"Orders, Lieutenant," called Corporal Singh, dug in about twenty feet away. "Hold as long as you can then fall back into the jungle."

Rain spattered against Lieutenant Shaffer's visor as his light blue eyes scanned the sky. He looked even younger than he was because of the freckles sprinkled across his nose. "So what else is new," he muttered. "Those are the same damn orders we had before. Silly bastards."

Even though the Haiken Maru were popping surveillance satellites like party balloons, a few were still in operation. They said an enemy shuttle was headed Shaffer's way and should break through the cloud cover any moment. Assuming the shuttle was Pact standard, it would hold about a hundred troops plus equipment. His twenty marines would be facing five times their numbers. Sure there were about thirty trolls in the surrounding jungle, but Shaffer didn't know if he could count on them or not.

A cold hand closed around his stomach and squeezed hard.

"Can't let it show," he told himself. "The troops are just as scared and depending on me to pull them through." Unlike their lieutenant, most of his troops were veterans. He didn't know if they were scared or not.

He sure hoped they were.

It wasn't a bad position, though. Thanks to the Haiken Maru, station 032 was well fortified against conventional ground attacks. Heavy equipment and chemical defoliants had cleared a free-fire zone all around the compound. Tons of earth had been scraped up into sloped embankments and topped with razor ribbon. But the Haiken Maru wanted the place back. . . .

Damned if Shaffer could see why. It was just a jumble of collapsed pre-fabs, a rusty derrick, and an overturned crawler.

He shrugged. "Ours is not to reason why, ours is to do or die. Or something like that." He couldn't remember who'd written the line, but chances were the poet had served in someone's army.

His AID spoke in his ear. "Sorry to bother you sir, but the shuttle will break through the clouds in thirty-one seconds, and its present approach suggests a strafing run. I wouldn't want to speak out of turn, but it seems to me that some sort of defensive action might be appropriate."

The damned thing's servile personality drove him crazy.

Shaffer activated the command channel. His fear was temporarily forgotten now that he had something to do. "Incoming aircraft. Into the tunnels, everybody."

He heard the roar of the shuttle dropping through the clouds to begin its strafing run. Cannon thumped; trees shook as explosive shells chewed their way through virgin jungle.

Shaffer waited for the last of his marines to duck into their bunkers. Then he turned, offered the incoming shuttle a one-fingered salute, and dropped down a ten-foot shaft into his own spacious tunnel.

The dirt under his hands and knees was cool and moist. Up above, the world became a flaming hell.

Wing Commander Marjorie Fox-Smith ran through her pre-flight check list with the ease of someone who's done it a thousand times before.

She had. She'd been a pilot for the last ten of her thirty-five years. During that time, she'd flown everything from gliders to smaller space craft. A halo of sandy brown hair surrounded her oval face; big green eyes scanned the computer check list; and perfect white teeth bit a full lower lip.

She regarded her looks as a curse sent to punish

her for some unknown sin. Women resented her, and men threw themselves at her with monotonous regularity. A waste of time, since only one man had ever captured her interest. And he was dead.

Fox-Smith watched her co-pilot from the corner of her eye. Melissa was a little pale, but otherwise OK.

"And," Fox-Smith thought, "she's got every right. After all, we're about to take twelve clumsy shuttles, and use them as interceptors. Not to mention being outnumbered fifty to one." A nifty little idea from a general who couldn't fly an aircar more than a hundred miles without crashing into the jungle.

In spite of that, Fox-Smith had a grudging admiration for General Merikur. The idea *was* kind of clever. Unless you were the one who had to carry it out, of course. But when you're a general, all snug in your bunker, what the hell do you care?

As usual the brass had planned for one kind of war and wound up fighting another. No one saw a need for aerospace fighters until the Haiken Maru fleet appeared—and by then it was too late. So, figuring shuttles were better than nothing, Merikur had stashed her wing in the jungle before sending the fleet to Augustine. And now they were supposed to make like an entire air force. If you asked Fox-Smith, which no one had, the whole thing sucked.

For the last week or so Fox-Smith, her pilots, and about a hundred ground crew had been concealed in the crater of a long extinct volcano. The heat created by underlying geothermal activity shielded the ships from orbital infrared sensors, while conventional camouflage took care of the rest.

At least they'd have the advantage of surprise. And so far there was no sign that the enemy had interceptors either.

"After all," she'd told her pilots, "the Haiken Maru wouldn't carry aerospace fighters in their merchant ships. That means shuttle-to-shuttle battles. And while the Haiken Maru have the numerical advantage, our training is better, and that should give us the edge."

As Fox-Smith checked her harness now, she hoped it was true.

She sub-vocalized. "Clear the launch area." Her AID relayed the order and a klaxon began to whoop.

"Cleared."

Forcing herself to relax Fox-Smith tilted her acceleration couch back and folded her hands across her stomach. Next to her Melissa did the same.

Wires snaked from the sensors in their pressure suits into the ship's computer. They'd fly the ship through the interface between their AIDs and the shuttle's computer. Through a combination of measured muscle response and verbal commands each pilot flew his or her ship without touching any controls. As a result there was almost no lag time between thought and action. The manual controls, such as they were, were more for crashing than flying.

Fox-Smith said in the verbal shorthand pilots used to communicate with their computer controls, "Exterior 180 pan."

A three-dimensional picture of the crater was projected on the inside surface of her visor. The image began to move from left to right, executing a 180° pan. Had she wished to, Fox-Smith could've controlled the speed of the pan by tensing one or the other forefinger.

The picture moved across camouflaged maintenance equipment, a couple of missle emplacements, and a crowd of techs waiting for the wing to lift. There were two shuttles in the foreground with the rest partially visible beyond. Everything shimmered in the warm air.

Enough screwing around, she thought to herself. "Command channel. All ships. Lift on me. Watch your wingmen. Let's do unto them before they do unto us."

With a mighty roar the twelve shuttles rode their repellors up and out of the crater. Dust billowed and sand blasted the watching techs. One, a balding noncom called "Pops," watched them lift and crossed himself. "Good luck, Margie," he whispered. "You're gonna need it."

Regardless of race, most soldiers agree that snipers are weird. They have to be.

Going out onto a rooftop or up into a tree all alone with the intention of shooting creatures who can shoot back is an act of intense courage. And it takes a little more courage each time you do it, because you know the odds are piling up against you, and eventually you will die.

Knowing that, but doing it anyway, has got to make you a bit strange. Buka was very strange indeed.

He was a good deal taller than the average Cernian, a fact which had caused him no small amount of grief in his younger days, and earned him nicknames like

"Stretch," and "Treetop." It wasn't long however, before Buka discovered that his larger size carried certain advantages, among which was the capacity to hurt those who made fun of him. This tendency towards violence, plus his increasingly antisocial personality, caused Buka to spend a great deal of time alone.

By the time Buka joined the army, he was already a confirmed loner and a violence-prone paranoid. Not the sort of person you'd want for a brother-in-law, but just right for a sniper.

During basic training, alert instructors put one and one together, and sent Buka off to sniper school. Needless to say, he took to sniper school like a nodank to water. After all, he had perfect vision, excellent hand-to-eye coordination, and actually liked to sit in trees.

More important was Buka's willingness to kill. It takes a special kind of person to draw a bead on a fellow sentient, coldly compute the ballistics, and squeeze the trigger. A person like Buka.

Like all Cernian snipers Buka was issued a rifle made just for him. It was a thing of beauty, a perfect fusion of wood, metal, and electronics. It fit his shoulder like another arm. It was the perfect weapon, but more than that, the perfect friend. It never called him names, it never made fun of him, and it never let him down.

From sniper school Buka went to a meaningless billet on a Cernian moon. The brass asked for volunteers one day; and, being bored, Buka hung his head, inviting their judgment. They found him worthy, put him through another school, and sent him off to kill humans.

He killed lots of humans. Now he was supposed to kill Cernians instead. It didn't make any sense . . . but hey . . . what did?

He could've touched the shuttles as they passed overhead, their drives screaming, the air displaced by their delta-shaped hulls pushing the foliage down and back. He felt naked and exposed in the tree even though he knew that between his camouflage uniform and green skin, he was almost invisible among the leaves.

Not so the two shuttles that touched down in the clearing. They were not only visible, but quite accomodating, landing right where Father Jomu wanted them to.

The shuttles hosed the jungle with automatic weapons, then dropped their ramps. Cernian troops poured out to take up positions around the shuttles.

Sweeping his weapon from right to left, Buka watched the uniforms drift through his crosshairs, and whispered "bang, bang, bang," as he pretended to pick them off. He knew others friendlies were dug in around the clearing, but he didn't much care. They'd fight their war and he'd fight his.

He touched his amulet and tried to relax.

The best way to survive a battle is to avoid fighting in it, and that was Larry's plan. He'd slipped away from his unit and was about to hole up in his girlfriend's apartment. Like most of Port City's citizens she'd been evacuated to the countryside.

"Too bad," he thought to himself. "I could've used some tender lovin' R & R."

Larry was not what recruiters call "prime material." In fact, the marine corps was something of a second career for Larry, the first being cut short by a judge who gave him a choice between enlistment and a vacation on an asteroid.

"Go with the flow," was Larry's motto, so he soon found himself in the Marine Corps. Basic was a pain; but once that was out of the way, Larry discovered the little scams which make military life worth living and settled in to enjoy them. Ending up dead wasn't part of his plan, so Larry had granted himself some extra time off. He was tall, thin, and given to wry humor.

Shrugging off the rack-pack and leaning his rocket launcher in a corner, Larry lay down on the bed and promptly went to sleep. Eventually he'd be forced to come up with a story to explain his absence; but, like the rest of his life, he'd figure that out later.

Cado frowned as Nola Rankoo buckled on her combat harness. His gear was already in place. "This isn't necessary," he growled. "We have others to perform such chores."

Rankoo looked at him and smiled. "I'm surprised, Cado. In the past you took pleasure in my kills."

"As I take pleasure in all that you accomplish," Cado replied gruffly. "But I don't think you should lead this assault."

Rankoo was pleased but careful not to show it. Her face was devoid of expression as she checked her personal weapons. "Computer analysis of their radio traffic shows their HQ is located just outside Port City. That's where we'll find Merikur and his staff. Kill the brain and you kill the beast. It's as simple as that."

"I know all that," Cado said stubbornly. "It's not your logic I question but your presence on the assault team. The firebase will be heavily defended. The loss of your leadership would delay victory."

Cado loved her and the knowledge made Rankoo warm inside. But she had a duty to fulfill and fulfill it she would. She tucked the last weapon into its holster and looked him in the eye. "What I eat I must kill."

For a long moment they just looked at each other. Then Cado shrugged and forced a smile. "Then let's kill Merikur and get it over with."

Chapter 12

Shaffer's ears were still ringing from the last explosion when he climbed up out of the tunnels. Confident that he'd sanitized the compound, the Haiken Maru pilot dropped his shuttle into the free-fire zone. A ramp fell and Cernian troops poured out.

Shaffer delivered his orders via hand signals. Helmets nodded and bodies went to work.

Keeping low Shaffer wiggled his way to the top of the embankment and swept the area with field glasses. The Cernians were spread out and advancing in good order, but their officers had decided to land them in the free-fire zone, an incredible mistake for which they were going to pay.

Shaffer looked over his shoulder and got the "go" sign from Sergeant Lang. She had a small console on her lap. A cable ran out the back of it and disappeared underground. Shaffer gave her a "standby" signal and took one more look at the Cernian troops.

The hostiles were damned close. Here and there troopers exchanged jokes in Cernian and were reprimanded by nervous NCO's. A few more minutes and they'd be sitting in his lap.

Mesker backed away and rolled over. Lang's eyes met his and he nodded. Grubby fingers tapped out a quick rhythm on the console. Explosions began to shake the ground like a string of Chinese fire crackers, one after another. Geysers of soil were thrown high into the air, Cernians were tossed about like rag dolls; the shuttle's port landing jack crumpled, causing a stubby wing to hit the ground.

The pilot panicked and tried to lift. Only the starboard repellors fired. The shuttle stalled and flipped over, crushing a dozen troops in the process.

By now the surviving Cernians had turned away from the compound and headed for the jungle. Another mistake. Concealed automatic weapons and mortars opened up and cut them to shreds. The rebels had come through all right—

But Shaffer's marines couldn't fire without raking the rebel positions. The idiots had placed themselves in direct line with the Cernians. Making matters worse, the rebels were marching mortar shells across the free-fire zone towards the compound.

"I still can't raise them, sir!" the com tech cried. Perhaps their com set was broken, maybe they just weren't listening.

Shaffer ordered his people into the tunnels, swearing a blue streak as he dived in after them.

The Cernians were unable to face the automatic weapons fire and turned once again. By now half of them were down and the rest were desperate. They ran towards the compound with only one thought in mind. Get in and escape the stuttering death which came from behind. They were just outside the razor ribbon before the rebels realized their error and stopped firing.

"Wire cutters! Whose got the fucking *wire* cutters!" someone shrieked. But nothing lasts forever; by the time Shaffer and his marines came up out of the tunnels, there were fifty crazed Cernians on top of the embankment, cutting through the ribbon and looking for someone to kill.

Fox-Smith swallowed hard as a radar display flashed onto the inside of her visor. There were more bogies than she cared to count. At least thirty, all loaded with troops, and all headed for Port City. The city was already under attack, so these were reinforcements. Once they arrived the defenders wouldn't stand a chance.

Well, that's what her team was here for.

Because both her ships and those of the Haiken Maru were Pact standard, and because all the intelligence reports swore that Merikur had no air force, Fox-Smith had been allowed to close on the larger formation without a challenge. She should receive one any moment now.

Meanwhile everything depended on an appearance of normalcy. "Easy does it," she said softly over the command channel. "Maintain formation until my command."

Her AID spoke in her ear. "I have a scrambled transmission on freq six. It orginates with the lead ship in the enemy formation. Request for I.D. 94 percent probable, issuance of orders 4 percent probable, all others 2 percent probable."

"Send the following in the clear," Fox-Smith ordered. "Can't descramble . . . modulator problems . . . please repeat last transmission in the clear." Just a few more seconds and they'd be in perfect position.

When the reply came, her AID relayed it through.

The voice was male and rather bored. "Group leader to twelve unknowns. A bum modulator's the least of your problems, sweet lips. Identify your unit and target."

Fox-Smith scanned the inside of her visor. Her ships were in perfect position above and slightly behind the Haiken Maru formation. "Give me the command channel. Here we go . . . good luck everyone. Send this in the clear. Sweet lips to group leader. Kiss your ass goodbye!"

Buka squeezed the trigger twice, watched the target jerk and fall; swung his rifle right and did it again. The other rebels hidden along the edges of the clearing opened up and turned the LZ into an abattoir. Cernian troopers dived right and left, searching for the slightest depression or smallest rock which might shelter them from incoming fire. A few bolted back toward the shuttles.

The shuttles lifted with a roar that cut off hope.

A brave officer stood, rallied a platoon of troops, and led them towards the jungle. Automatic weapons ripped them in a crossfire. The officer fell, a long line of her troops dying with her.

Buka grinned. He'd never had so many targets before. His scope slid across the clearing to a medic bent over a trooper with a sucking chest wound. Each time the casualty took a breath, he pumped out a small geyser of blood. The medic slapped a piece of sterile plastic over the wound and taped it down.

Buka smiled as the tiny micro-processor in his rifle computed distance, windage, and velocity.

"Each medic is worth six troopers."

It was one of the catch phrases they taught in sniper's school. For every medic killed, six wounded troopers will die. Therefore it's a sniper's job to make sure lots of medics die.

Buka had just started to squeeze the trigger when an invisible club smashed into his left shoulder and threw him back against his safety line. The rifle spun out of his hands and fell four feet to the end of its lanyard. Damn! Just his luck to catch a wild round.

Then the invisible club hit him again, in the right leg this time, and now Buka knew it was no accident. It was a fellow sniper, a graduate of the same schools he'd been to, and a sadistic bastard at that. Anyone who could shoot that well could've killed him, if not with the first shot, then with the second. The fug sucker was playing with him.

Buka ignored the pain as he pulled himself around the huge tree trunk. It would shelter him from the clearing. Fumbling fingers sought and found the first aid kit, pulled out a handful of dressings and stuck them between his teeth. Buka rested his weight against the safety line and treated his leg first.

He placed pressure bandages on both entry and exit wounds, bound the whole thing in place with roller bandage, and slapped a two-ounce package of blood-volume expander over the large distributor vein on his right thigh. Seconds later the package convulsed and injected a chemically balanced liquid into his bloodstream.

Then Buka stuffed more dressings against his shoulder, waited a moment while they sealed themselves in place, and took a stabilizer capsule to fend off shock. Feeling a good deal better, he peeked around the tree trunk.

Things had improved for the Cernian regulars. Although some were still pinned down in the clearing, the survivors had made it to the edge of the jungle and were locked in a desperate struggle with the rebels. Something slid along the left side of Buka's head followed by a sharp pain. The bastard had done it again! Only this time he'd tried to finish the job and failed.

Gritting his teeth, Buka loosened his safety line, winced as he put some of his weight on his wounded leg, and eased himself downwards. On three different occasions branches forced him to stop, unclip his safety line, and resecure it further on down. It was annoying but necessary. Given the way he felt, it would be easy to screw up and fall.

Fifteen feet down the tree, Buka entered an area of thick foliage. His wounds hurt like hell, so he stopped to take a rest. Wrapping some roller gauze around his head, he stopped the bleeding from his latest wound.

Then, careful not to disturb the surrounding leaves, he used the lanyard to pull his rifle up. Taking his time, he eased it onto a convenient branch and found a comfortable position.

Infrared was useless with so many bodies around, so he switched to high mag optical and squinted into the scope. Working from right to left he quartered the clearing. Somehow, he wasn't sure why, he knew the bastard was in the LZ.

A wave of dizziness rolled over Buka, forcing him to close his eyes. He waited till the spasm passed. Bringing his eye back to the scope, he resumed his search. The bastard would have to show himself eventually, and when he did, Buka would send one more penitent to the gods.

The heavy thumping awoke Larry.

It took him a foggy moment to place the noise: Guns. Big ones. Artillery or tanks. Now he heard the rumble of powerful engines, the squeal of metal treads, and the chatter of automatic weapons.

He rolled off the bed and scrambled over to a window. The small apartment was on the top floor of an older building, offering a good view of the central city.

Even though he knew what to expect, Larry was still surprised. There were two monster tanks rolling up Commerce Street. As they moved, their turret guns swiveled right and left like long noses searching out a scent. Every twenty yards or so the tankers fired their ball mounted automatics. Windows shattered, walls disintegrated, and buildings burst into flames.

Marines looking like stick figures popped up to spray the lumbering machines with repulsor fire, then darted into doorways or alleys.

"Come on," Larry said to himself. "Get a tube tech up there. Repulsors won't even scratch their paint."

The lead tank kept rolling but its stabilized cannon froze, then flared light. The crash shook the walls of Larry's building. Two blocks away, at the head of Commerce Street, a whole warehouse caved in. Company HQ gone in a wink of the eye.

"Shit! They weren't supposed to do that!" Everybody'd said they wouldn't blow up their own property. But either the bastards didn't care, or things were so desperate they were willing to accept the damage.

The reasons didn't matter to Larry. He was about to leave the window, gather up his stuff, and head for healthier climes when movement caught his eye.

Two marines dashed into the middle of Commerce street. One carried a stubby launcher and the other had a rack pack with five extra rockets. The stupid bastards had decided the only way they'd get a clear shot at the tank beyond the arming distance of their fuzes was to break cover.

Blond hair fluffed from beneath the helmet of the one with the rocket launcher. Cissy, no question, so the other one had to be Purdy; the two of them were inseparable.

But neither was worth a shit with a launcher. Larry was the best tube tech around. Everyone knew that. Somehow they'd drawn his assignment. His thoughts froze as Cissy knelt, aimed, and squeezed the trigger.

The rocket flew straight and true as it raced down Commerce Street—glanced off the sloped surface of the tank's turret, flew across the street, hit a five-story building. Blew up.

Tons of rubble fell on the tank. For a moment, Larry thought the shattered building had finished what the rocket had started.

Main battle tanks are built to take punishment. This one shrugged off the avalanche of concrete and rolled out of the dust spitting death. Purdy was still loading a second rocket into Cissy's launcher when the beads hit and bounced them down the street like kick balls.

Nobody heard Larry's scream of rage and self-loathing. His fingers furrowed in his face. He was lead tube. They were dead because they were as good as the company had left.

He grabbed his launcher and kicked out the window. Stepped onto the tiny balcony, he filled his sight with tank. Panning to match the vehicle's movement below him, he placed the offset crosshairs on the seam between the tank's turret and the main part of its hull. That was one of the few weak points on a tank and Larry's elevation gave him a better angle on the sloped armor. He pressed the "ready" button and gave the little missile a peek at its target. When he pressed "fire," he lurched slightly as the missile left the tube and accelerated downwards.

There's no subtle way to take a firebase. Knowing that, Nola Rankoo began the job with saturation bombing.

Flight after flight of shuttles came in low, dropped their bombs, and chewed up the ground with cannon fire. Ground vehicles exploded, pre-fabs melted, and the craters multiplied until they overlapped each other.

But Merikur's marines still lived. For days rebel miners, trained by the Haiken Maru and using company equipment, had worked to extend the system of tunnels and bunkers already started by the marines. At the first sign of trouble most of Merikur's marines had retreated underground.

But even though most of the marines stayed underground and no air force opposed them, the Haiken Maru still took some lumps.

Rebels in the jungle used to good effect the one-shot shoulder launched ground-to-air missiles supplied by Merikur. To attack the firebase the shuttles were forced to come in low over the surrounding jungle, the little heat seeking missiles screamed up out of the trees searching for targets.

The shuttles jinked, dumped hot chaff, and occasionally aborted runs. Most of them escaped.

Most, but not all. The rebels claimed two confirmed kills and a probable that trailed black smoke towards the low lying hills and then disappeared.

The marine air-defense missile launchers hidden around the perimeter of the firebase were completely automatic and armed with a full array of heat and radar-seeking missiles. They were designed for point defense and didn't do much damage until the Haiken Maru shuttles were almost overhead, but then they took quite a toll. Five shuttles disintegrated in mid-air, one crashed into the firebase, and two more were badly damaged.

It was easy to track the missiles back to their source, so each time a shuttle blew up, another missile launcher was located and destroyed. But it was still a good bargain from Merikur's point of view.

Not that he could spend much time on any one area of conflict. He had the whole planet to consider and things didn't look good. The Haiken Maru were trying to retake a number of important mining stations, Port City was under attack by enemy armor, and the firebase was taking a beating as well.

Merikur felt the ground shake as a five-hundred-pound smart bomb hit the compound and tried to dig its way down to the main power plant. It didn't quite make it, but the lights dimmed for a moment as a smaller generator went belly up and a back-up came on-line.

Dirt showered from the ceiling to dust Merikur's hair and dribble down his neck. He swore as he brushed it off. The com techs grinned. They'd had the foresight to shelter themselves and their equipment under a sheet of plastic.

Fouts appeared at his side. She wore full armor with her helmet visor up. "Time to bail out, sir. Gopher One reports shuttles down with Haiken Maru infantry on the way."

Merikur snapped on his body armor. "Thank you, Major. Let's go topside and welcome our guests."

"One other thing, sir."

"Yes?"

"It looks like they sent us human security forces instead of Cernian regulars."

"Interesting," Merikur mused. "An officer who doesn't like aliens perhaps? Well, we'll soon find out. Bethany?" He turned looking for his wife and found her standing right behind him.

"Yes, my lord?" She wore a smile, full body armor, and cradled an auto repulsor in her arms.

"You know how to use that thing?"

"Of course," she replied serenely. "We learned a little bit of everything in finishing school."

For a moment Merikur tried to think of some way to protect her, to hide her away, but the look in her eyes stopped him.

He nodded. "Good. But I expect you to follow orders. Consider yourself part of my personal bodyguard." At least that way they could stay together. He looked around.

The techs had abandoned their equipment and strapped on body armor. He knew it was the same everywhere. When the chips are down there aren't any cooks, com techs or medics. Just marines.

He pulled his visor down and activated the command channel. "All right people . . . let's go up there and kick some ass!"

"Fire!" The order was unnecessary. The Cernians who'd cut through the razor ribbon were charging the compound.

As the marines opened up, their weapons made a rolling thunder of sound. Cernian troopers jerked and fell. Others returned fire as they ran.

A marine threw up his hands and fell backwards, a hole where his nose used to be. Another threw a grenade and took a burst through the chest.

"Fall back!" Shaffer screamed. "Make for the tunnels!"

He didn't need to say it twice. The marines fell back, firing from the hip, dragging their wounded with them. In ones, twos and threes they dropped down the short vertical shafts. Scrambling on hands and knees they entered tunnels and headed for the distant jungle. They had two tunnels to choose from, both constructed by the rebels as a way to get in.

Sergeant Lang stood in front of a drop shaft, her repulsor burping. "Come on, Lieutenant! They're all down!"

Shaffer continued to fire, inserting his words between ten-round bursts. "Go ahead, Sergeant! You're gonna need some time to reach the jungle!"

"Bullshit, sir! I'm not leaving till you do!"

"That's an order, Sergeant." Shaffer swung towards her and squeezed the trigger. Glass balls dug up the dirt in front of her feet. Surprised, Lang fell over backwards and into the vertical shaft.

Shaffer had decided some time ago that there was only one way his troops would have a chance of making it all the way. He screamed an incoherent war cry and charged the Cernians. His weapon sprayed without his conscious awareness. Something hit him hard.

He was flat on his back with rain pattering in his face. Something hurt real bad and he knew he'd messed his pants. Damn. They'd find him lying there with shit in his pants like a little kid. It wasn't fair. He began to cry.

A familiar voice filled his ears. It was his AID. "Don't cry, sir. I called for reinforcements. They'll be here any moment, sir. I'm sorry I couldn't get them here earlier, sir, but . . ."

Shaffer stopped crying. He was furious. "Cut the crap!"

"Sir?"

"I said cut the crap. I've been meaning to talk to you about this for a long time. I'm dying, for god's sake, and you're busy kissing my ass. Do me a favor . . ."

"Sir?" Silence. "Sir? Talk to me, sir . . . I'm sorry if I did anything wrong. Don't worry sir . . . everything will be all right."

But things wouldn't be all right, and the AID knew it. Shaffer was dead, and things would never be all right again. He'd died talking to the AID like a real person, something he'd never done before, and asking for a favor.

Oh, it would give anything, *anything*, if only, only Shaffer would come back to life.

A blob of heat suddenly filled the AID's electronic awareness. The blob was a 99.9 percent match with Cernian body type and hummed on freq twelve. It grew larger as it bent over Shaffer's body. The AID screamed "Don't you dare touch him!" but no one heard.

The Cernian noticed the wavy black line on Shaffer's shoulder tabs. A human officer! The trooper felt around the corpse's waist ignoring the coils of pink viscera spilling out through the hole in the abdomen. It had to be here somewhere, the small computer command wanted so much, the one they'd give a hundred dru for. Wait a minute . . . here it was . . . covered with blood but still intact. The trooper cut the AID free with his combat knife and brought it up into the light. A simple black box. Why the big deal?

But the question was never answered, because when the AID said, "I love you, Lieutenant Shaffer," the Cernian couldn't hear.

Then the AID melted itself down. They almost always did.

Fox-Smith and her pilots had the advantage of surprise and made the most of it. Eight Haiken Maru shuttles went down in the first forty-five seconds of combat. Five of the victims carried troops, which meant five hundred fewer reinforcements for the attack on Port City. It was quite a victory—as far as it went. Even with eight hostiles down the marines were still outnumbered almost two to one.

Patterns flickered across the inside of Fox-Smith's visor as her AID and the shuttle's computer fed her information. The enemy formation had broken; individual ships were going off in every direction. Some, those loaded with equipment and supplies, stayed to fight. Others ran, knowing high-G combat would turn their passengers into green paste.

Those were the targets Fox-Smith wanted most. Every additional trooper killed in the air was one less they'd have to kill on the ground. "Don't let 'em get away," she ordered. "It's the troop ships we want."

A chorus of "rogers" filled her ears as the marine pilots broke formation and headed off in pursuit of the fleeing Haiken Maru ships.

Flexing certain muscles in her right arm, Fox-Smith banked right and kicked in more power by moving her right foot. Ahead and below, nubbly green jungle swept through the targeting grid as she overtook a fleeing shuttle. Because it was empty, her ship was faster. Clenching and then loosening her left fist, she swung the LCS to port and flattened her pursuit curve. "Two missiles . . . activate."

Two lights came on in the upper right-hand corner of her visor informing Fox-Smith that two stubby missiles were armed and ready. A few more seconds and the Haiken Maru shuttle would be dead meat.

"Shit . . . we've got one on our tail." Melissa must be scared because she never swore.

Fox-Smith dumped chaff.

"Roger." They weren't going to lose this target. Closer . . . closer . . . closer . . . now. "Fire missiles."

As the shuttle quivered with missile release, Fox-Smith broke left. It was too late. Melissa's voice was shaky but under control. The array on her visor showed that the Haiken Maru shuttle had readied a missile and was ready to fire. "They have missile lock-on. Chaff ineffective."

"Kill confirmed." The voice belonged to Fox-Smith's AID. The ship's sensors had witnessed her kill and the AID had recorded their input. Handy if you're keeping score, but pretty damn meaningless if you're about to get nailed yourself.

Fox-Smith was only dimly aware of the AID's words and what they meant. She jinked right, then left, the smell of her own sweat filling her nostrils.

"They still have missile lock-on," Melissa croaked. "Estimated time to impact twenty point five seconds."

A distant part of Fox-Smith's mind marvelled at Melissa's ability to control her fear. The woman had guts. A closer, more involved part gave the order. "Prepare for emergency separation. Execute."

Explosive bolts blew, slamming down into her couch as the control compartment separated from the hull. The hull kept on going, faithfully obeying the last orders she'd given it. The missiles hit with a mind-numbing roar, showering the jungle with fire.

The bottom of Fox-Smith's stomach dropped out as the main chute popped open and jerked them upwards. Moments later they were falling again, but more slowly now, giving her a chance to think.

Thanks to her AID and the on-board computer, Fox-Smith's visor was still functional. She scanned it for any sign of attack. If the Haiken Maru pilot wanted to kill them, the control compartment would be easy meat.

Nothing. The pilot was either giving them a break or had other priorities.

Like shooting down the rest of her wing for example. Fox-Smith bit her lip. "Give me the wing freq."

She listened. Where there should have been constant chatter she heard nothing but static. "Wing Commander Fox-Smith to wing. Report." More static. She sighed. Every single ship was either dead or down.

The control compartment hit the top layer of the jungle canopy and broke through. Hundreds of birds took to the air.

The control compartment fell fifty feet before the main chute caught on a branch and jerked them to a halt. As they swung gently back and forth, Fox-Smith was reminded of the hammock she'd played in as a girl. It had been her retreat, the place she'd gone to be alone. She made no effort to release her harness and begin the business of survival. There would be plenty of time for that. For the moment it felt good to lie there and think.

Melissa was the first to speak. "We're alive." There was awe in her voice.

Fox-Smith smiled behind her visor. She let out a deep breath, and suddenly realized she'd been holding it for a long time. "Yes," she agreed. "We're alive."

The Cernians came close to breaking out of the LZ three different times, but the rebels had forced them back. Now the pinned-down attackers were screaming for air support and reinforcements.

Nothing came. Automatic weapons fire was a constant, intermittently punctuated by the thump of mortars. The rebels were softening up the LZ for an assault. In half an hour, an hour at most, they'd sweep across the open area and wipe the Cernians out.

None of this mattered to Buka. He was waiting for the other sniper. He swept the powerful scope across the LZ for the hundredth time, dipping where it dipped, pausing wherever there was the slightest bit of cover. Nothing. But wait, what was that? A slightly different shade of green? He jerked the rifle back and grinned. Gottcha!

The slimy bastard was lying in a small depression screened by low growth. All Buka could see was the top of the sniper's head and a section of his back.

He slipped the safety off, snuggling the rifle to his shoulder. He was adjusting the fine focus on the scope when his opponent looked up.

Buka couldn't believe it. He knew the bastard! It was Father Pola, his favorite instructor in sniper school, and maybe the best sniper in the Cernian army! Apparently they'd rotated Pola back to a line unit.

Pola brought his rifle up and Buka found himself looking right down the weapon's bore. He smiled. The old geezer was still looking for him. Maybe when this was all over they could get together over a meal. Pulling some branches aside he stuck his head out and waved.

Pola squeezed the trigger and watched Buka's face disappear. He shook his head angrily. Buka had shown promise in school. Could these kids never learn? Then, motionless save for his questing eyes, Pola searched for a new target.

Larry's missile hit the tank with a brilliant flash of light. The explosion shook the balcony and the rest of Larry's building as well.

But the tank kept on coming.

He thought it was undamaged at first, but then he saw it was turning slightly, as it moved with no hand at the controls.

It didn't even slow down when it hit the building. A wall caved in. Still the tank's engines roared as they tried to drive the machine through the building and out the other side.

Glass balls deafeningly sprayed the wall over Larry's head showering him with chips of hot concrete. The other tank was trying to cancel his ticket!

Diving inside the apartment, Larry grabbed the rack-pack and headed for the back stairs. He was halfway down when the cannon shell exploded inside the apartment and tore it apart. Man, Suzy would be pissed. Then he laughed, realizing he'd be dead, and it wouldn't make any difference what she thought.

Another cannon shell exploded, lower now, and the displaced air heaved Larry out the door and onto a side street. He shoved a rocket into the launcher as he ran up the sidewalk towards Commerce.

He stepped out onto the pavement. He didn't give a shit whether the tank saw him or not. Either way they'd pay.

Larry passed Cissy's body as he jogged down Commerce, jumped over Purdy, and stopped when the huge tank was a hundred yards away. He brought the launcher up to his shoulder and pressed "ready." He couldn't miss. The tank filled his sight but it didn't make much difference. In spite of his earlier success, the bow of a main battle tank is well protected and almost impervious to shoulder launched missiles.

Now they'd seen him and were bringing the cannon to bear. The bore looked big enough to walk through.

What the hell. Why not?

He pressed "fire," and felt the slight jerk as the missile sailed down the street.

There was a stuttering roar as the tank fired its automatics and cut Larry's legs out from under him. As his body toppled the tank came apart with a gigantic explosion, hurling jagged metal in every direction. The missile had struck the cannon's bore squarely, and there was a fuzed round right there waiting for it.

Larry passed out. When he woke up, a medic was bending over him. He was black and wore a big grin. "Welcome back, Private. Not that you'll be here long. They've got nice clean hospital beds for heroes like you. The company CO says he's puttin' you in for a medal, and I agree with him. The way you cooked that tank was something to see."

Larry struggled to speak, to tell the medic he wasn't a hero, that Cissy and Purdy were, but the fellow wouldn't listen. He smiled and slapped an injector against Larry's arm. Antibiotics, painkillers, and a sedative shot through the pores in Larry's skin and into his blood stream.

The medic wondered why Larry was crying; in a month he'd have a new set of legs—but what the hell, if he'd gone one-on-one with a tank, maybe he'd cry too.

Chapter 13

By the time Merikur reached the surface, Nola Rankoo controlled a quarter of the firebase. All the missile batteries had been silenced and Rankoo's shuttles were nearly unopposed. The rebels launched the occasional missile from the jungle, and the marines did likewise from the compound, but these were not sufficient to drive the shuttles off. Rankoo was able to use her air and ground forces in combination.

First Rankoo's shuttles would strafe an area just beyond her position. Then, while the marines were still in their bunkers, the shuttles would break off the attack and her ground troops would sweep across the new ground.

As they advanced, the Haiken Maru troops dropped grenades into every bunker they could find. When the marines opened up from the next set of prepared positions Rankoo's forces would disengage. Moments later the shuttles were back and the whole thing started over.

Merikur knew he could order his marines up and out of the tunnels during a strafing run and break the cycle. Casualties would be heavy, but the survivors would push the security forces back. But was it worth the cost? Merikur found himself stalling because he couldn't answer that question . . . and if he stalled much longer Rankoo would win. Where was she anyway? In orbit or on the ground?

Anson Merikur no longer had a useful role as general. The battle had degenerated into a series of bunker assaults—that would end within minutes when the Marine line of engagement ran out of ammunition —with resupply cut off by the constant air attacks.

Merikur waved his com tech forward.

"Sir?"

"Try their surface freqs. Tell 'em I want to speak with Nola Rankoo."

"Yes, sir."

Merikur waited while the com tech ran through a number of freqs. Most were either jammed or full of non-stop code. Finally he got a response and forwarded Merikur's request. He listened for a moment, said something in reply, and looked up.

"They told us to wait one, sir."

Merikur nodded. He used the moment to sweep ahead with his field glasses. Damn. The Haiken Maru troops were taking a beating but they kept on coming."

"Nola Rankoo on freq three, sir."

Merikur nodded and took the handset. He did his best to sound casual. "General Merikur here."

"This is Nola Rankoo, General. I've been expecting your call. Surrender *is* the wisest choice."

"Oh, I don't know," Merikur replied casually. "I'd say your troops are doing fairly well. You shouldn't surrender yet. You might still be able to pull off a retreat."

Rankoo was impatient. "If you want something, spit it out."

"All right," Merikur said reasonably, as Eitor and Bethany listened dumbfounded. "I've got a proposal. Both sides are taking heavy casualties. Even if you win you will lose half your force. Let's settle this through personal combat. You and me. Winner take all."

"One moment." There was a *click* and the speaker stopped humming.

The silence was broken first by Bethany. "Have you lost your *mind*? Why should she accept? They're beating us. And if she does accept—she's a monster; she'll break you in half. Besides, her forces would never honor the deal even if by some miracle you won!"

"Oh, she'll accept," Merikur replied. "Rankoo is not just a monster; she's a *lunatic* monster. She'll think the lost time is a cheap price to pay; the chance to tear me apart in front of an audience will be irresistible." Despite himself Merikur shuddered slightly. "She's paying. We're buying. Time."

"Time for what?" asked Eitor.

"Time to breathe," Merikur replied. "Time to re-supply the forward bunkers. Time for hope, maybe." He turned to Bethany, who had turned inward on herself. "Hey, you know, maybe I'll give her a surprise. Could happen."

Speechless, Bethany smiled bravely, falsely, at her second lost love.

The speaker snarled back to life. "General Merikur, I accept your offer of personal combat. On my home world disputes are often settled in this manner. What weapons will we use?"

Merikur thought fast. Bethany was right. Rankoo could probably break him in half. In fact she was probably counting on it. Repulsors were out, chances were they'd both wind up dead, and any sort of edged weapon would give her a bigger advantage. "Why, none, Manager Rankoo. I understand you stay in shape by practicing unarmed combat. I do likewise. We should be a perfect match."

He used his free hand to hold the field glasses. "There's a large bomb crater a hundred yards forward of your present position. I'll meet you in the middle of it in five minutes."

"Understood," Rankoo replied and she was gone.

Orders were passed, and moments later both outgoing and incoming fire dwindled away to nothing.

"I still don't like it," Bethany said desperately. "There's got to be a better way."

Merikur shrugged and placed a hand on her shoulder. *I love you too.* Aloud he said, "Maybe so, but I'll be damned if I know what it is. We've got the time we need to resupply the forward bunkers.

"Eitor, contact Major Fouts, I think she's inspecting the western permimeter. Tell her what I'm doing, and tell her Rankoo agreed too easily, she's up to something. I want Fouts to find and stop it.

"Bethany, keep that lunatic Cado from shooting me in the back."

"Count on it," Bethany replied grimly as she worked the action on her auto repulsor. "All he has to do is *breathe* funny."

"Good," Merikur replied, stripping off his body

armor and shirt. "See you shortly." He gave her a salute which was a good deal more jaunty than he felt and strode off in the direction of the bomb crater.

The sky was cloudy. The raindrops felt cold as they splattered against his bare chest. Every sound, every sight, every smell was crisp and clear. After days in the command bunker, it felt good to do something himself instead of working through someone else.

By now his marines had heard about the coming contest, and were filtering out of their bunkers and fox holes in twos and threes, all drifting towards the crater. Merikur didn't approve but he'd have to let Fouts handle such matters.

As Merikur passed through the marines a cheer went up and he found himself smiling and nodding in response. This was something he hadn't anticipated, a partisan crowd, and one which wouldn't forget his performance, good or bad.

There were other spectators as well. Looking towards the far side of the giant crater Merikur saw Rankoo, and behind her, a crowd of security troops also eager to see the match.

As he approached the edge of the crater, and descended its steep sides in a series of short jumps, his AID said, "Well, your generalship, you've really done it this time."

"Done what?"

"Been sucked into a no-win situation."

"Thanks for the vote of confidence. As the old saying goes, if you don't have something positive to say, don't say anything at all."

"Or as another old saying goes," the AID replied,

"bullshit. You don't realize it yet . . . but I'm your secret weapon."

Both were interrupted as Merikur reached the center of the crater and faced Rankoo. She wore a brown cape and a golden replica of the Haiken Maru logo at her throat. She reached up to touch it and the cape fell away. Rankoo wore an olive drab bra and a pair of shorts under the cape. She was a beautiful woman, with breasts that were full, but not overfull, a narrow waist, and long slim legs.

But Merikur barely noticed. All he saw was rippling muscle, a long reach, and steel-shod boots. Beating her wouldn't be easy.

Not that it mattered. His troops didn't need *him*, they needed ammo for the next round. And they'd have that ammo even though their late general lay in a bomb crater with his back broken. . . .

A cheer went up from the security forces, and was quickly matched by an answering cheer from the marines. The crater had become an amphitheatre with seating all around the rim. Where the two groups came together bets were placed, insults were shouted, and rough laughter followed.

The carnival atmosphere would make a wonderful distraction for some sleight of hand. Merikur hoped Eitor and Fouts were paying close attention to the rest of the base. And then such thoughts were gone as Nola Rankoo claimed all of his attention.

"Prepare to die, General," Rankoo said casually. It was clear she had no doubts about the outcome.

Merikur smiled, opening his mouth slightly as if getting ready to speak, and trapped her eyes with his. By the time she saw the kick, it was too close to avoid. Merikur's right combat boot hit her in the stomach.

It was like kicking a cement wall.

Rankoo staggered backwards but didn't fall. The marines cheered, but Merikur knew better. All he'd done was make her mad.

Rankoo came straight at him. Nothing subtle, nothing tricky, just a straight charge. Merikur went in to meet her and soon regretted his decision. She hit him three times before he was close enough to respond. Then, after his single ineffectual blow, she picked him up and threw him down. The impact knocked the breath out of him and blurred his vision.

Rankoo didn't even bother to follow up. Instead she stood there enjoying the cheers from her troops and the moans from Merikur's marines.

"Nice moves," his AID said cheerfully. "I assume you're trying to make her overconfident. Keep it up. I think it's working."

"Screw you," Merikur growled as he rolled over and got to his feet. Rankoo was about twenty feet away. He ran the first ten feet and dived into a series of forward somersaults just as Eitor had taught him. It had the desired effect.

Unsure of how to meet this unorthodox attack, Rankoo did nothing at first, which gave Merikur the opening he needed. He landed in front of her and clapped his hands Cernian style. Pain lanced through her head.

Rankoo brought her hands up towards the source of her pain. Merikur delivered two quick blows to her stomach and jumped back out of reach. A loud cheer went up from the marines.

As Rankoo moved forward, her eyes narrowed. Most opponents never hurt her at all. She didn't approve of Merikur's methods, but she was willing to wait. He could somersault all he liked, but eventually he'd tire, and then she'd break him in two.

Cado drifted along the edge of the crater like a ghost, stopping occasionally to watch the fight, but always moving on. Somewhere along the rim he'd find the perfect spot. Finally he found it, a place where a thick gathering of Haiken Maru security forces would shield him from view, and where he'd have a good angle on Merikur. No one thought it unusual when he set up the tripod-mounted telescope. He was just another officer using his rank to get a better view of the fight.

Encouraged by his success, Merikur tried the same attack again. This time Rankoo was ready for him. She accepted the twin blows to her head, grabbed him, and crushed him against her chest.

For one split second he thought it was funny and then he began to suffocate.

"So hot shot," his AID inquired, "how are you doing now?"

"Just great," Merikur subvocalized. "She'll give up any second now."

"Right," his AID replied dryly. "Meanwhile, why not hurry things along? Go limp, then try for a head butt."

Having no better idea, Merikur did as the AID suggested, going limp and lunging upwards as Rankoo loosened her grip. The top of his head made a solid thumping sound as it connected with her chin. Her eyes were slightly out of focus as she fell over backwards.

Merikur sucked oxygen and wondered if her jaw ached as much as his head did. If so, she was really hurting.

However his AID was quite cheerful. "A successful ploy, was it not?"

"Yeah," Merikur grunted under his breath, "a few more successes like that and she won't need to kill me. I'll kill myself."

Both combatants edged through the rough floor of the crater. After two minutes of this, neither had closed to grapple.

Knowing he was there to buy time, Merikur was grateful for the big woman's hesitation. Then, as if on a signal, Rankoo's actions became more determined.

Bethany had covered her body armor with a nondescript rain poncho. Gradually she drifted away from the cheering marines and into the mob of security troops. By now a few marines had done likewise. No one gave her a second glance.

It took awhile, but eventually she found Cado looking through his telescope and pretending to cheer. Fading into the surrounding crowd she surreptitiously checked her auto repulsor and watched him from the corner of her eye.

"Watch out! She's throwing a rock!"

Merikur dived to the side as a heavy object passed through the space he'd just occupied and thumped into the dirt beyond. It was a piece of bomb casing rather than a rock, but under the circumstances Merikur decided to be magnanimous and ignore the AID's mistake.

When Rankoo roared her anger and charged, he was still trying to get up. Her heavy boot caught him in the side and flipped him over. He rolled away and scrambled to his feet. The searing pain down his right side suggested broken ribs. If so, he was in deep trouble. No more trying to buy time; he needed to end the fight, and end it fast.

Rankoo charged once again but tripped on the piece of bomb casing she'd thrown earlier and sprawled forward.

"Jump her!" the AID urged, and Merikur obeyed. He placed a knee on her spine, grabbed her hair, and pulled her head back. Rankoo tried to throw him off but failed. A little more pressure and her neck would snap like a dry stick.

Cado's lips were drawn back in a snarl as he placed the cross hairs on Merikur's back and armed the laser. The instrument in his hands was more than a fancy telescope. It was an industrial spot welder designed for situations in which the operator couldn't or shouldn't get too close to his work. It would slice through a man as if he weren't there.

Bethany's auto repulsor touched Cado's right ear. "Hold," she said, "or die."

Cado's finger was tightening on the firing stud when five shuttles roared in to hang over the compound.

The roar of their drives nearly drowned out the voice which boomed through their external speakers.

"Attention below. This is Captain Von Oy, Pact Naval Forces, Cluster Command. By order of Governor Anthony Windsor, all Haiken Maru forces will lay down their arms and surrender. The alternative is death."

Captain Yamaguchi's wardroom was full to overflowing. A long buffet table was loaded with rich food. The bar was open and the buzz of conversation filled the air. Uniforms, both human and Cernian dominated the room, but there was lots of bright civilian garb as well. Now that the battle was over, and Windsor had won, the civilian population was eager to court the Governor's favor. They surrounded him like a flock of colorful birds vying to display their plumage.

Merikur had his own group of admirers. Some were genuine, and some were false, but all smiled with equal enthusiasm. What with that, his uncomfortable dress uniform, his aching ribs, and his hatred for social situations, Merikur could have been quite unhappy.

But he wasn't. Much to his own surprise, Merikur was having a good time.

He'd won.

And then there was Bethany, a radiant presence at his side. She wore a gown of shimmering white and was easily the most beautiful woman in the room. In her he had found the friend and lover he'd been waiting for all his life.

So Merikur was a happy man, though his eyes were a bit glazed, as Yamaguchi's executive officer droned on about a recent control rod realignment to the ship's main drives. Out of self-defense, Merikur's mind drifted elsewhere, reviewing his present happiness and how it had come about.

Captain Von Oy had started work on the relief force as soon as Merikur's ships emerged from hyperspace and radioed Augustine. By working his staff around the clock, Von Oy managed to round up three hundred marines, plus four hundred members of the local militia. They were loaded aboard a small fleet of ships and were ready to go within a few hours. Then, with Windsor pacing restlessly back and forth across the bridge of his flagship, Von Oy had blasted for Teller.

Faced with a fleet of warships, the Haiken Maru transports surrendered without firing a shot.

The subsequent arrival of Von Oy's shuttles over the firebase was part luck and part Fouts. While Merikur fought Rankoo and Bethany watched Cado, Fouts worked on the assumption that the Haiken Maru had a trick up their sleeves.

Having carefully limited the number of marines allowed to watch the fight, Fouts ordered the rest to search the compound. Outside the razor ribbon, Jomu's rebels did likewise.

It was the rebels who'd found the hidden shuttle and the company of Cernian regulars, moving in on the east side of the base.

The Cernians were badly outnumbered. The survivors surrendered after a brief fire fight.

Meanwhile Von Oy's fleet had dropped into orbit. Seeing a chance to end the conflict with an overwhelming show of force, Fouts requested five shuttles. The shuttles burned every reg in the books as they dropped through the atmosphere and swept in over the jungle.

So Nola Rankoo was still alive, as was Cado, as was Merikur himself. While Merikur celebrated, the other two were locked up dirtside. The only thing that bothered him about that was the possibility that they might go free someday.

The room fell silent as someone tapped a spoon against crystal. Windsor stepped forward and raised his glass. He looked regal in his suit and formal cape. "Gentle beings . . . I'd like to propose a toast. To the gallant General and his lovely bride!"

"Hear, hear!" All over the wardroom glasses were raised to Merikur and Bethany.

As the noise died down, Merikur raised his glass and said, "To Governor Windsor, to his vision, and to those who died making it come true."

The eyes of the two men met across the length of the room. An oath was taken, loyalty was offered and accepted, all without a word being spoken.

Meanwhile the crowd went wild. "Speech! Speech!" they cried.

As the applause finally died away, Windsor stepped forward to look around the room. He allowed the moment to build until every eye in the room was on him. When he spoke there was passion in his voice.

"Thanks to those gathered in this room, and those buried in the soil below, a new day has dawned. Not just on Teller, and not just for one race, but for every planet and sentient in the Harmony Cluster."

Several started to cheer but Windsor raised his hands for silence. "As we bury our dead, let us also bury the hate and fear which led to their deaths, and affirm the birth of something better. From this day forward, all the sentients within Harmony Cluster will be equal before the law, equally represented within government, and equally entitled to the protection of that government."

This time the applause was deafening and continued on and on.

When it finally died away, Merikur found himself sharing in Windsor's popularity as people came up to pound him on the back or shake his hand. He was too busy to notice the com tech step into the wardroom and talk to Tenly, or see Tenly whisper in Windsor's ear, or watch as all three slipped out of the room.

Half an hour later Eitor and Jomu sidled up to Merikur, wearing their upside down grins and Cernian finery, short jackets trimmed with gold brocade, and pleated skirts. "We've been summoned to the Captain's day cabin," Eitor said. "Some kind of get together. You and Bethany are invited as well."

"So, are you coming peacefully, or must we use force?" Jomu asked, doing his best to look menacing.

Bethany laughed. "Peacefully, I think. We wouldn't want to anger the dreaded Jomu."

"A wise decision," Jomu said, offering Bethany his arm. "Here, you can walk with me, while Anson and Eitor attempt to hold each other up."

Merikur was feeling a bit light-headed as they headed towards the bridge. And why not? He'd been drinking, the war was over, and he'd won. Or so it seemed until they entered Yamaguchi's day cabin, which looked as he'd seen it last, though considerably more crowded.

Yamaguchi was there with Von Oy, Tenly, Windsor and two aliens of a species Merikur hadn't seen before. Both were tall, pale, and draped over with robes of cartilage. They looked like ghosts wearing shrouds of white. The aliens bowed as the foursome entered.

Merikur tried to clear his alcohol-fogged brain as he bowed in return. This was more than the private celebration he'd expected. Judging from the look on Windsor's face, much more. Merikur straightened as the Governor spoke.

"Ambassador Relfenzig, Sub-ambassador Dolwinzer, I would like to introduce my niece, Bethany Windsor-Merikur, her husband, General Merikur, my principal political advisor, Eitor Senda, and his brother, Jomu Senda, a Commander in the Cernian Army."

Because Relfenzig's eyes were big and shiny, and his face hung in long loose folds, he had what most humans would consider a sad, lugubrious look. His mouth was hidden behind a drapery of tissue so that when he spoke his voice was somewhat muffled. "It's an honor to meet you, gentle beings. May the soil break softly before your plow."

Windsor gestured towards the empty chairs crammed against one wall. "If you'll find seats, I'd like to hold a short meeting. I'm sorry to pull you away from the party, but as you'll see, this is something of an emergency."

Merikur took a seat and accepted a cup of coffee from Yamaguchi. As he sipped the coffee Merikur wondered what was going on. Why were the aliens here, and what did they want?

Windsor stood and looked around the room. "Am-

bassador Relfenzig and Sub-ambassador Dolwinzer
bring us important news. They come from the planet
Strya in the Apex Cluster. Though independent, Strya
had benefit of Pact protection, but fell into arrears on
its taxes. As a result, human administrators were
appointed to run the planet's economy, and a force of
human overseers were brought in to supervise production. I'll let Ambassador Relfenzig tell you the
rest in his own words."

Ambassador Relfenzig stood and bowed formally.
"What I say will sound like slander on your kind, and
for that I apologize in advance; but Governor Windsor assures me I must tell the truth. And the truth is
that with rare exceptions the human overseers have
been cruel to my people.

"Under their orders all Stryans over the age of ten
must work in the fields. Those caught hiding children or parents are killed. Each year new quotas are
announced and they are always higher. Failure to
meet a quota means death for every fifth person in
that particular village."

"And unfortunately," Dolwinzer added, "this has
happened many times,"

"Most of us accepted the situation in spite of this
and tried to meet the quotas," Relfenzig continued.
"By working hard, we believed we could earn enough
to pay off the back taxes and get rid of the administrators. A few favored an armed uprising. They pointed
out that in spite of their superior weapons, the overseers were few in number and could be overwhelmed.
But in the long run, while we might kill the overseers, more humans would come, and we would
suffer grievous consequences."

"And that is how things remained until twenty-three Styran days ago, when disaster struck the village of Dantha. This is a nine year, the time when the Mangdabla stage their cyclical emergence and lay waste to our crops. It is our practice to put part of the seven-and eight-year harvests aside to see us through the ninth, but this time, in an effort to make its quotas, the village of Dantha didn't, couldn't. And its crop was not merely decimated; it was entirely wiped out. Not only would the village be unable to meet its quotas, most of its citizens would starve as well.

"To most this would seem punishment enough, but the overseers chose Dantha for a special example. All the children under the age of ten were placed in the empty storehouse. Then the overseers locked the doors and soaked the thatch with liquid fuel. A man called Larkin lit the fire with his cigar and laughed while our children burned."

Here Relfenzig turned his back on them and Sub-ambassador Dolwinzer stood. His, or perhaps her voice was lighter somehow, though still muffled like Relfenzig's. "Please forgive Ambassador Relfenzig. He means no discourtesy. His youngest son was among those burned in the storehouse and he has not yet recovered.

"You must understand that after the storehouse burned there was a time of great killing. The human called Larkin was the first to die, crucified in Dantha's town square. But he was not the last. Word spread quickly, racing from village to village like a terrible wind, and wherever it went humans died. They fought and their terrible weapons killed thousands; but eventually they died. For days the stench of their dying filled every square on Strya."

Dolwinzer was silent for a moment as if considering her next words. "You must understand that our revolt was not planned out in advance, or if it was, only a few knew, so a few humans escaped; by now the Governor of Apex Cluster knows." Dolwinzer sounded regretful, though it wasn't clear whether her sadness flowed from the human deaths, or the fact that some had managed to escape.

"Yes," Relfenzig agreed turning to face them once more. "And now the Governor will send his fleet, not simply to punish us, but to annihilate us. That is why we went first to Augustine, and then here. Governor Windsor proclaims that all should be equal before the law. We sought his justice and protection."

Chapter 14

When the *Bremerton* jumped for Strya the resulting blackness matched Merikur's thoughts. So black was his mood, he'd sought out a little-used observation dome in which to be by himself and think. Back on Teller, Jomu, Nugumbe, Von Oy and Fouts were sorting things out, restoring order, and preparing for Rankoo's eventual trial. Sure, they were capable— but Harmony Cluster was *his* responsibility, and that's where he wanted to be.

Yes, the Stryans needed help. Yes, they'd been abused. Yes, their plight demanded justice—

But so did a dozen situations within Harmony Cluster. *If* the battle for Teller were five years in the past, *if* racial equality were an accomplished fact, *if* all of Harmony Cluster were secure, things would be different.

But Teller was an open wound, racial equality was no more than a pronouncement by the governor, and there were other problems as well. There were good reasons why Windsor should consolidate his gains before conquering new territory.

231

Tenly and Eitor echoed Merikur's views, pleading with Windsor to give the matter more thought and pointing out all the potential problems which might result if he didn't.

Windsor allowed them their say. When they were finished, he met their eyes one at a time. His voice was weary as if their arguments weighed a ton each and had worn him out.

"We aren't discussing some fine point of law, or the ability of humans and Cernians to work side by side in a factory, we're talking about the death of a planet. And by *God* I won't allow it!" He shook his head. "I won't allow you to tell me that saving the Stryans isn't convenient right now, or that it might cause problems in the Senate, or any other goddamn thing! Is that clear?"

It *was* clear, and equally clear was the fact that Windsor was disappointed, saddened by their lack of courage and vision. They'd seen the hills and ignored the mountains beyond.

Merikur could understand the Governor's point of view—but what if the Apex Cluster ignored Windsor's attempts to intercede? What if they attempted to destroy Strya?

More immediately, what would Merikur do if Windsor ordered him to attack Apex naval vessels? To attack them was to attack the Pact itself, the very thing he and Windsor were sworn to protect.

Merikur was suddenly reminded of Citizen Ritt and the Kona Tatsu. Had they managed to anticipate his dilemma? Known in advance that Windsor's beliefs would lead him into conflict with the Pact? And if so, what would they want Merikur to do?

The answer came as swiftly as the question. They'd want Merikur to stop him. More than that, they'd *expect* Merikur to stop him. Looking back, Merikur realized his jump to general, his assignment to Windsor's staff, had all been arranged with this kind of situation in mind.

He was their back-up system, their fail-safe, the final check on Windsor's eccentric personality. Merikur wouldn't question the Pact's authority, Merikur wouldn't turn his back on his duty.

Merikur wouldn't do anything unpredictable.

Merikur's lips twisted into a sour smile. *Their* Merikur wouldn't be in this situation. *He'd* have lost the battle for Teller; and without that victory, Windsor wouldn't be sticking his nose into the Apex Cluster.

The choice remained nonetheless. If forced to decide, which would he choose, Windsor and a race of ghostly aliens? Or the Pact he was sworn to uphold? Merikur stared up through armored plastic but there were no answers in the blackness beyond.

Two days later Merikur's fleet dropped out of hyperspace. His larger ships launched scouts as they picked up speed and headed for Strya.

The vedettes spread out like hunting dogs in search of game. This game could shoot back, should they find and corner it.

Merikur waited aboard the *Bremerton* to see what kind of hand he'd been dealt. Was the system swarming with Apex Cluster naval forces? If so, how would they feel about his incursion on their territory, and what would Windsor order him to do? Most of the possibilities weren't very good.

Reports began to filter in. A small freighter heading in-system with a cargo of farm machinery, a scientific outpost on a rogue asteroid, a private yacht headed out-system. But no sign of naval vessels.

Merikur heaved a sigh of relief. Apparently he'd lucked out; the Apex Command ships hadn't arrived yet. Merikur was on thin legal ice as it was, but the presence of Apex Command Vessels would've forced an instant confrontation and destroyed any hope of cooperation. Now at least he could position his units as friendly forces coming to the aid of a neighboring cluster. Such a mission was unlikely, give the eternal shortage of ships, but not clearly illegal.

And upon that hook Merikur hung his hope. Maybe he could find a way to satisfy both Windsor and Pact Command.

Windsor was distant and aloof—sympathetic to Merikur's efforts, but preoccupied by inner conflict.

Windsor wondered if he'd made the right decision. More than once he opened his mouth to order the fleet home; each time, the thought of disruptor bombs, exploding over farming villages froze the words in his throat and forced him to remain silent. So, while the fleet moved forward under his orders, Windsor struggled to decide if it should.

Bethany was caught in the middle. She had a natural sympathy for her uncle and his goals, but she understood Merikur's position as well. She thought Merikur was right—but the decision was the Governors' to make. She did her best to stay out of the conflict, and be supportive.

Also she had to admit to herself, she was loathe to

take a stand that would make her, however indirectly, responsible for a planet-wide slaughter.

Bethany wasn't the only one caught in the middle. All the senior officers knew of the conflict—and knew that their careers, even their lives could depend on the outcome. Because he was the man he was, mostly their loyalties were with Windsor, but they dreaded the thought of fighting Pact forces.

The atmosphere on the *Bremerton's* bridge was tense, with none of the good natured banter that normally passed for silence among military types. Eyes were locked on screens, fingers searched for something to do, and conversation was minimal.

Windsor sat towards the rear of the bridge, a dark presence lost in dark thoughts, while Merikur waited with hands clasped behind his back. The initial reports were good, but that didn't mean they were in the clear; a whole fleet might be hidden by Strya's sister planet or lost within a nearby asteroid belt. But time passed and eventually the more obvious possibilities were ruled out. So far so good. It was time to move.

"Captain Yamaguchi."

"Sir?"

"Order the DE's to make for Strya at top speed. Once dirtside they will disembark their troops and lift ASAP. I want them in space in case company arrives."

"Yes, sir." Yamaguchi turned to a com tech who contacted the DE's.

A few minutes later two destroyer escorts broke formation and blasted for Strya. They were small ships, similar to Merikur's first command, and right now each was packed to overflowing with two hundred and fifty marines. Because the DE's were faster than the rest of Merikur's ships, they would land on Strya hours before the rest of the fleet arrived, and that could make an important difference. Once on the ground, the marines would extend Windsor's authority dirtside and force Apex Command to negotiate.

But speed was of the essence. The marines would become an important bargaining chip when they were on the ground, but en-route they were nothing but potential missile fodder.

Eitor, Ambassador Relfenzig, and Sub-ambassador Dolwinzer were aboard the DE's as well.

It would be their task to convince the citizens of Strya that they should surrender to Windsor. Though sympathetic to their situation, Windsor would no more approve mass murder of humans by Stryans than the reverse. But if the Stryans had already submitted themselves to his judgment before the Apex Command ships arrived, it would strengthen Windsor's position immensely; a *fait accompli* would minimize the chance of violence. Relfenzig and Dolwinzer had been urged to work fast. But they couldn't do anything until they arrived, and that was hours away.

The plans were complete and being executed by the personnel whose job they had become. Until the situation changed, Merikur himself could only get in the way.

Windsor retreated to his cabin, so Merikur did likewise, knowing Yamaguchi and the bridge crew couldn't relax until both of them were out of sight. Bethany put up with his pacing for an hour, then headed for the gym.

Finding the cabin lonely, Merikur headed for the fire-control center, supposedly looking for his briefcase, but actually sneaking a look at their small plot tank. The DE's were closer, but still had a ways to go.

Engineering was the next section to receive an unexpected visit from Merikur. Surprised techs looked up from their tasks to see a general striding through, nodding agreeably and stopping to talk to those he knew. From there Merikur wandered through hydroponics, medical, and the wardroom. Eventually he arrived back on the bridge.

Reports had been dribbling in from all over the ship for hours now. "General Merikur just arrived in engineering; General Merikur just left medical; General Merikur's headed for the bridge." Yamaguchi had plenty of warning.

"Well, Captain, how are we doing?"

In spite of her own tension, Yamaguchi had to supress a smile. She knew what the real question was and answered accordingly.

"Just fine, sir. The DE's have landed and are unloading troops."

"Excellent," Merikur replied, his spirits rising. "Has the Governor been notified?"

"No sir, but we'll inform him now."

"Captain . . ." The voice belonged to a Chief Petty Officer with the flashes of an electronic tech on her sleeve. "We've got five unknowns coming out of hyper between us and Strya. The computer says they're a ninety-eight percent match to Pact design."

"Continue to track," Yamaguchi ordered.

"Damn," Merikur muttered to himself. He watched the five new arrows in the plot tank. Whoever commanded the Apex ships had cut it close, coming out of hyperspace just beyond Strya's gravitational domain. Risky enough for a single ship and foolhardy with a fleet. Nonetheless, whoever was in charge had unknowingly blocked Merikur's ships, and given the Apex forces a tactical advantage.

That was the bad news. The good news, if you could call it that, were the marines now on the surface.

"Ship-to-ship audio and video on freq six, Captain," a com tech said, "Standard challenge and request for I.D."

Yamaguchi looked at Merikur and he nodded. "Standard response with codes," Yamaguchi replied.

"Aye, aye ma'am."

"Captain Yamaguchi."

"Sir?"

"Where are the DE's now? I don't see them in the plot tank."

"I believe they're on the far side of Strya sir, lifting, or just about to."

"Tell them to lift, but to keep the planet between them and us. And Captain . . ."

"Yes, sir?"

"Use a *Harmony* code rather than Pact standard."

"Yes, sir." If Yamaguchi was curious, she hid it well, relaying his orders in a flat unemotional voice.

The DE's weren't much; but something was better than nothing.

"The Apex forces have acknowledged our signals,"

the com tech said. "A Governor Kalbrand wishes to speak with our commanding officer."

"If General Merikur has no objection, I'll take that call," Windsor said as he strode onto the bridge. He wore a smile and seemed his normal self again. His private battle was apparently won.

Merikur smiled, glad to have Windsor back. "By all means, sir. Take that seat over there."

Windsor slipped into the chair and a confident smile at the same time. Moments later the com screen faded up from black and Windsor was face to face with the governor of the Apex Cluster.

Governor Kalbrand was completely bald. The top of his head was a tracery of raised scar tissue acquired during the rites of manhood on his native Kristen. Bushy eyebrows cast deep shadows down over his eyes and a long sharp nose split his face.

In spite of Kalbrand's intimidating appearance, his voice was smooth and mellow. Windsor knew immediately that this was no unreasoning bully. Whatever else Kalbrand might be, he was first and foremost a practicing politician. "Governor Kalbrand here . . . whom have I the pleasure of addressing?"

"It's a pleasure to meet you, Governor Kalbrand," Windsor replied. "The name's Windsor . . . I'm governor of Harmony Cluster."

"Ah," Kalbrand said knowingly, "formerly Senator Windsor."

Windsor nodded. "A pleasure to meet the Plenipotentiary Kalbrand who negotiated the treaty of Valpar."

Kalbrand nodded, obviously pleased. "I had some help; but yes, I pride myself on that success. Now

. . . allow me to welcome you to Apex Cluster. I hope you won't be offended if I ask what the hell you're doing here?" The last was said with a slight smile.

"Not at all," Windsor said equably. "Were our situations reversed I'd be asking you the same question." Without further ado, Windsor provided Kalbrand with a somewhat sanitized account of the massacre on Strya, the Stryan appeal for help, and his subsequent decision to come to Kalbrand's aid.

Merikur smiled when he heard the part about coming to Kalbrand's aid. It didn't exactly square with the rest of the explanation, but if the Apex governor noticed he gave no sign of it.

"So," Windsor said as he wrapped things up, "while my mission is somewhat unusual, we're all members of the Pact, and I think we should support each other."

"Very commendable," Kalbrand replied glibly. "And I'll send the president of the senate a note to that effect. But as you can see, I have sufficient force to deal with the situation, and won't need further assistance."

Windsor appeared to ignore Kalbrand's comment, asking instead, "Out of curiosity, Govenor Kalbrand, how *will* you deal with the situation? Lacking your experience at negotiation perhaps I could learn something."

"First of all," Kalbrand replied calmly, "there will be no negotiations. Since Strya is an agricultural planet with only a small annual surplus, and of no particular political or strategic value, I'll destroy it as an example for others. The first rule of negotiations is, don't, unless the other party has something you want. Strya doesn't. This way we avoid endless investigations, trials, and God knows what else. We'll just drop a few disruptor bombs." He smiled. "End of problem."

The way Kalbrand said it he might have been discussing the price of bread.

What amazed Merikur was Kalbrand's lack of passion. If the man were stricken with grief over the loss of human life, or furious because of Stryan cruelty, Merikur could've understood his decision. Not approved, but understood. Instead Kalbrand regarded the murder of an entire race as nothing more than the most expedient way to solve an administrative problem.

Suddenly Merikur understood Windsor's unwillingness to compromise in the face of such evil. Convenient or not.

Windsor shook his head sadly. "I'm sorry, Governor Kalbrand . . . but I'm afraid I can't allow that."

Kalbrand's bushy eyebrows shot up in surprise. "What did you say?"

"I said I can't allow you to destroy an entire planet filled with living, thinking beings for the sake of political expedience," Windsor replied calmly.

Kalbrand shook his head in amazement. "What they say about you is true. You do love aliens."

Windsor smiled. "The truth is that I love humans *and* aliens alike."

Kalbrand frowned. "You realize that if you use your fleet against me, the Pact will hunt you down like a common criminal."

Windsor shrugged. "I realize that's a possibility.

On the other hand there are those who feel as I do, that murder is murder, regardless of the victim's race. Should you destroy Strya, they might hunt *you* down like a common criminal."

Kalbrand laughed cynically, "I think you'll find little support from that direction. Besides, Strya will soon be nothing more than glazed rock, and that will render the whole matter academic."

Yamaguchi touched Merikur's arm. "General . . . two of their destroyers have started towards Strya. The rest of their ships are redeploying to block us from the planet."

Merikur swallowed. The moment of decision had arrived. He could have Windsor arrested and confined to quarters. His general orders, his fellow officers, and Governor Kalbrand would all support him.

Meanwhile, a once-living world of glazed rock would orbit slowly around its sun. . . .

When Merikur gave the order, it sounded no more important than thousands of others he'd given over the years. "Send this to the DE's. Approaching vessels are hostile. Take them out. Repeat. Flash the destroyers now." The battle for Strya had begun.

Chapter 15

Governor Kalbrand looked off camera and then back, a snarl forming on his face.

The screen faded to black.

Windsor swiveled to face Merikur. Their eyes met in silence. Finally Windsor spoke. "It's begun."

"Yes, sir," Merikur replied, "Indeed it has."

Second later Windsor was gone and Merikur was struggling into his space armor. The rest of the bridge crew had already put theirs on. If the hull were breached, the space armor could save their lives. Briefly.

In the meantime, the suits would provide them with communications, food, and if necessary, basic first aid.

Thanks to Yamaguchi, the Harmony squadron was already at general quarters, air-tight compartments sealed, weapons on line and tracking. They were in standard V-formation, with Yamaguchi's cruiser at the point of the V, and the other ships strung out along either side.

"Launch torpedos, Captain," Merikur said, as he sealed his suit.

"Aye, aye, sir."

There was an almost imperceptible delay as Yamaguchi repeated Merikur's orders over another channel. Then she was back. "Torpedos away and locked on. We're at extreme range, sir."

Merikur smiled behind his visor. Yamaguchi was worried that he'd fired the torpedos too early; the other fleet would have plenty of time to destroy them. "I realize we won't hit anything, Captain, but we'll get their attention. Right now that's very desirable."

With luck the torpedos would keep the Apex ships busy long enough for the DE's to get into position. As it had turned out, the DE's, not the marines, were his ace in the hole.

Of course two destroyer escorts against two tin cans wasn't a fair match, but Merikur hoped that the element of surprise would make the vital difference.

There were tiny flashes in the plot tank as the enemy fleet picked off the incoming torpedos. Merikur took a moment to analyze the Apex fleet.

Even though his ships outnumbered the Apex fleet eight to five, Merikur's fleet was still out-gunned. The Apex fleet included two battleships; Merikur had none. He'd left the *Nike* back in Harmony Cluster in case of trouble there. The *Bremerton*, a cruiser, was his largest and most heavily-armed ship.

In addition, Merikur had the two DE's, two destroyers, and two troop ships. The latter were more of a liability than an advantage; they were lightly armed and therefore quite vulnerable. Yamaguchi had correctly placed them at the rear of the formation.

With two battleships, a heavy cruiser, and the two destroyers now racing for Strya, Kalbrand had a considerable advantage.

"The DE's are about to engage, sir." Yamaguchi's voice was tight but controlled.

Merikur shifted his attention from the enemy fleet to the planet beyond. Strya appeared in the plot tank as a three dimensional globe. Two moons circled the planet, blocking, then revealing portions of its surface.

As Merikur watched, the destroyer escorts appeared over Strya's north pole and accelerated. Merikur imagined what it would be like. The G-forces pushing you down into your acceleration couch, the sweat trickling down your spine, praying it would be the other guy and not you.

Merikur's DE's were facing greatly superior opponents—but the Apex destroyers, already deep into their bombing runs, were caught in a nightmare of their own.

The destroyers' radar began tracking the DE's as soon as the Harmony vessels came out of the planet's shadow. Before the DE's began to launch missiles, alarms went off on the destroyers. Their chimes called the changed situation to the attention of the whole crew, even the personnel who were most involved in targeting procedures for the ground attack.

For almost a minute, the destroyers knew they were under attack—without being able to do anything about it. Each had deployed its payload of disruptor bombs in clusters harnessed to the vessels by spiderweb lattices of tubing and control cables.

The destroyers could neither attack with their own missiles, nor defend by using their secondary batteries against the incoming salvoes, until they managed to jettison the bomb clusters. Nothing the Harmony vessels could do would match the destruction a destroyer would achieve by detonating a disruptor bomb thirty meters from its hull with an unlucky "defensive" bolt.

The leading destroyer was far enough into its engagement sequence that, by rippling off its disruptors without their final course corrections, it was able to clear its secondary batteries in time to survive. The bombs vaporized in Strya's atmosphere as harmlessly as any other bits of space junk—but the oncoming missiles vaporized as well, clawed out of space by plasma bolts and concentrated volleys from the destroyer's barbette-mounted repulsors.

The second Apex vessel attempted to abort its run, but the bomb deployment system was checked and cross-checked with a variety of fail-safes. The design team hadn't wanted to be responsible for the loss of a ship which attempted to recover a lattice whose disruptors were still armed. Twelve seconds after the lead destroyer was out of danger and maneuvering in Strya's gravity well to pursue the DE's, a Harmony missile intersected the second ship.

Those on the destroyer's bridge knew they were all going to die in the next microsecond.

And they did.

On the bridge of the Harmony destroyer-escort *Oliphant,* Ensign Laurin Murphy began whooping from her acceleration couch, "We got 'em, Captain! We got 'em!"

"Yup," said Lieutenant Harkesh Sizbo, commanding officer of the *Oliphant*. "And if you hadn't stole the bottle outa my couch here, I'd have something useful t' do before they get *us*."

Sizbo was seventeen years in grade—if you counted from the first time he'd made Senior Lieutenant as a young officer on the way up fast. He'd been able to party all night, then solve tactical problems with a ruthless brilliance that astounded scoring officers as well as his fellows who'd tried to prepare in more pedestrian ways.

Sizbo was a commander awaiting promotion to captain the night he was found too drunk to rouse when Delavart rebels hit Hachima Base in a desperate attempt to get weapons. This time there were no scoring officers for Sizbo, only a Board of Inquiry.

And the need to explain the twenty-three naval personnel killed in the disaster.

The Board broke Sizbo two grades, with a jacket notation that guaranteed he would never again be promoted. Many of Sizbo's fellow officers—never his equals, but now his superiors—expected him to commit suicide.

And maybe they were right; but instead of a gun, Sizbo decided to finish himself with the weapon that had already killed his career. His junior officers over the years had made that more difficult, by quietly finding and flushing the bottles that Sizbo concealed on the bridge.

"But Captain," Murphy protested, "we got one. Now—"

"Now the other one eats the both of us for breakfast!" Sizbo snapped. "Don't they teach you little turds t' *count* at the Academy anymore?"

As Sizbo spoke, his fingers input control changes through the pressure-sensitive pad on his right armrest. In the holographic plot tank in the center of the bridge, the DE's paired courses were narrow blue lines curving toward Strya's inner moon while the orange track of the destroyer showed it was using both the atmosphere and gravity of Strya to enhance its forced orbit back to the action.

"But there's two—"

"And *one* bleedin' destroyer has 60 percent greater throw weight than *both* these bleedin' DE's together," Sizbo interrupted with a logic as remorseless as that of a missile guidance system. "As well as a higher power-to-weight ratio and twice the initial velocity—which they will use to run us down before—"

The *Oliphant* lurched as her side-thrusters kicked in with violent determination.

"Ha!" Sizbo snarled at the plot. "Foxed ye, ye bastard!" The *Oliphant*'s course jogged, while that of her sister ship, the *Porpentine*, conformed as nearly as possible. The difference between the original curve and that with the added correction was slight, but it took the DE's into the moon radar shadow just before their pursuer could achieve a missile lock.

"Sir, could we lead them back to our own—" Murphy began.

"Shit, there it goes," Sizbo muttered.

"Sir?" Murphy asked. Then she saw the blips of missiles separate from the destroyer and realized what her senior had known when he saw the orange track twitch like a dog coming out of the rain. A slight change in the destroyer's mass and weight distribution; of no importance unless you know you're the target for the mass being ejected from your pursuer's missile batteries.

"Eighteen seconds for the *Porpentine*," Sizbo said matter-of-factly. " 'Bout a hundred and forty-seven fer us, I make it."

Sizbo grimaced. "Missile Room," he said, the words keying the artificial intelligence that routed the vessel's communications.

"Roger."

"Dribble 'em out, Duncan," Sizbo said while his hand fumbled between the cushions of his acceleration couch. His bottle was still gone. "One every three seconds."

"Sir, unless we volley all we've got at once, we won't get through their—"

"Duncan," Sizbo interrupted calmly, "we *ain't* getting through their secondaries; period, so stop dreamin'. But we can let 'em take out some of their own hardware while they're stoppin' ours. So we live a few seconds longer."

"Roger, sir." The *Oliphant*'s hull rang as a single missile left its launch cradle.

"Sizbo out," the captain said.

Then, as if someone had thrown a switch in his drink-sodden mind, he said, "Shit. Shit! *Shit!*"

Again, with apparent calm, "Angie was a friend a mine, y'know, kid. Much as a drunken old fart's got friends, I mean."

"Maybe Lieutenant Angell will abandon—" Murphy said, then stopped as the line of the *Porpentine*'s course ended in a ball of blue light that expanded and dissipated in the plot.

The *Oliphant*'s secondaries hammered briefly. The missiles they destroyed were only those late-comers which passed through where the *Porpentine* had been, but found nothing remaining which was large enough to detonate their warheads.

"Shit," Sizbo repeated softly.

His fingers continued to play on the command console. Pearly lines and beads—alternate courses, alternate impact points—flickered their ghost-lives across the plot.

The secondaries began continuous fire, while the *Oliphant*'s own occasional missiles shuddered loose like drops attempting to titrate a solution of death.

"Commo," ordered Sizbo. "Flagship, Priority One."

"Ready," responded the AI when it had the *Bremerton*'s Ready to Receive signal.

"Offset Point Twelve," Sizbo said, "Five-five-three, one-seven-nine, nine-zed-niner. All you bleedin' got. Out."

"I don't understand," Murphy cried as her eyes shifted between her CO and the plotted intersection points, finding no hope either place.

"Merikur will," Sizbo grunted. "Or he's another dumb bastard." After a moment he added. "Wisht you'd left me the bottle this once, girlie."

"He got the offset point wrong," snapped the *Bremerton*'s Missile Control Officer. "That'd put them—"

"Captain Yamaguchi," Merikur said with his eyes on the plot, "I would be grateful if you ordered a three-salvo launch to those coordinates."

"Missiles control," said Merikur's flag captain. "Plotted coordinates. Battery three—launch!"

"Aye, aye, sir!" said the Missile Control Officer through tight lips. The first salvo rippled off within two seconds, aimed at a point in empty space. The loading cradles cycled, pulsed as another dozen missiles fired, and cycled again.

"If I may point out, Captain," said the Missile Control Officer coldly, his eyes carefully averted from General Merikur—his superior's superior. "The target chosen is beyond the burn range of our missile. They'll be on ballistic courses at that point, unable to manuever even in the event that a target chooses to manifest itself."

"They won't need to maneuver," said Merikur, continuing to stare at the plot.

"With all respect, sir—" the Missile Control Officer continued.

The blip of the *Oliphant* shuddered. Not a hit; not quite. One of the DE's missiles had detonated a hostile weapon within a hundred meters of the *Oliphant*. The doubled blast shook the little vessel's hull, voiding a cloud of gas and fragments which looked, for a moment, as if the Apex missile had gotten lethally home.

"Oh," said the Missile Control Officer suddenly.

"Yeah," agreed Merikur. "Sizbo's running a course reciprocal to the missile plot he gave us. Captain Sizbo. That's why he's sure where the destroyer's going to be."

"He'll, ah . . . ," Yamaguchi suggested. " . . . take evasive action at the last . . . ?"

"No, he won't," Merikur said simply. "If I know

Siz—Captain Sizbo, he already knows exactly where the missiles will get through the *Oliphant*'s forcefield and secondaries. By the time she reaches the plot point he gave us, she'll be a cloud of vapor good for nothing except screening *our* salvoes from the destroyer's sensors."

"She's going," someone on the bridge muttered, but they could all see it happening. A twitch in the line of the *Oliphant*'s course as a missile warhead injected sidethrust. Three more missiles, striking almost simultaneously after the first knocked out the DE's fire control.

Half a dozen escape capsules separated from the ravaged *Oliphant*. They had enough mass to activate the seeker heads of the remaining Apex missiles in multiple pinpricks of light that faded almost at once from the plot.

The *Bremerton*'s missiles stabbed through the gaseous remains of the DE and intersected with the *Oliphant*'s slayer. The Apex destroyer vanished utterly.

"Wow!" said the Missile Control Officer.

Merikur swallowed. "Must still have had disruptors in her hold," he said, trying to keep the catch out of his voice. Harshly he added, "Gentlemen, we have a battle to fight!"

Miles below, Dolang Prelder, paused stolidly behind his plow to watch the ball of fire race across the sky. He didn't know it was an Apex destroyer, didn't know people had died defending him from it, and didn't know the battle still raged on.

Such things were beyond his comprehension. There was harrowing to complete. Even with the stench of the dead overseers only recently gone, there would still be quotas to fill. If not theirs, then someone else's. That's how it had always been, and that's how it would always be. Prelder clucked to his draft nanders and continued across the field.

The bridge crew cheered as the second Apex destroyer went down. Everyone except Merikur, whose mouth formed a hard straight line. The loss of two DE's and God knows how many people was nothing to cheer about. But at least they had delayed delivery of the disruptor bombs. That was something. But at the cost of killing their own. There would never be a time to cheer about that.

The surviving vessels of both squadrons had reformed. The Apex battleships cruised side by side about fifty or sixty miles apart. Any ship which ran the gauntlet between them would be caught in a lethal crossfire. The enemy cruiser matched vectors and velocity to the rear, the third point of an equilateral triangle.

The individual ships were strong, but they were too few to provide interlocking support. Harmony attacks on either flank would face only those missile and plasma batteries on a single Apex battleship. The battleships had launched twenty four-interceptors, but that wasn't sufficient screen to blunt the thrusts Merikur's force could make.

Merikur had split his force into two elements: one made up of the *Bremerton* and the carrier, the other consisting of the two destroyers and two troop ships.

The second element had orders to hang back, staying out of the conflict altogether if possible. The

destroyers were no match for the massive battlewag-
ons, but they should be able to protect the troop-
ships from enemy interceptors.

So it was up to a single cruiser and carrier to take
on two ships-of-the-line and a cruiser. Merikur knew
that it looked worse than it really was. In terms of
pure destructive power, his carrier was almost the
equal of a battleship. She carried a hundred and
fourteen operational aerospace interceptors inside her
hull, each capable of killing a battleship with a lucky
shot, and each a separate target for the enemy to
track and worry about.

Merikur had held them back till now in an effort to
conserve the fuel his interceptors drank in such enormous quantities. If launched too soon, they'd have to
refuel in the middle of the battle.

Meanwhile the missile and torpedo duel had grown
worse. Each of the opposing battleships could ripple
three times the throw weight of the *Bremerton*. If
Merikur didn't launch interceptors soon, the cruiser
would be quickly overwhelmed.

The deck shuddered under his feet as if to empha-
size that point. They'd taken a direct hit from a
nuclear torpedo. The force field must have held or
he'd be dead.

If two more torpedos hit simultaneously, he would
be.

Turning, Merikur found Yamaguchi's troubled eyes
already on him. "Hold thirty interceptors back for
fuel rotation and reserve. Launch the rest."

"Aye, aye sir," Yamaguchi said, and the orders
went out.

*   *   *

A hot launch is akin to climbing into a bullet and being fired downrange. The only difference is that ten miles after you leave a launch tube, you get to steer the bullet. If you're smart enough, fast enough, and crazy enough.

Jessie was all three, or she had been once. Now it was anyone's guess.

It doesn't happen often, but when it does, a training accident can be worse than actual combat. In combat you expect to get creamed. Sure, you think it'll be the other guy, in fact you pray it'll be the other guy. But somewhere in the back of your head is the knowledge that it could be you instead. So if you cop one in combat it's no surprise. You're pissed, literally sometimes, and it hurts like hell if you've got anything left to hurt with, but you're not surprised.

Training accidents are almost always a surprise. They're not supposed to happen. The whole idea is to simulate danger, *not* create it. It works for the most part, but every once in awhile something goes wrong as it had for Jessie, and then the shock can be worse than the pain. It can rob you of your self-confidence, your speed, and your courage.

That's why Jessie's wingman disappeared ten seconds after launch. He matched vectors with the orange element, leaving Blue One—Jessie—on a course of her own. It was against regs, but what the hell, he knew Jessie wouldn't report him, and if someone else did, well, too bad. He could claim he'd lost her in all the confusion.

Or they could court martial his ass if they wanted to, but *he* wasn't flying alongside a head case. Damn, the brass were throwing everything but the kitchen sink into this one, psychos included.

Jessie couldn't blame Blue Two. Her hands were shaking, her stomach felt like a bottomless pit, and she wanted to scream. She remembered the impact as Dolf's interceptor slammed into hers, the sickening spin, and the heavy G's as her cockpit module blasted away and tumbled through space.

The doctors had managed to repair her broken body, but they couldn't bring Dolf back to life or restore Jessie's shattered confidence. She made a fist and the little ship turned out and away from the oncoming ships.

Her visor was filled with blackness now, pierced here and there by pinpoints of light, distant stars to which she could journey. Never mind that her interceptor would run out of fuel long before she got there, or that the trip would take thousands of years; the stars were bright and pure, a worthy destination whether she arrived or not.

But behind her the battle still raged, and even though Jessie couldn't see it, she could hear it via her radio. "Blue one . . . Blue one . . . where the hell are you going?" "Forget her, Oscar one . . . the bitch is psycho." "Delta leader to delta five . . . break right . . . you've got one on your tail." "C'mon sucker . . . jus' a little more . . . gotcha!" "Alright ladies and gentlemen, buy the numbers, let's show these Apex assholes how it's done." "Oh shit . . . it hurts! It hurts so bad! Please don't let me die in here, please!" "Shut up. Mag . . . you're on the command frequency."

Something broke inside Jessie as she listened to Mag die. Tears began to flow down her cheeks and gather around her neck gasket.

She hadn't cried since the accident. Her fingers made a fist; the interceptor changed attitude, accelerated again.

Then, as suddenly as they'd come, the tears were gone. They'd killed Mag. Jessie didn't like Mag, *those* bastards had no right to kill her. No right to make someone suffer like Mag had, like Jessie had. No right at all.

She switched her visor to the plot mode. The larger ships were shooting at each other with everything they had. Light strobed as plasma batteries fired in sequence, explosions blossomed as missiles hit enemy force fields, and the huge hulls performed a slow motion ballet.

The interceptors attacked their flanks rather than run the gauntlet between the two battleships—though the flank approach was no joyride either. As they came in, the interceptors faced everything from missiles to enemy interceptors.

Though badly outnumbered, the Apex interceptors had given a good account of themselves, breaking up the initial Harmony attack wave. But now there were only ten of the defensive screen left, and soon they too would be overwhelmed. Nonetheless, the battleships were only slightly damaged and the cruiser was untouched.

Jessie's eyes narrowed at the sight of the cruiser. Why should that asshole sit there untouched?

She tumbled her interceptor on both the pitch and

yaw axes, then dumped all systems and went inert. Hopefully the computers on both sides would assume she'd been hit and destroyed.

Seconds passed, and then minutes, of gut wrenching spins—as the interceptor continued off its plotted course. There was no sign that she'd been discovered. She touched the attitude controls, stabilizing her rotation in what she prayed were undetectable increments.

Strya filled half Jessie's main viewscreen, a large yellow globe overlaid with patches of white cloud. The awesome shape of a battleship was silhouetted against the planet. It grew steadily larger until most of the planet was hidden behind it. Light rippled along the battlewagon's far side as interceptors attacked and plasma batteries fired in response.

It reminded her of distant lightning on Terra, something that you watched in eerie silence, as if it were part of someone else's world and not yours. The other battleship was discernible only by the corona of fire from its far side, a blackness blacker than the black around it.

And straight ahead there was the cruiser.

It lashed out lazily as the occasional interceptor tried her defenses, satisfied to sit back and let others do her work.

Jessie's interceptor sailed through the heart of the Apex formation. The three ships could've fried her a million times over, but to them she was only one more bit of space junk.

It would work or it wouldn't. She was totally detached, even as she thought of the countless missiles and cannon muzzles, pointed her way and ready to fire.

Time. The cruiser was almost on her. Muscles tensed; the heads-up display reappeared on her visor as she powered her systems.

Jesse kicked in full thrust and toggled off her payload as her interceptor raced up towards the cruiser's belly. Four nuclear torpedos, sixteen high explosive missiles, and thousands of rounds of repulsor fire all hit the cruiser's force field at once.

The defensive force field overloaded when the four nuclear warheads exploded together. Jessie spiked onward, through the dissipating fireballs.

Mag had been a real bitch. Thinking about it, she was glad that Mag'd bought the farm.

The interceptor had become a three-ton missile, still accelerating as the cruiser's repulsors chewed vainly out of it.

Jessie hit the cruiser towards the stern. The added velocities were enough to convert part of the mass to plasma, a bright flare that announced the death of the cruiser and everyone aboard her.

"Blessed spirits! Did you see that?" Yamaguchi demanded. "Somebody *just rammed* the cruiser! Did you *see* that?"

Merikur had. That single action might throw the battle their way.

But it made him cold all over to think of anybody doing *that*. Take a risk, sure. . . . But not *that*. *That* was crazy.

There wasn't any time to give the matter further thought because a missile hit the *Bremerton's* bridge and the starboard bulkhead disappeared and with it a full third of the bridge crew. Everything loose was sucked through the hole and out into space. Merikur felt himself pulled towards the hole and then jerked to a stop by his safety strap.

Yamaguchi was likewise saved. Her voice was grim inside his helmet. "Medical party to the bridge. We've lost hull integrity and argrav. Estimate thirty percent casualties. The weapons section was hardest hit. If any weapons failed to make the shift to manual control, then shut them down. All stations report."

"Drive room closed up on manuals. No casualties." "Sick bay closed up on manuals. Medical party enroute." "Fire control closed up and running off back-up computers. No casualties."

And so it went until all departments had reported in. The bridge had taken the worst of it. A good deal of the ship's primary weapon control system had been destroyed, along with some long-range sensors. That wasn't good, but the rest of the ship was functional and, with the exception of the mess deck, was still airtight.

It was strange to see a ragged pattern of stars where a section of bulkhead ought to be, although it made little difference to the ship or its ability to fight. Humans needed artificial gravity and bulkheads, but the ship didn't. Thanks to a multiplicity of back-up systems, the *Bremerton* would continue to function with or without them. As for the bridge crew, their space armor would provide them with life support for six hours, and by that time the battle would be over.

The medical party cycled through the mini-lock separating the bridge from the main corridor. They were systematically searching the wreckage for wounded and doing what they could to clean up the mess. The members of the bridge crew were too busy to notice. Later they would count their dead. Later they would wonder why someone else and not them. Later they would get drunk, tell stories, and cry.

But this was now and the battle was still underway. A cheer went up. It overmodulated the speakers in Merikur's helmet and forced the volume down.

Yamaguchi's eyes were bright behind her visor. "Our interceptors report damage to target one, General. They managed to slip a torp into her starboard drive room. Her port drives are untouched but she's using them to maintain her force field."

"Excellent," Merikur replied. "If target one can't manuever that cuts our problems in half. Keep the pressure on her but shift most of the interceptors to target two."

Yamaguchi gave the necessary orders while Merikur pondered his next move. Kalbrand was aboard target two and they hadn't heard a peep out of him so far. He was down to a single battlewagon. What would it take to beat him into submission?

"General! Target two's turning!" Looking at the plot tank Merikur saw it was true.

The remaining battleship was dropping towards Strya. It'd be suicide to attempt a landing while under attack.

The bastards were planning to bomb the planet!

"Order the destroyers to attack," Merikur said, "and put us alongside the battleship's main hatch." By throwing the tin cans into the fray, Merikur was stripping the troop transports of protection; but he couldn't help it. At least most of the Apex interceptors had been destroyed and the rest were too low on fuel and stores to be a serious threat.

He prayed they were too low on fuel and stores. . . .

The cruiser picked up speed as Chief Engineer Baines goosed the ship's drives. Baines was a big man, well over seven feet tall, and the boarding axe looked like a toy in his hands. Word was out that Merikur planned to board the battleship and Baines planned to go along.

The engineer grinned as he checked the weapon's edge and swung it around his head. Others could have their repulsors and needle guns. Baines believed there was nothing like a bloody great wedge of razor sharp steel to make room in an armored crowd.

The next half hour was a living hell as the *Bremerton* accepted the punishment necessary in order to close with the Apex battleship. Missile after missile penetrated the ship's force field, opening huge holes in her hull. Ravening plasma charges lighted the force field into a coruscant globe.

In the background there was the constant drone of damage and casualty reports which documented each stage of the ship's slow death.

For Merikur the hardest part was the helpless inactivity while Yamaguchi fought to keep her ship alive.

It was Merikur's role to set strategy, to look at the big picture, to give orders and then stay out of the way. He found it very hard to do.

At some point, he wasn't sure when, Bethany had appeared by his side. She didn't say anything and didn't need to.

They would die together.

But in spite of everything the battleship threw at them, the *Bremerton* survived.

Merikur could see the battleship through the shattered bulkhead: the cooling fins along the top of its hull, the shot-up radiant panels, and the repulsor batteries which still spewed death.

"Baines says he can't give us much more," Yamaguchi said calmly. "The drives are going down."

"Understood," Merikur replied. "Tell him to give us one last surge of power. Then put us alongside. We're going aboard. Pass the word for everyone to tie something white around their left arm. There'll be enough people trying to shoot us without our killing each other."

Yamaguchi turned with a look of horror. "*What*? I assumed we were going to slide a nuke through a hole in their hull and cast off."

Merikur gave a quick toss of his head—a gesture which blended acknowledgement with denial. "Kalbrand's aboard the battlewagon."

"Yes, of course," Yamaguchi agreed. "Eliminating him will surely cause the other battleship to surrender."

"*Killing* the Governor of Apex Cluster," Merikur said harshly, "will surely be treated as rebellion against the Pact—no matter what our justifications. We'll board."

"Aye, aye sir." Yamaguchi passed the word.

The *Bremerton* matched velocities—a fraction—with the battlewagon. A moment later they touched.

With half its control systems shot away the *Bremerton* was barely under control. The contact was more a collision than a docking maneuver, jerking Merikur and Bethany to the ends of their safety lines.

Merikur grabbed a handhold and chinned the command frequency. It was an order he'd never expected to give. "Boarders away! Go for her drives! I repeat, go for her drives!"

Bethany was right behind him as he left the bridge. Like him, she wore a white bandage around her left arm. She saw his glance and gave him a thumbs up.

He wished he could tell her he loved her, but that would mean telling a thousand other people as well.

He too settled for a thumbs up.

With the argrav gone, the boarders had to swim towards the main hatch using handholds. In spite of the people around him, Merikur knew there weren't near enough to take a battleship whose crew outnumbered his about three to one.

Merikur had to concentrate, and he was ignoring the bridge in favor of the drives. The controls were on the bridge; but without the drives the controls were meaningless, and the ship couldn't bomb Strya.

By the time Merikur reached the main lock, Yamaguchi's marines had blown the battleship's hatch and surged inside. As he followed, Merikur felt the battleship's argrav tug him towards the floor. He twisted and managed to land feet first.

Most of the battleship's crew were still tied up fighting off the interceptor and destroyer attacks. The platoon of marines who tried to defend the main hatch suffered heavy casualties and were quickly dispersed by the boarders.

They fought well, and it pained Merikur to see them fall, knowing they were doing their duty.

But so was he. Merikur screamed with all the rest when they broke out of the battleship's lock and charged down the main corridor.

Baines led the way swinging his battle-ax and yelling with joy as another group of Apex marines came to meet them. Even a battleship's corridor made a small, ugly place to fight. Battle-axes split armor, repulsors vaporized visors, and people from both sides boiled inside their suits. The radio was full of urgent talk and occasional screams.

"Behind you Slim . . . damn that was close." "Burn him! Burn the bastard!" "Oh God I'm hit . . . I've got a leak . . . aaahhhh!"

"This way, sir," the chief engineer grunted. "I served on one of these my first enlistment."

Merikur sidestepped a boarding pike, shot an Apex marine through the visor, and followed Baines around a corner. Thank God he'd decided to go for the drives. The bridge was literally miles away through a maze of corridors.

Baines' head vaporized. Light flashed past Merikur's visor. Half blinded, Merikur sprayed the corridor with glass. At his side Bethany did likewise. Armored figures stumbled backwards as the vacuum sucked them through the holes in their suits.

Slipping, falling, then scrambling to his feet Merikur staggered toward a hatch. The sign said "Engineering Section" and he couldn't believe it when the hatch slid open.

Two men in armor stepped out.

Merikur knew he was going to die. Even as he brought the repulsor upwards he knew he'd never make it in time.

The figures were gone in an incandescent flash. A marine sergeant stepped up from behind. He had a mini-launcher propped up on one shoulder. "Sorry to ruin your fun sir . . . but I couldn't resist."

"Apology accepted, Sergeant," Merikur replied. "You owe me a drink."

"Aye, aye sir," the sergeant said, stepping through the hatch, "but first I'm gonna give these swabbies a surprise inspection."

Ten minutes later it was all over. The engineering section was secure, a survivor from the *Bremerton* had dumped the drives, and the main corridor was under their control.

Windsor arrived a few minutes later, surrounded by members of the elite guard. Tenly followed, obviously hesitant.

Kalbrand looked tired when he came up on the drive-room screen. He wore armor, but his helmet was tucked under one arm. The bridge was still pressurized. Tired or not, his cynical smile was still in place. "Well Windsor, it looks like this round falls to you."

Kalbrand looked around as if surveying the damage off screen, then back to Windsor. "But it's far from over. From here it will spread. Planet after planet, cluster after cluster, until the Pact exists no more."

Windsor was silent for a moment. When he answered his voice was little more than a whisper. "I didn't want this, Kalbrand, but you and those like you left me no choice. Whatever comes is as much yours as mine."

To Merikur's surprise Kalbrand nodded his agreement. "Yes, cause and effect must always walk hand in hand. One of us will go down in history as a great hero, and the other as a great villain. I wonder which *you'll* be?"

Chapter 16

Merikur was tired, his uniform felt tight, and people kept asking him stupid questions.

"How did it feel to attack the Apex fleet? What was your wife wearing? Space armor? How uncomfortable. Poor dear, I can't imagine how she could stand it. I'd kill Herbert if he even suggested such a thing."

As always Merikur did his best to smile, to hear over the loud music, and to say something reasonable in response. The last few weeks had been a whirl of activity, and while he could understand the political value of holding a governor's ball, he hated the reality of actually attending it.

Winning battles makes more work, not less. It's the victor who has to deal with the casualties, repair the damage, and try to hold onto what's been won.

After Kalbrand's surrender, Windsor and his staff spent a lot of time and energy deciding what to do. In the absence of faster-than-ship communication, it would take time for the news to reach Earth; but

269

eventually it would, and then all hell would break loose.

In the end Windsor did what politicians do best: he compromised, not once but numerous times. First he loaded Kalbrand onto one of Merikur's troop ships and allowed him to return home. It was tempting to hold him prisoner, but Windsor was in enough trouble without that.

By releasing Kalbrand, he could defend his intervention on legal as well as moral grounds. He would claim that Kalbrand's plan to destroy Strya was not only an act of unmitigated barbarism but a violation of Pact law as well, since the power to destroy planets for punitive reasons resided in the Senate alone.

Kalbrand would try to justify his actions under the broad emergency powers granted to governors; but he'd be on the defensive, and the whole thing would descend into the kind of political bickering the Senate was famous for.

As an ex-senator himself, Windsor felt sure he could guide the matter to successful conclusion. They'd censure him, or give him some other slap on the wrist, and he'd be back in business. The main thing was to avoid any appearance of annexation—

Because that would amount to rebellion, and there was a long list of dead governors who'd tried that.

But there were more immediate problems as well. Kalbrand had committed most but not all of his fleet to the Strya operation. Once he got home, the Apex governor might gather the rest of his force and return. To defend against that possibility, Yamaguchi had assumed command of the surviving ships and positioned them to defend Strya.

With a fleet of damaged ships, hundreds of casualties, and a planetful of accused murderers to deal with, Yamaguchi didn't need crews of doubtful loyalty as well. Therefore all of the Apex naval personnel were loaded aboard the troop ships and sent home with Kalbrand.

The battleships were in orbit around Strya where they could serve as weapons platforms while Yamaguchi's personnel carried out temporary repairs. What was left of the *Bremerton* supplied spare parts and hull metal.

Meanwhile the battleships, damaged though they were, plus Merikur's carrier and one of his destroyers, would be more than equal to any ships Kalbrand might have in reserve.

Jomu had agreed to stay on Strya's surface and conduct a murder investigation. Even with a large contingent of marines at his disposal, it would be no easy task.

Windsor was adamant: murder was murder, no matter how well deserved, and those responsible must be brought to justice.

The problem was that the entire population of Strya had the motive, the opportunity, and the means. Jomu would have to sift through five million suspects to find those responsible.

Fortunately, he had the help of Strya's leadership. They were so pleased to have a neutral third party conduct the investigation that two regional governors confessed immediately, and the rest promised to help in any way they could. Jomu hoped that between the leaders' help and the temporary suspension of capital punishment, others would step forward as well.

Merikur didn't envy Jomu his task, he didn't much care for his own, either. He and Eitor were supposed to hold things together while Windsor traveled to Earth. By going there of his own volition, Windsor hoped to preempt the inevitable summons and any appearance of sedition. The combination victory and going away party was now in full swing.

The governor's mansion was full to overflowing with uniformed men and gowned women once again, but this time there was an even larger number of aliens than before. They were clad either in exotic finery or utilitarian atmospheric support suits.

One enterprising soul had combined the two by covering his four-armed environment suit with sequins. An envoy from Lavorian III, if Merikur remembered correctly. Bethany had greeted the alien in its own tongue while Merikur's AID provided him with a translation.

"Fellow sentients . . . I could talk for hours about this man's accomplishments . . . but unlike most politicians his actions speak louder than words. So without further ado it is my pleasure to present Governor Anthony Windsor!"

There was loud applause followed by cries of "Speech!" "Speech!"

Windsor raised his hands and waited for the applause to die down. When he spoke his voice easily filled the room. "Fellow sentients . . . thank you. To those of you who have supported me through the last few months I offer my heartfelt gratitude. I truly could not have accomplished anything without you. But please, don't rest on your laurels, the journey has just begun and a rough road lies ahead.

"As you know I leave for Terra in the morning. Once there I will plead Strya's case, and the case for alien equality in general. I wish I could assure you that the Senate will accept my arguments, that justice will be forthcoming, that no further lives will be lost in our cause. But I can't. I know only that the journey must be made, that our voices must be heard, that the Senate must be given an opportunity to decide.

"Many of you have asked what I'll do if they refuse me, and in all truth I'm not sure. But this I do know. I will never renounce the concept of equality, I will never act in the interest of tyranny, and I will never betray your trust."

And the Lavorian wasn't alone. Word of Windsor's accomplishments had leaked from system to system and cluster to cluster. All sorts of governments, both human and alien, had sent representatives to pay their respects and get a feel for where Windsor was headed.

Who was the man? A crackpot with a few lucky wins—or the leader many were waiting for, the man who could take the crumbling Pact and breathe new lift into it.

Laughter exploded on the other side of the room as Windsor cracked a joke. The crowd swirled and parted, allowing Windsor to mount a low platform. He would deliver a short speech and then invite the crowd to eat.

Merikur was worried about security, but wherever he looked he saw members of the Governor's Hundred, shielding Windsor with their armored bodies and scanning the crowd for any signs of trouble.

Good. There must be no repeat of the last party. A critical eye could still see where blood had seeped into and stained the marble floor.

Merikur ran a finger around the inside of his collar and drifted towards the speaker's platform. It was hot and crowded. Bethany was a short distance away. He caught her eye and pointed towards the platform. She nodded, made her excuses to an elderly dowager, and eased her way through the crowd. Tenly called for silence as the two of them arrived at the platform.

The applause was so loud that Merikur didn't even hear the shot.

Windsor was falling with a hole through his chest.

The body was still in motion when Tenly jumped to the platform and threw down this repulsor. "You have just witnessed an official execution by the Kona Tatsu," he shouted. "This action was considered and approved by the full Senate. Any attempt to harm me will be interpreted as an attack on the Senate itself."

A lot of things happened at once. The Governor's Hundred closed in on Tenly, one of them scooping up the repulsor as they looked towards Merikur for instructions. Someone shouted for a medic; Bethany and Eitor knelt beside Windsor's body.

The crowd surged forward to get a better view.

A combination of anger and sadness flooded through Merikur as he met Tenly's eyes. Of course. A back-up.

Merikur had assumed that *he* was the back-up, the safety, the Kona Tatsu's final check on Windsor. But he should have known there would be others. Tenly to watch him, someone to watch Tenly, on and on without end. All to maintain the status quo.

They were afraid of equality, afraid that they might lose their power . . . so they had tried and convicted Windsor in secret. Word of the public execution would spread quickly, and anyone who had sympathized with Windsor would have second thoughts.

The ideals Windsor had died for would die with him. They were sure of that.

Tenly ignored the guards, his eyes on Merikur alone. "Ladies and gentlemen, by order of the Senate I give you Governor pro-tem, Anson Merikur. Governor Merikur will accept responsibility for governing Harmony Cluster until a suitable replacement has been chosen by the Senate. Though a member of Windsor's staff, General Merikur opposed Windsor's insane attack on the Apex Cluster but was bound to follow the Governor's orders. Governor Merikur, would you care to say a few words?"

It was clever. Merikur had to hand them that. They knew he'd supported Windsor in the end but were giving him a way out. They were afraid of him too. Even dead, Windsor had some loyal followers. They might rebel against the Pact—

But they wouldn't rebel against Anson Merikur.

Merikur felt the weight of their stares as he stepped up onto the stage. The Governor's Hundred waiting for orders to kill, Bethany and Eitor waiting to see what he'd do, the crowd waiting for some sort of catharsis.

Tenly smiled.

The repulsor was light as a feather and seemed to

streak upwards on its own. The glass beads erased Tenly's arrogant smile and the rest of his face as well.

Eitor was on his left and Bethany on his right as Merikur looked out over the sea of shocked and curious faces. They wanted him to say something profound. Wanted him to explain what it meant, tell them what to do, offer them some sort of consolation.

Words wouldn't come. Words were for politicians, not soldiers like Anson Merikur.

But as the tears ran down his cheeks, Merikur remembered what Governor Kalbrand had said.

Facing the crowd that was only a blur of color to him, Merikur said, "This is just the beginning. From here it will spread. Planet after planet, cluster after cluster, until the Pact exists no more. I pray to God we'll build something better."

Have You Missed?

DRAKE, DAVID
At Any Price
Hammer's Slammers are back—and Baen Books has them!
Now the 23rd-century armored division faces its deadliest
enemies ever: aliens who *teleport* into combat.
55978-8 $3.50

DRAKE, DAVID
Hammer's Slammers
A special *expanded* edition of the book that began the
legend of Colonel Alois Hammer. Now the toughest, meanest mercs who ever killed for a dollar or wrecked a world
for pay have come home—to Baen Books—and they've
brought a secret weapon: "The Tank Lords," a brand-new
short novel, included in this special Baen edition of *Hammer's Slammers*. **65632-5 $3.50**

DRAKE, DAVID
Lacey and His Friends
In Jed Lacey's time the United States computers scan
every citizen, every hour of the day. When crime is detected, it's Lacey's turn. There are a few things worse than
having him come after you, but they're not survivable
either. But things aren't really that bad—not for Lacey and
his friends. By the author of *Hammer's Slammers* and *At
Any Price*. **65593-0 $3.50**

**CARD, ORSON SCOTT; DRAKE, DAVID;
& BUJOLD, LOIS MCMASTER**
(edited by Elizabeth Mitchell)
Free Lancers (Alien Stars, Vol. IV)
Three short novels about mercenary soldiers—never be-
fore in print! Card's hero leads a ragtag group of scientific
refugees to sanctuary in Utah; Drake contributes a new
"Hammer's Slammers" story; Bujold tells a new tale of
Miles Vorkosigan, hero of *The Warrior's Apprentice*.
65352-0 $2.95

DRAKE, DAVID
Birds of Prey
The time: 262 A.D. The place: Imperial Rome. There had
never been a greater empire, but now it is dying. Everywhere its armies are in retreat, and what had been civiliza-
tion seethes with riots and bizarre cults. Against the
imminent fall of the Long Night stands Aulus Perennius,
an Imperial secret agent as tough and ruthless as the age
in which he lives. But he stands alone—until a traveller
from Earth's far future recruits him for a mission so strange
it cannot be disclosed.

55912-5 (trade paper) $7.95
55909-5 (hardcover) $14.95

DRAKE, DAVID
Ranks of Bronze
Disguised alien traders bought captured Roman soldiers
on the slave market because they needed troops who
could win battles without high-tech weaponry. The leigion-
aires provided victories, smashing barbarian armies with
the swords, javelins, and discipline that had won a world.
But the worlds on which they now fought were strange
ones, and the spoils of victory did not include freedom. If
the legionaires went home, it would be through the use of
the beam weapons and force screens of their ruthless alien
owners. It's been 2000 years—and now they want to go
home.   65568-X $3.50

DRAKE, DAVID, & WAGNER, KARL EDWARD
Killer
Vonones and Lycon capture wild animals to sell for
bloodsport in ancient Rome. A vicious animal sold to them
by a trader turns out to be more than they bargained
for—it is the sole survivor of the crash of an alien space-
craft. Possessed of intelligence nearly human, it has two
goals in life: to breed and to kill.

55931-1 $2.95

DAVID DRAKE

"Drake has distinguished himself as the master of the mercenary sf novel."—Rave Reviews

ENTER A NEW WORLD
OF FANTASY ...

Sometimes an author grows in stature so steadily that it seems as if he has always been a master. Such a one is David Drake, whose rise to fame has been driven equally by his archetypal creation, Colonel Alois Hammer's armored brigade of future mercenaries, and his non-series science fiction novels such as **Ranks of Bronze**, and **Fortress**.

Now Drake commences a new literary Quest, this time in the universe of fantasy. Just as he has become the acknowledged peer of such authors as Jerry Pournelle and Gordon R. Dickson in military and historically oriented science fiction, he will now take his place as a leading proponent of fantasy adventure. So enter now . . .

AUGUST 1988 65424-1 352 PP. $3.95

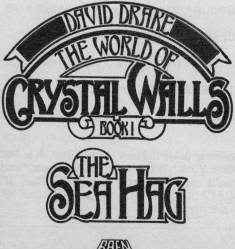

DAVID DRAKE
THE WORLD OF
CRYSTAL WALLS
BOOK I
THE SEA HAG

BAEN BOOKS